DAVID UTT,

ROM

WALES

CW00521728

Warscape

Warscape

Pauline Hunter Blair

CHURCH FARM
HOUSE BOOKS

British Library Cataloguing in Publication Data
A catalogue record for this book is available from the British
Library

ISBN   0-9536317-2-9

Typeset by Amolibros, Watchet, Somerset
This book production has been managed by Amolibros
Printed and bound by T J International Ltd, Padstow, Cornwall, UK

To DKC in loving and delightful memory

So off I go, funnily enough, to enter the world of The Spy," Laura said caustically to her mother. The sharp tone concealed nerves.

"The spy!" Kitty's tone was uncomprehending. It was ludicrously unlikely, looking at the girl: whose current style of hairdressing and general air of sensibility made her look a little like a Victorian poetess.

"Sorting reports from spies. About enemy sources of supply, in their engineering industry. What's that if it's not the world of the spy?"

"They'll be brave locals in occupied Europe, not 'spies'. Perhaps you'll find it exciting." Kitty sounded dubious.

"Engineering supplies exciting? And suppose they're in German? I don't know any."

"But they'll be in French, surely! Do go, you'll miss that train."

"I don't want to go, I feel nervous."

"I know, darling. You needn't. You'll be told what's expected of you. Do go."

"It's so utterly different from anything I know about."

"I can't, I can't," Kitty heard in her mind, the voice of her younger daughter when little. She smiled. Laura smiled back, made a face, waved, and went.

Kitty Cardew watched her, slim, tall and neat, walking over the grass, going off to the first proper job she had ever had. Laura's clothes and hair were usually pretty and neat. The precise back and swinging movement hid a deal of nervous tension. Kitty was aware that she had deep, deep feelings: and that though she would often be frenetically merry with those she knew, the natural tenour of her mind was reflective and melancholy. Laura's face, not beautiful, but often pretty, and full of feeling, with the dark straight hair, the deep-set violet-grey eyes, had always expressed a star-crossed, longing quality, as of somebody searching, searching for the unattainable. In little-girlhood, freckled and shorthaired in summer, or framed with fur caps in winter, Kitty had always wanted to comfort it with kisses. For part of the expression was a fearful timidity of what was in store. In her young womanhood there was a conscious sadness added, which often made the countenance heartbreaking. Partly, Kitty knew, it was the wretched debacle of their family unhappiness and break-up. Then the catastrophes of the war which, without saying much, she took to her heart. Now added, was the sorrow of an impossible love for a married don about ten years older than she, who had wisely and firmly fended her off, Kitty suspected, but not before showing a response to her affection. The negation of this passion had laid Laura waste, she had been for a time like a field no longer fruitful to the seeds of love. Kitty trusted to the job, the London life, the new people, and her older faithful friends who loved her, to replenish her daughter. Though there were times when she wanted to shake her at this perverse waste of emotion, Kitty nevertheless mourned the kind of pain her daughter evidently suffered from the ill-starred happening. Was any man, she wondered, worth this distress? And knew, romantic as she herself was, that she had to answer Yes: if you love him.

The day happened to be All Saints' Day, 1943. Laura's three years at the university seemed gone in a flash. The war was now four years old and felt endless.

Laura proceeded nervously to their station on the southern railway, bought a green cardboard return ticket at the up-line and sat in a carriage with five workers congealed into each side and at a guess six standing in the middle, give or take a few, trying to pretend they were not inconvenienced.

"Excuse me."

"Can't, I'm sorry."

"You could get off my foot I mean."

"Oh pardon."

It was a smoker (most were) which Laura thought she might avoid in future. Fortunately only one plutocrat had the wherewithal (and the gall) to smoke so wantonly early.

It was not a bad day, quite bright for November, so at Victoria she crossed the local bus bays and made for the Buckingham Palace road and the Park. These bus bays had recently been divided by pavements for the queuers to queue on, their kerbs still presenting the most terrible series of booby-traps for the unwary in the black-out: umbrellas, brief-cases and bowler hats would clatter in all directions as benighted home-goers fell over not one but several in their dash over the bus space for the evening trains beyond.

The Park, where some distant mounds betokened air-raid shelters or leaf-strewn static-water-tanks, was nevertheless still the Park. It was easier to walk across it than change tubes. Once across Piccadilly, she soon found herself marching with others down the slope into the square.

The twentieth century had defaced the historic square with various monstrous buildings including the immense block of flats towards which Laura made her way now. The square still held a few jigsaw-barked plane trees in its centre.

There was a lift. There was also a uniformed commissionaire, kept on for the duration perhaps because of faithful service and his advanced age. Little else was recognisable of the past (questionable) splendour of the luxury flats. Each according to size had become a grander or lesser domain for the denizens of the ministry, those important enough retaining carpets once prized by past inhabitants, upon which stood proper desks of imposing proportions; those of lesser size reduced to bare boards over which the typists' heels knocked, and trestle tables of familiar temporary civil-service type prone to give splinters and to creak with the pressure of working thought. Varnished collapsible chairs drew up to them with a hideous squeal or judder. Dark green light-shades directed low on to the tables helped preserve the blackout on winter afternoons. Cubbyholes that had been kitchens were stocked with mugs, kettles, quarters of tea, tins of coffee and milk powder. Lavatories with no outlet to the world, their air-conditioning long since broken and unmended, smelt of lavatory. Their Government Issue toilet rolls were like a poor kind of emery paper. Their shallow "luxury" washbasins were seldom free from scum.

"I'm Laura Cardew, good morning."

"Oh here you are, Miss Cardew, good morning."

Mr Cook, tall, gingerish and fifty, pawed Laura in kindly welcome, a gesture she was used to in all men who were the age her father should have been (he was much older) and which she would politely put up with until it proved itself more lascivious than kind.

"You know what you'll be doing?"

"I'm to be a research assistant, aren't I?"

Laura's memory of her interview some weeks ago had been made vague by anxiety: only the notion of the "spy" reports which she had mentioned to her mother, remaining.

"That's it. Well, we get reports you see, intelligence reports. About what the enemy are making and where, and how they get their raw materials. We'll soon hear which section you're for. It's all engineering. Know about engineering, do you?"

"Not at all, but I remember Mr Wheedon saying so. What kind of engineering?"

"It's all war vehicles. Or their components. You'll pick it up. You'll be helping sort out the intelligence reports, on whatever product they give you."

Laura's mind could only willingly picture, amongst all this about vehicles, the people and their reports: it was this, which had settled in her imagination.

"Who sends the reports?"

"People over there. Secretly. From the occupied countries."

"How do we get them?"

"That would be telling. Even if I knew."

He made what he hoped was a comforting clutch at her shoulder.

Laura had never harboured overwhelming feeling for any kind of motor vehicle, the only cars her father had possessed when she was a child being an old navy Standard with a discoloured sun-roof; and a thing called a Trojan? Spartan? Swift? She could not even remember—long since out of production and causing trouble with its spare parts and also with the more caustic of their boy neighbours. She hoped she looked enthralled.

"We try to pinpoint the factories. For the People Upstairs," he went on enigmatically. The People Upstairs, said with capital letters but with a kind of cringing casualness that implied their superior importance, were, she learnt eventually, connected with Bomber Command. But so shrouded in respect were they, or so unaware was she, that it was some months before she realised their significance.

Not far away, Laura learned, the Americans had soon set up a counterpart or rival establishment covering the same ground in what they no doubt considered to be superior techniques. (The Allies were not noted for unequivocal admiration of each other's methods, in the HQ, the office, the backroom, the air or the field.) This must have been repetitious and probably wasteful. From time to time, members of the one would visit the other, to probe, to compare, to criticise or to corroborate. The Americans heated their building to eighty degrees (causing the often freezing British to gnaw their blue knuckles in rage), wore open-necked short-sleeved shirts all the year, and still in 1943 exuded an after-shave sense of fresh superiority, engendered by their relatively late entry into hostilities, which washed over the weary British like so much hydrochloric acid. All over London their servicemen, with pants of superior, smooth, khaki cloth stretched tight over bulging buttocks, irritated the natives they had invaded with their boredom, their unconcealed lechery, their oily well-being and their wastefulness. In every hotel, restaurant or dive piles of rejected food, chicken casserole sometimes even in the best hotels revealing rabbit bones, tough steak which wags suggested was Derby winner, cardboard pies, curled sandwiches, wet lettuce, but none the less *food*—were scraped off American plates for the lurking pig outside the confines of the city. Hungry Londoners noted this and it inflamed dislike, being so far from their own war-strained, angular endurance of privation.

5

Propitious first meetings are often forgotten in the splendour of full acquaintance. Of the two young women destined to become such friends, Laura had arrived at the ministry first, by a day.

The next day, All Souls' Day, came Prudence. Prudence Kyle bounced over the common to the tube still looking as if she should have been in a gym tunic, immensely tall, her wild, curled glorious gold hair, her pink cheeks, her honey hazel eyes and ample bosom above an otherwise slim body, striking longing and admiration into several meno-pausal travellers of both sexes. Laura noted them too, with the inevitable envy of one kind of colouring and looks for another. (No woman, had declaimed one of her boyfriends in exasperation, is ever content with her own body. Why not?) Delighted to have a friend with the same history and background, as was immediately obvious to them both, each studied the other prepared to be pleased. Yet theirs was an ordinary everyday first meeting: no star shone, no sense of meaning glowed.

"Hullo, you must be Prudence, I'm Laura Cardew. Got here yesterday, Mr Cook said you were coming."

"Hullo! Yes, I'm Prudence Kyle."

"Do you live near?"

"Fairly. Do you? I live at home."

"Me too. Have you been waiting ages for a job?"

"Since I came down from Cambridge. In June."

"So have I. Feeling guilty. Shall we be interested in this? What did you read?"

"History."

"Mm. And me." Consternation. Laura's brows went up. Prudence laughed, a small spurt of amused, apologetic laughter, which Laura grew soon to wait for, her friend's kind, objective commentary upon the absurdity of life.

Prudence, for whom life in Cambridge had not been enough to detach her yet from the bosom of her adored and adoring family, saw a slightly less tall, thinner, delicate creature, small breasted but obviously athletic, dark-haired, violet-eyed and underlain by a sad anxiety which was foreign to her experience as yet and not at once recognised. It was weeks likewise before Laura, a "sound second" from Oxford, discovered that this surprising near tomboy was an intellectual, that a research studentship awaited her in medieval French History: for Prudence was so very modest that her achievements, invisible to herself, were naturally so to her acquaintances.

Meanwhile whenever the disappearance of Mr Cook (who glided with a slight stoop like someone on a dance floor to the typing pool) left them safely alone, they set about rapidly filling in the landscapes of each other's lives, so that by the end of the morning they were familiar enough to prattle with ease.

"There's not a bad canteen," said Mr Cook, quite sorry from his own point of view to see the two young ladies so magnetised, for he had thought he might have lunch with the dark one, who had cleverly evaded him yesterday. "I'll show you."

An immense clatter reigned. Worse than college, being vaster and heterosexual. Worse than school, where determined female staff banged knives on the high table to quell the riot at intervals. It was partly its vastness and an echoing quality due to many windows so high up. And the crashing down of handfuls of newly washed steel knives, forks and spoons into metal holders by seemingly furious washers-up. The scraping and squeaking of numberless crowded chairs. The banging of metal food lids on to empty containers by equally provoked servers, no doubt peckish themselves.

A great deal of bad temper was manifested in everyday life, most of it from people who had least reason, and who were quick to blame the circumstance of war: canteen helpers, shop assistants, post office people: safe, but discontented with wartime difficulties, they were taking hell out of those they were supposed to serve.

"You've filled the form in wrong. Look, there," an irritable finger. "I'll give you another. You'll have to go to the back of the queue."

"But it'll only take a second!"

"Stand aside please. Yes, sir?" A crook of the bullying neck.

There was no counting, either, the occasions of sloth and laziness, the evidences of dirtiness and sloppiness; of shortages triumphantly made excuses of in shops by assistants operating in a sellers' market.

"It's not a *pair*, the colour's different."

"Well, take it or leave it."

"Would *you* wear not a pair?"

"It's up to you."

"Will you have more in?"

"No. Very lucky to get *those*."

Prudence and Laura had collected their food.

"What a noise," Laura shouted.

It was difficult to talk. The food was heavy. Cheapness was its advantage. Soon they were to take lighter meals in smaller places: or sample less governmental recipes in Oxford Street department stores. Soon lunch times became their haven, their main time of meeting: for Prudence was placed in a section dealing with trucks, caterpillar tractors, lorries and the like, while Laura was introduced to the ubiquitous ball-bearing, a product needing a far more esoteric knowledge of engineering than she possessed to appreciate its all-embracing functions. For girls who had done arts degrees there was difficulty in making the work seem colourful.

A week or two later, they sat once more considering lunch.

"Omelette's safest."

"It'll be dried egg. Leather."

"Yes. Chips may be all right."

(In war as in peace the only ingredients needed for good chips are potatoes, hot oil and a modicum of skill: and perhaps this accounts for their rise to universal prominence in the war, the chips-with-everything syndrome.) They were in a little dive briefly and cruelly known as the Wop shop.

The term summed up harshly the prevailing attitude of the British to the Italians. Mussolini had been toppled from his position in July by King Victor Emmanuel, who had ordered his arrest and imprisonment, and had replaced him with General Badoglio. Italian Fascism disappeared with him. But after a month or so Mussolini had escaped, rescued by a German SS detachment, and had been flown to meet Hitler in Munich. He had been restored to a puppet's power and now operated under the giant dictator. Badoglio made speedy peace with the Allies: Italy Surrenders, shouted the *Evening News Late Extra*, of September the eighth. Unconditional Capitulation of all her Armed Forces. Whereupon the Germans in Rome disarmed the Italian troops and took over the city, and all other strategic points in Italy they could still defend. The Italian fleet surrendered too and entered Malta dramatically flying black pennants. With the Allied invasions of Salerno and Taranto in the following days, the long struggle for Italy had begun. No backbone, no backbone shrugged the average Englishman, of the traditionally peace-loving Italian soldier: and knowing nothing of the Italian resistance in the north.

The Italian girl in the Wop shop was as pale as a dishcloth. Here was she, cut off in what was till recently enemy country, living virtually below ground, cooking-oil her element. Now the Allies were pushing their way through her country and the Germans who had over-run it, destroying as they went. She could speak only café English: it was no wonder she could not smile at all. (Long after the war, Laura would recall her limp, sad face and hope she was a happy grandmother in the sun of her native land.)

"Two omelette. Ships," said this unsmiling girl, setting down their food.

"When am I going to meet your wonderful Mrs Wicklow?" Laura asked.

It was Prudence who had first met Mrs Wicklow, they were in the same room. When her conversation had been laced with warm references to this lady for several weeks, Laura's interest was impatient.

"We'll have lunch here, next week," Prudence promised.

Imogen Wicklow, Laura came soon to think, was the most beautiful, enviable, good-humoured, courageous married woman, of an age somewhere between the middle and late fifties that she had yet met. Ah, the truth was, everyone felt it, she was a superbly happy woman and her element was gratitude. Yet she was a widow. She was not tall, and had the soft amplitude of motherhood, her face and her plump hands still dimpled. Abundant heavy hair of a remarkable silvery brightness at the sides and in front was swept up to surmount a shapely neck. Her creamy, squarish face was of such characterful beauty that those who knew her waited, rapt, for the green eyes to light and sparkle below black humorously raised brows, the small straight nose to wrinkle at the nostrils, the red lips to be pursed into a most beguiling pout, before the whole countenance broke into abandoned laughter, and the teeth flashed as white as a child's. Her hair, one could tell from the back of her head, had been of that wiry raven black, with eagle glints, which graces many Scotto-Irish. Her tongue was still entrancingly Irish, her love and loyalty totally British. Left alone, with two sons fighting, a daughter working in England and another married, marooned in India, she must needs come to serve her country and help the war effort.

"*Four* months," Laura once exclaimed, "for four months Prudence and I sat about, waiting for our country to need us."

"Much more difficult when you're educated," said Mrs Wicklow with a pout. "You need to be uneducated. Like me," her laughter pealed. "No qualifications but goodwill," she said, out of her urbane, polished, privileged, cosmopolitan experience. Her husband had been in the Indian Civil Service, important and valued.

This, she reflected, was her main asset. He had been her main asset from start to finish, she thought (just as he would have affirmed that she was his). Their love, their wonderful, exciting, colourful life, their children, the eldest born in Patna; the people out there, both English and Indians that they had known! Yes, you made me, she still told him, I know it, I bless you, I love you. And hear him say, looking back on his life, nonsense it was you, my beautiful wife, who made us. In fact, they had made each other. He had been dead for several years now but never dead to her.

Imogen Wicklow came to love both the young women rather as she loved her own children. She loved their youth, their intelligence (it was true, all her education was acquired from a convent school or from life itself), their seriousness, even their terrible gloom, into which they would pull each other like devotees of some dark devilish power, interested and often amused her. They were so young: they enjoyed their gloom. To explode their gloom was unconsciously part of her war-effort. Out of her great contentment she kept her spirits undaunted, knowing how fortunate she had been. Out of her religion she drew unassailable hope and broadcast a kind of merry charity over the whole dreary, suffocating, seemingly pointless repetition of their office days.

She was shy and rather over-awed by these men put over her; modest, well aware that she was not clever in an office way, thinking that she was on sufferance in this world, perhaps because of her husband's service. As she padded along corridors in her flat-heeled soft leather slippers she would suddenly marvel that this was she, who had been visited by Rajahs carried upon elephants, and be grateful for this very different but diverting company.

For it was diverting, and endlessly diverse.

There was Daisy, who made the coffee with sparse teaspoonsful as if it had been tea, adding cold milk and proffering the resultant grey brew with a serious glance from pale blue eyes. "Have to spin it out," would apologise Daisy. There was cross-faced little Marie with a cap of fair hair, neat and charming as to body, who often typed for them and who was much older than one at first thought. "Well, I'll try. But not before lunch," grudged Marie. And the men, where had they come from, all these engineers, were they evicted from small firms turned over to the war effort, not amongst the lucky younger ones to be kept on? It was difficult to avoid this conclusion. Some boasted of what they had been engaged on earlier in the war. "More enlivening designing anti-aircraft missiles," said Alex Harvald with a proud sneer, whose hair was so fair that it was almost white. Some covered the knowledge that they were not first-rate by tight-lipped looks, silent and wise. Ted Watson, for instance. "We must ponder that possibility very well indeed," he would say, biting at his cigarette-holder even when it was empty, to aid thought, and disclosing small brown teeth in the smile of a conspirator. (There were times when he looked remarkably like Herr Hitler.) Irene Wainewright caught many of his smiles, perhaps because her father was an engineering magnate, perhaps because Mr Watson and she were alike for size. They used to walk out arm-in-arm for lunch like two dolls from a twin box, but the one more than twice the age of the other. "Hell, I don't know what I'm doing here, for God's sake," Irene Wainewright would very often drawl.

The head himself, Mr Wheedon, was a shadowy figure too important to emerge, seen only in interview, or upon rare meetings of the whole department when he would oil his cogs along towards greater efficiency.

"I sometimes think of you…I'd like you to think of yourselves, as my smooth-running, well-oiled, multiple machine tool," smiled Mr Wheedon.

At which metaphor Laura looked at Prudence with incomprehension turning to horror: and Prudence smiled her gentle, conciliatory, amused, detached smile.

11

After about six weeks they were slubbed into a clumsy fabric with all the other curiously different bundles of temperament and capability, enmeshed in an artificial wartime weave supposed to be achieving something. Sorting out numberless typed slips of paper, intelligence messages with sources "reliable", "new", "doubtful", "poor", from places all along the northern coast of the continent, in Belgium and Holland and France: names which one recognised as resorts, where before both wars wheeled machines with striped awnings carried becostumed ladies and shivering little girls into the sea: or names which were centres of industry in the 'thirties: names of districts, or remote villages, acquiring because of this traffic a perverse, frightening romance. Laura would shudder at the vision of a humble countryman in a village such as theirs had been in Suffolk, risking his neck to hand on observations, spied on by a smart collaborator, seized, tortured by the Gestapo, her mind winced with the terror of it. While Prudence who sometimes floated a dream of research in Paris after the war, wondered if she would ever pass these places in the train, freed and innocent once more, and think, there lived that persistent fellow who told us the same thing every time. They developed an instinct for when a report was a repeat.

Meanwhile they sorted, synthesised, indexed; were asked to present overall pictures of material already known about; had these reports typed and retyped, gave them to their superiors who sent them upstairs or to the Americans: forgot about them, went on to something else. Increasingly often, there was not enough to do. (Matthew Tate, it was said, on the floor above them, was writing a novel under his blotter.) A regular, dull office existence. About matters of life and death.

For it could not be said in late 1943 that the tide had yet properly turned. Buoyed up by belief in their cause, by Churchill's staunchness and rhetoric, by judicious propaganda, and by the sagacious under-emphasis of disasters which all protagonists practised, the Allies knew they were going to win the war but knew it by faith. They had known it thus from the start.

Day shuttled after day, weaving unlikely relationships as people shared offices, lunches, shopping trips or evening entertainments. Miss Richardson on her thin legs and rather large feet had approached Laura soon after her arrival and smiling said, "Will you have lunch with me today? I know a nice place off Oxford Street." Miss Richardson twisted her long yellow nose like the mandible of some monkey as she nervously laughed. She lived alone it seemed, and on evenings when she could afford it she went to a certain restaurant, people had seen her there, to worship the performer of the saxophone with whom she dreamed herself passionately in love.

It was appalling how mean life was to so many. Mrs Patricia Tripp, for instance, as well. Exiled from sunny Malta. Mourning it with repeated wailing. Particularly on days like this one, not long before Christmas, of a deep, bone-searching, desolating grey.

"Oh this grey," burst out poor Mrs Tripp in a real rage, slamming down some typing late in the morning. "I wish I were in Malta! Always, nearly always sunny, however brisk you know!"

"Poor you," said Laura.

Her husband had leapt into the air force, tugging her along too. She seldom saw him, she might just as well have stayed in the sun. With her parents, who were ageing. She had no children. But she was fiercely, volubly, proud of him. A pilot.

The phone rang. Secret glances at watches. Twelve-thirty. Marie. Who had come in from the typing room by chance. No one took it, so she supposed she had better. Her face unscrewed.

"Yes," she said. "About one."

The minute she put it down it pounced again, lying in wait. "Miss Cardew?" it said.

"Yes she's here, Mr Wheedon," Marie said deferentially.

"Ask Miss Cardew if she will kindly step along and see me before lunch," it said, clicking itself off magisterially.

"Wants to see you. Now," Marie said to Laura.

"Why on earth?" Laura asked them, going

"Come in, sit down," said he. "How are you getting on?"

"All right, thank you," Laura said, noncommittally.

"Finding it interesting?"

What a suggestion. "Oh yes," Laura lied.

"So now I want to take you off it," he said, perversely jokish, "to something much more vital. But secret. Top secret. I want to put you on the secret weapon."

A fascinating ride, thought Laura. He enlarged upon what they all knew about it. Two weapons, there were, would be, stories had got into the papers. Had not Hitler, even at the invasion of Poland, threatened the use of secret weapons?

"I must be sure though that you won't speak of this work at any time to anyone, not even within your family. What does your family consist of, Miss Cardew?"

"My mother and my sister. She's in the army."

"Then she will perfectly understand. I have to have your assurance now as well as that general undertaking when you joined. And are you willing to work over Christmas? They all are," he threatened. Christmas was the weekend after next. Flattered, and amused thereby, Laura gave her assurances without considering.

"Good. The People Upstairs have already managed to identify and bomb some of the launching sites. We shall be pressing on with this as top priority. The secret band is in the room opposite yours. Join them on Monday. Thank you, Miss Cardew," said he.

"I hear we're losing you," said Mr Watson to Laura, oh very knowingly, winking a slow wink as he went into Irene's room to take her to lunch. Laura remained clamped shut, wink or no wink, she felt as if she would never speak again.

"Why don't you take the General?" Kitty Cardew said, over breakfast, rather late, on the Saturday before Christmas, afraid that Laura would make heavy weather of it. Laura did.

"Oh, Mamma," looking at her watch.

"You've kept saying you will, you never have, he'd so love to see him." The General was the ageing family dog. It seemed to be all that she could suggest that might give pleasure. All she could offer, which was so odd and sad. Laura looked at the General, tawny like a lion, lying in a minute square of sun near the cooker, all the sun there was on his silk ears. The dog had started off as a wild, highly-strung rapscallion of a Welsh sheep dog crossed with collie, his sober character as the General had developed with age.

Laura was going to see her father. They usually worked on Saturday mornings, but by dint of overtime each evening, and all the more now in view of Christmas, Laura was taking the morning off to go and see poor Papa who would have goodness knows what sort of Christmas. (He would protest he did not mind, it was all in his view overdone, a pagan festival, a Roman festival, a Teutonic festival, what you will, it varied with Papa's current obsession: the Christian part submerged.)

"It must be three and a half years," her mother said, doing the sum unnecessarily yet again. "Since he saw him."

"All right. I will. Gamage," she said in the exciting high voice, which meant promise. "You're coming!" General Gamage's claws slithered upon the lino as he leapt up.

"Shall I get a bus or a tube to Gunnersbury?"

"A tube. To Acton Town," said Kitty, who knew her London since her girlhood.

"Goodbye darling," Kitty said, as the dog jostled the girl out of the gate by the mulberry tree. She wished Laura would kiss her. "It's no good my sending any messages."

"No. Goodbye, darling," Laura called, aware of not being able to kiss her mother. She could kiss no one lately, she wanted only one person's kisses and he the man she had loved and lost. "Can't think when home," she sang shorthandedly.

In the train, the General though large made himself small against her knee like a sack of coal, heavy. Various people admired him. I wonder if he knows. Who he is going to see. Animals are so psychic, I wonder if he knows. Papa, Papa, Papa: the train in a rhythmic rattle. Laura, the dog heavy at her knee, wondering what they should talk about. Well, there were presents for him, a few minor things. There was the good old General. Not her new work, silence, total. The office, otherwise? Her friend, Prudence? A little. Mrs Imogen Wicklow? A charming Irishwoman, two sons fighting, a Roman Catholic, she screamed in her mind. Outrage. A Roman Catholic? Fury. Mrs Wicklow would not do. It was difficult working out what to talk to Papa about. So many subjects aroused fury, scorn, outrage, so much was taboo.

It was better to leave it to chance.

It was sad, it was pathetic, yes, but it was of his own making. Was it? It depended in what proportions you thought people were at the mercy of their inherited qualities, their upbringing, and their circumstances. Despite quite conscious attempts not to become bitter about the long, slow, inescapable spoiling of their family life, the iron unfreedom of their childhood (for it all went back as far as she and Marian could remember and further) Laura was aware of a kind of brittle, comical cynicism about her father, in uneasy harness with the certain love engendered in childhood, now wryly inhibited and disillusioned, but still love. Why otherwise did she journey towards their meeting in such helpless pain? For as they grew up, when they became reasonable creatures detached from their cage, moving amongst friends with normal families, happy parents, they had so often to explain their father's old-fashioned, hide-bound, unreasonable attitudes: and in self-defence resorted to the comic and cynical. But, as Laura increasingly knew, her father's situation was not comical.

Laurence Cardew, handsome, passionate, sensitive, artistic and endowed with more intelligence than his sparse education had ever uncovered, was the victim of a religious absolutism implanted in him in late teens by a much older devotee, who being captivated by the young man's charms had found him empty, open, searching, idealistic. Laurence's parents were nominally Church of England but uncaring, and their attitude had not allowed him the higher education which would have produced enlightenment and liberal-mindedness. His sisters they educated not at all after their dame schools, save in sewing and domesticity, while their son went early into his father's printing business in a small Suffolk town. While there, before he had time to pursue and enlarge his own education, in fields such as literature and history and poetry and painting which would have delighted him, he fell under the power of this bearded patron, a Victorian prude, an evangelical die-hard, an un-denominational man who nonetheless flirted with most brands of non-conformity, allying himself briefly here and there while he attacked deadness in the Church of England, worldliness, heresy and far worse in the Church of Rome, the Whore of Babylon, the Scarlet Woman. All this, as he lacked any other, became the motive force of Laurence's life. His authoritarian God towered over him, demanding a narrow, definable, stringent right. As he grew older he became the definer of this rightness for everyone in his world. When anyone questioned his right to define right, he turned and snarled, and dealt with the situation very speedily by dropping them. The rightness was not simply to do with what one thought about religion, God, Christianity, which in any event by Laurence's day could never be simple and in fact never had been. It was to do with common life. Very little was found to be right except an extreme puritan simplicity, a great deal was wrong, was taboo. Worldliness of any kind was wrong, which covered most things: high living was wrong, fine clothes were wrong, drinking and smoking were wrong, all kinds of acting were wrong, so it followed that the cinema was wrong, and even dressing-up was (almost) wrong; novels (except Dickens) were usually wrong, paintings (particularly nudes) were shamingly wrong, poetry was mostly suspect, anything pleasurable must be examined carefully to find out where it was wrong: (for it assuredly would be). Sex was the worst wrong of all.

No one knew, Kitty could not reconstruct, his two daughters had not the detailed material of his early life to investigate, to define, as they grew older, the complex reasons for Laurence's fascination, fear, horror of and revulsion towards sex. But those reasons must be more than just the attitudes of his late Victorian boyhood.

One could suggest many reasons. Laura thought he had a buried homosexuality he was never aware of.

Beautiful Kitty, gentle, loving and talented, early fatherless and taught no profession, counted off the boys she had known, slaughtered in the First World War, upon her ten fingers. She married Laurence towards the end of it, fifteen years older than she, and very soon realised her mistake. A living, sparse, was always made from the printing, and all the more when Laurence's parents died early. But Kitty discovered a talent for storytelling and supplemented the family income, keeping herself independent, by the spinning of thousands of romantic, or humorous, or touching or homely tales for newspapers and women's magazines. The two girls went to the grammar school in the town. Kitty paid the fees.

Laura always thought what brought things to a head in June 1940 was the fact that she, the youngest, was soon to leave school and home; moreover, the jolly trio of warm East Enders, evacuated at such trouble and expense to their Suffolk village with hundreds more in 1939, who had cut across Laurence's defences by loving him, dashing at him, treating him like an older father, a granddad perhaps, taking his affection (long dammed-up) for granted, were now to be whisked away because this was too near the coast. This would leave him alone with Kitty. Also, surely, he was fearful, he was panic-stricken, at the thought of the possible invasion. As the Spitfires over the east coast screamed chalky splintered trails in the blue 1940 sky, his whole life full of fears and depressions came at him screaming. Laurence left the printing works to his good manager Mr Butt, but continued to live upon it; left his family to their own (evil) devices (for a very long time his wife had been to him the enemy, the persecutor, the perpetrator of evil) and retreated to one London suburb after another, pursued by suppressed guilt and bombs. Laura and Marian tried to keep in touch with him. Laura managed best, as he had always been gentler to her. Laura suffered much resentment on her mother's account, yet felt how terrible it was to be her father, wandering in this wilderness, at bay, in this self-made implacable trap. (For her mother was not an enemy at all, was as sweet as honey, full of love, and with no wish to persecute.) Her mother was invincibly romantic, not only because of her Edwardian girlhood, all Tolstoy and Francis Thompson, but because of the make of her, an unworldly shine upon her. He had let all her expectations down. She now accepted that he could not help it, and went on believing in romantic love, wrote it into her stories and prayed for it for her daughters.

A year or two later, she left the Suffolk village and came to London herself, to another suburb, because it would be easier to find different work to supplement the story-telling, as all the magazines dwindled with the dwindling of paper.

Laura saw him before he saw her (she did not yet know how punctual the lonely always are) standing on the grass near to the old golf course by the chestnuts. She and Marian had trailed round caddying for Uncle Miles and Papa, rewarded only by the chestnuts, bright, damp, rich brown treasure. This was long ago, when they used to stay with Uncle Miles's family, before Papa more or less dropped Mamma's brother Uncle Miles. He looked trim and upright as he always did, in the mushroom-coloured Burberry over his dark suit, the grey trilby with the black band.

He looked round. His tawny hair as she first remembered it had long been grey, now it was white. He was not expecting her to be with the dog. He soon recognised them. The dog was taut like steel, pulling. He began to yelp. Within a few paces she dropped the lead.

The dog flew in one bound. He leapt. Waist high. Shoulder high. He leapt. To the brim of the hat. His great flapping red tongue all over Papa's face, Papa laughing, warding him off but welcoming. Papa's very blue eyes glittering.

"All right, all right, down, down old fellow. Hullo," said Papa, shy, blustery, laughing. Laura's eyes glittered too. Oh why cannot I fling myself at Papa and hug him as a child? She longed for the animal's simplicity.

"Hullo. Isn't he pleased?" The dog danced and shrieked, panting.

"You didn't say you were bringing him."

"Mamma suggested it, last minute."

"How is she, how's your mother?"

"All right, thanks."

Years later Marian said to Laura, you know why, don't you, you know why Gamage loved Pa so much? He rescued him. That time he was giving those lectures, some ghastly Christian lectures, in north London. He saw him from the top of the bus, week after week, in a tiny yard, tied up. We went and offered to buy him, I was staying with Uncle Miles. They just let us buy him. You must remember. Laura remembered the dog's arrival, his wild unruly joy at being free; she remembered that he had been rescued. But this sharp, vivid picture like a film shot, of the dog in the yard from the top of the bus, and Marian's part in it, she did not remember hearing. Strange lacunae occur in communications within the closest families.

After their walk, they went out to a place for lunch. (Last Christmas she and Marian had come together, as Marian had convenient leave. They had walked up Piccadilly, Laura lithe and dark, Marian taller and pale, with her copper beech hair, one on each side of the handsome man in the grey trilby. Everybody had looked at them, swinging with the same walk along the bright clean pavement, the same family face, all three tall, yet the man too old surely to be the girls' father. They had walked right along to Kensington, to the Serpentine, to feed the seagulls. Not the ducks, Papa stipulated, they got everything. The seagulls. With sprats, thrown in the air. Just like when they were children, staying with Uncle Miles. It must have reminded him of earlier days, he must surely have thought of it.)

"Well, how's your work?"

"So secret I can't tell you! Got to work over Christmas too."

"Really?" He was pleased. "Any more interesting?"

"In a horrid way."

Laura told him funny things about the office, how two of the men had a feud, shouted at each other; they talked of her aunt, his eldest sister, whom she regularly saw but had not seen lately.

And of other members of the family on Mamma's side with whom he had not yet quarrelled. He was busy, writing pamphlets, he had always written pamphlets, so handy to be able to print them himself. He was giving a few lectures. He thought of writing another book. (His book had been full of polemic, anti-everything, Laura had been paid one farthing per mistake, reading the proofs at the age of eight.)

"I hope you're not working yourself to death," she said.

"Why not? Quite the best way to die," said Papa. "Drop in one's tracks."

He was proud of her, with her degree, though he never said so. If you have any brains they're mine, he once declared. He was uneasily convinced that Oxford would contaminate her, ruin her "faith": which it had. He did not know the first blows had already been delivered well before Oxford, which perfected the process. She was wily in concealing the fact. This was one reason why they got on all right, Laura's diplomacy.

⚜

Prudence sat waiting for the telephone, for when Laura was ready. This Thursday they were to have their Christmas lunch, for she was taking tomorrow off (feeling guilty because of Laura working). She hoped she would hear about Laura's meeting with her father.

Laura rang.

"Prudence. I feel so ill. I've got iller and iller. I left it till now, I hoped I'd feel all right, but I think I'm light-headed, I feel hot."

"Goods heavens. You're getting this flu."

"I'm so sorry, I shall have to go home. Oh, *Prudence*. A happy Christmas."

"Thank you. Shall I come with you to Victoria, poor thing? It's no good my wishing *you* one. Either way," said Prudence, in brisk comical summary.

"No, I'll manage. Oh Prudence, I'm so sorry. Goodbye."

Up the hill she walked in a daze behind ancient, slow Mr Simpson, thin as a stick, yellow as parchment, his pointed nose always hung with a dewdrop. It was, even now.

"Merry Christmas," said Laura, hustling past him.

"The same to you," quavered Dewdrop accusingly. It was his magnifying spectacles that produced this impression. Also his evident mistrust of youth.

By the bus stop beyond the sobered Ritz, Mr Gorzinska hovered, Mr Gorzinska, never happy, and worse since Katyn, which froze his heart but not his manners.

In a forest near the Polish village of Katyn in April this year, the occupying Germans announced they had found the bodies of thousands of Polish officers, shot in the head, their hands tied, and claimed these must be victims of the Soviet secret police. The Russians preserved silence but would have nothing to do with the Red Cross enquiry the Polish government appealed for, and broke off relations. They blamed the Germans. Most Poles blamed the Russians. No one knew the cold truth.

Very soon after this a desperate last battle had been fought by a small band of Jews in the Warsaw ghetto against the systematic destruction and deportation of their fellows. They had fought for almost a month in the cellars and sewers of the city. They were necessarily overwhelmed. They died fighting or were shot, and the remaining thousands of Polish Jews were sent off to labour or concentration camps.

The rumours of these terrible events had wounded Mr Gorzinska to his heart, which seemed now only to be occupied by a silent scream. But he had mourned with actual sudden tears the death of General Sikorski (prime minister of the exiled Polish government in London and a hero to him) when he was killed in an air crash off Gibraltar.

Laura tripped, clumsily hurrying. He caught her.

"Miss Cardew, take care, you look ill, my dear young lady. What is it?"

"I *feel* ill. I feel so ill, Mr Gorzinska, I'm going home. And I'm supposed to be working over Christmas," she panted.

"I think not. Which bus? This one, good."

He helped her on, a hand under her arm. He bowed, at the flushed face turning to say thank you. He was immensely, classically handsome, modestly debonair; Laura was too ill to notice how he sprang forward as the bus swung away. It was his bus too. He shrugged his shoulders sadly and turned to walk over the park.

At Clapham Junction she ran, up the stairs and down again, she was missing a connection. She dashed to the train hearing the whistle, some kind man opened a door, her feet were on the step, her hands clutched the door, but her bag! Her bag had slipped from her shoulder, was wedged between left foot and train. She could not move the foot to get in without her bag dropping on to the line. The train was gathering speed, the occupants of the carriage could not see the difficulty. The guard blew the whistle again, and ran furiously along as the train stopped. Oh, what an awful thing to happen. She felt so ill she could not even feel foolish, or diminished by the condemnatory stares of other passengers. She sat with her head in her collar, her wretched bag on her knees, her eyes closed, feeling at a remove from everything.

"Lolly!" said Kitty, astonished. "You do look ill."

Into the semi-sleep that engulfed her, over-heated by Kitty's hot-water bottles and made nightmarish with compulsive re-enactments of running for the train and *not* dropping the bag—into this burrowed the telephone bell like a horrifying yellow caterpillar. Kitty came creeping up the stairs.

"Are you awake? It's that Tom, that rather nice Canadian fellow—"

Laura groaned.

"I'll tell him you're too ill, shall I?"

"I'll come. Make him hold on."

Violent heat overcame her, she flung off the clothes: violent chill set in as she put her feet to the ground. She pulled the eiderdown round her and descended.

"Tom—"

"Laura! You sound terrible—You shouldn't have got out of bed— I'm sorry—"

"I'm practical delirium delirious—"

"Lord. It was just to suggest a Christmas drink—"

"I'm meant to be working all over Christmas—"

"Not a hope. Go back at once—"

"Ring again soon?"

"Sure. Is that your teeth I hear chattering? Go back girl, go back, sorry I called just now. Goodbye." He rang off quickly.

Laura's demented dreams took for a while a new turn. Tom, Rosamund Turner's quiet, comical, amused Canadian cousin. Presiding over them all, the only man, much older than they, at Rose's twenty-first party. Six excited young women being plied with wine in the Mitre before going to *The Magic Flute*. A good dinner, melon came into it, oh don't think of sickening food. Crimson shaded lamps, suddenly blurring and swaying. Up some stairs somewhere, a table for seven, the waiter chasing up and down, Tom with his centurion's face twinkling at them all, steel-rimmed spectacles, very black hair, very pale olive-skinned face, a thin Roman nose, straight lips over brilliant regular teeth. Tom, don't give me any more I think I'm drunk. What! Look at me, by golly, so you are, your pupils! Rosy, black coffee for all. Watch out going down those old-world stairs. I'll take this one, what's her name, Laura, I'll take Laura. Up came the stairs at one, most extraordinary. The first time I ever was drunk swinging about with the crimson lamps at Rosamund's party. Fair Rosamund and Henry the Second and the maze at Godstowe. A story, I made up a story for us fire-watchers huddled on camp-beds in the belly of the Bodleian, blue lights, dusty smell, metal book-racks. But it is Gavin helping me down the stairs, these are his long, gentle fingers beneath my armpit! If I turn now, I want to turn now, to lay my head on his breast, it will be beloved Gavin; my clever, affectionate teacher, for whom I long, I long with passion, and cannot have.

The memory of Gavin awoke her, she groaned. Saw him rush up the dusty stairs two at a time, she waiting outside the door: saw him sweep off the mortar board (had he been at some committee? More likely lecturing), swish the gown in a Walter Ralegh gesture of apology. My dear, my dear girl, I'm so sorry. Felt his hand between her shoulder blades, propelling her gently into his rooms. There, five minutes late, forfeit, pay five kisses. It was the first time the light and frivolous kisses had been bestowed upon her cheek. The remembered joy welled within her and came out in a great sob.

Kitty heard the sob. "Lolly? Are you all right?" she called.

"Feel so ill," Laura sobbed helplessly like a child.

Laura had never had 'flu. She ached for three days as she had never ached before, deciding that no Christmas and the secret weapon would have been much better than this.

"You are not to pump her about the work," Kitty said to Marian, when Laura was better, "it isn't fair."

"I'll get it out of her," said Marian, determined. But she failed.

24

3

Tea," explained Edwin Kyle, knocking at his daughter's bedroom door with the excessively modest tap, the fingernail dance, which his Scottish sense of propriety and shyness afforded her since she was eight years old.

"Tea," he repeated in a low tone, once more, entering. She looked scarcely older now, her round sweet face very pink, her burnished Botticelli hair all over the pillow in its wavy long strands, her breathing deep, quiet, scarcely audible. Fast asleep. Never seen her faster. Tired, with this office trek every day.

"Tea," he said more loudly. He stood for a long half-minute, for sometimes another presence at hand worked. It did not. What should he do? Lay hands on her any longer, as in the delicious girl-child days, he would not. Much as he longed to, would enjoy it, the pleasure of tickling her. But she was a woman. He looked round the comfortable room, and coughed. His eye fell on a piece of headgear she had worn as the White Rabbit. Long floppy ears. Not big enough but all the more ridiculous, made him feel in the mood.

Edwin Kyle, rigid, sombre, and caustic, escaped from the repression of a Wee Free childhood near Oban by virtue of his fairly formidable intelligence, loved slapstick. Loved to be jolted into laughter, nothing he liked more than a farce at the theatre, opening his tight-shut laughter like a jack-in-the-box.

"Chairmany calling, this is Chairmany calling," he began, in the much loathed, singsong Irish genteel of Lord Haw Haw.

Prudence stirred, then relapsed.

"Chairmany calling, this is Chairmany calling, how many more times must Chairmany call?"

Prudence began to shake, to open her eyes, to splutter. Pop, in the rabbit head.

"He doesn't have fur ears," she gasped through her giggles.

"There's no knowing what he has. Wake up. Don't go off again. Tea. Then *get up*."

She groaned.

"Oh I can't. Must I? Do I have to?"

"If you can engage in polemic you're awake."

Now she lay laughing the helpless amused laugh he waited for.

The things he said, how they tickled her. She modelled her own repartee on them, unaware.

He flung the rabbit head at her and stalked stiffly out in his shirtsleeves, thin and taut. Then a huge laugh burst out, which Margery heard from the kitchen.

"Eddie? What is it?"

"Waking Prudence."

Margery giggled over the cooker. She liked it when he laughed, he did it so seldom. His angular granite face which gave away nothing, his sparkling grey eye that gave away much. They would have breakfast together before they left her. If only Donald were here, not in the training camp.

Prudence went in on a bus. Pop had gone by tube a quarter of an hour before her. To the Board of Trade. She clambered up to the top by the metal stairs, heels clattering. There was only one seat left, she almost turned to go down. But the bus had started, and was swaying. She sat down next to a thick, soft RAF overcoat spread over most of the seat.

"I'm sorry," he said, "these things make us much fatter than we are." And gathered it in. "A good thing you are so slim." The compliment was uncalculating, natural, in a gentle, deprecatory voice.

Prudence smiled her sweet shy smile, told him not to worry.

"And what do you do, in this battle to the death? Forgive me, I always talk to people, do you mind? It feels a waste not to."

Prudence was startled at his first sentence: it was as if it came from miles away and he stood calmly outside it all.

"Intelligence," she said. "Enemy production." Surely that did not break her pledge.

"Ah. I daresay you tell our boys what to bomb."

"Are you a bomber pilot?"

"Fighter." He did not say so, but in fact he was one of the very rare survivors, one of the first of the few. His profile was composed, ageless. He was not young as she was young. His hair was light brown and chunky. Prudence, very reserved, seldom talked to people travelling. But,

"You're all so brave," she blurted.

"No, I'm very un-brave. But I believe in what we fight for. I believe in freedom, truth. And all. I believe in God. Or I couldn't be any good at it, couldn't think it worth it." He spoke assessingly. This she could not answer. What an innocent, pristine, serious girl. Her thoughts were on her face. From the Kyle household God—(that Wee Free God, head of the remnant of a supposedly Free Church of Scotland, the most unfree organisation ever invented Edwin would spit out)—God had been excluded. Real freedom, yes, truth, yes, the strictest, noblest, ethical principles in all directions. But God?

"How can you be so sure?" She realised he waited.

"About what?"

"About God."

"I know that my Redeemer liveth," said he. But it did not sound like a quotation (which she thought it was). He said it in a low tone for which she was grateful, and conversationally. Yet with some excitement.

"What did you do before the intelligence?"

"A degree. History, mostly medieval."

"Then not knowing about God must have bothered you."

She giggled, touché. He was pleased.

"*Arsenic and Old Lace*," he said next, seeing a poster of the West End show, "have you seen it?"

"My father heard it's very funny."

"My great-aunt, on the other hand, a considerable age, could stick no more than the first act. She screwed up her face at me and said *Owch*, no." He turned his head and performed the imitation very comically, which made Prudence laugh.

"Oh, I hope it's funny. Pop so loves to be made to laugh."

"A good thing, to laugh." He spoke as if all these things had been consciously given up already. Relinquished. That was it, he had got himself ready to die, Prudence thought with a sense of coldness.

"I was going to offer to take you," he said, "since I never saw the last two acts."

"Oh, how kind of you. Pop's taking us," she said simply. She did not even think to herself that Laura would have concealed this fact. They talked of other shows. He, too, enjoyed Robertson Hare, as her father did. They talked of the war, of the Allies stuck at the Gustav line.

"It's a pity we can't seem to make Rome," he said, "despite of Anzio. What will you do? After the war?" He asked the question as if it were of profound interest, an urgent question. As if he built up a picture of a place where he would never be.

"Research first."

"Ah, then, you're clever. What about?"

"Not sure yet. It'll be someone, something in the twelfth century. Not Peter Abelard," she said, for most people knew him as a landmark, "but a little later."

"Ah." He sighed. "As you're clever, you must believe 'in the supernatural striving of a mind'?"

Prudence half turned. "Of course. Though what exactly does it mean? It's John Pudney, isn't it?" she said.

"Of course," he echoed. "Our air force voice."

Laura had lent her the last book of poems, published the year before: not a great poet, but a poet who spoke quite astonishingly accurately for a whole group.

"I like the one about the radio word, too."

"Truth in every season there must speak steadfast"?

"That's the one," she said. "I get off here," she added apologetically.

"Goodbye. Thank you for talking to me," he smiled his calm smile. "I shall remember it."

"Goodbye," she said, moved.

When I die, he thought, as I assuredly must soon, this luck can't go on, I shall remember you, golden girl, you and your companions for whom I fight. (But when it came to it, there was not time, he remembered only his parents and his God.)

He lingered, he lingered in Prudence's mind. His face kept re-appearing all through the morning, with its bright calmness that was not resignation, but readiness, a positive quality. She did not think she would be able to tell Mum and Pop. It wanted talking about, even for self-contained Prudence.

"I met the most beautiful RAF man on the bus," suddenly stated Prudence, seeing Mrs Wicklow sitting back, gathering her papers, preparing for lunch. She looked at Prudence over her half-spectacles, her amused mouth red and pursed.

"So," she said. "Go on."

"A fighter pilot. He said I know that my Redeemer liveth. He said he couldn't do any of it if he didn't believe in God."

Mrs Wicklow could not be expected to be surprised. She looked at Prudence smiling.

"Of course not."

"I think he knew he was going to die."

Laura had come in to fetch Prudence and was listening.

"They many of them do," Imogen said. "It is on their faces."

Loyalty to her father came at Prudence like a hot wind.

"But I don't know how you can be a Christian," said Prudence flushed and worried, all the horrors of Christian history assaulting her. Mrs Wicklow's square cream face, Laura noted, looked momentarily affronted. Then it broke into smiles, and a peal of laughter followed.

"I don't know how you can't," she told them, motherly. "Where are you off to?"

"Myra Hess. Will you come?"

"No, meeting Willy. Off you go."

From all over London people converged upon the National Gallery, sacrificing their lunch, or gobbling a sandwich, to have the healing joy of hearing Myra Hess play Bach. Other noble soloists gave lunch-time concerts to weary Londoners, but perhaps the most memorable were these.

"Let's walk," Laura said. "Who were you telling Mrs Wicklow about?"

Prudence told Laura about him too.

"But how wonderful," Laura said, delighted at the pilot's faith. Laura was to spend most of her life delighted by other people's faith. Battening on it, in lieu of her own. Looking at the stars had cut Laura off from the intimate, simple faith of her childhood and her parents. Looking at the stars one summer night, as on so many innocent nights before. But suddenly, seventeen and still at school, filled with wonder and reduced to a pin-prick, the stars severed her, snip, with a pair of silver scissors from any sense of that comfort, stranded her at a vast distance away from it on her own, as she sensed her child's "God" recede yet not unkindly, like a receding star: implanting in her for ever the thirst and necessity to search. For whatever truth was. To get back. This by no means resulted in her no longer believing in "God": simply that the subject presented itself as a dark, perpetual magnetic mystery, not a near-at-hand source of comfort, strength or guidance capable of being familiarly known. She and Marian thought it was the result of having God thrust upon them.

Whereas, Prudence had grown up almost being forbidden God, certainly being deprived of God. Within a framework of strict rectitude, duty, neighbourliness, and family affection. With the highest ethics, a clinical, antiseptic absence of God prevailed. Her studies, as the flying officer said, made her wonder. There was a kind of aching emptiness, she sensed, behind her parents' lives. Both young women now occupied a stance of bewildered slightly pained agnosticism. (Once when Laura sent Prudence an illuminated manuscript card of a small dejected medieval lady in a cheerless cart, depicting the soul on its journey through life, Prudence was entranced: I know the feeling so well, she wrote.) When they realised they had reached the same place from opposite ends of experience they were mildly amused.

"What was his name? I hope you're seeing him again?" Laura said.

Prudence tossed her gold head, laughed into the air. Laura's absorbed interest in men made her laugh, but lovingly. She had not reached it, herself. She supposed she would marry sometime: it did not concern her yet.

'I don't know his name. He tried to take me to *Arsenic*, but Pop's taking us.'

"Prudence," Laura said shocked. "What a waste."

They looked down upon the depleted pigeons waddling below, short of food, and up to Nelson brooding upon his country's fate, again in the balance: then walked up the steps, to the gallery where the concerts were held.

Gavin Kitto saw them come, his surprise rose in his throat almost aloud, but caution made him quickly shrink into his corner seat, ready to bow his head or raise his newspaper, to take evading tactics. Laura Cardew. Little Laura. No doubt of it, but much thinner, much paler, with already that war-tired look. He had always thought she looked melancholy, which was why the blaze of joy he had unwittingly caused had so moved and flattered him. Well. It was not so surprising to see her, he believed she lived near London, she probably worked here. She was with a taller, fair girl. He longed just to stride quickly over and say Laura! How good to see you, how are you, what are you doing…all brisk and warm and casual. Caution prevented him and the concert began. With a conscious effort he stopped remembering Laura and listened attentively to Bach who heals all. He had grown up playing, his mother was a pianist, but his talent was not great enough and too much else intervened.

She was going to play to them several of the preludes and fugues, they stepped off quietly into the first and it was a park and a Palladian building, or perhaps a series of Palladian buildings. In his mind Gavin found himself walking up flights of wonderful shallow marble steps, the kind of steps which lead up to Italian cathedrals, modest roseate cathedrals in little towns, not overwhelming, but warmly gracious. Now he was approaching a fine country house with regular windows and curved steps up from each side to the open door on the first floor; smooth stone balusters, stone parapets above top windows with architraves. And water, water falling with controlled energy over shallow, stepped falls, water rampant, water flying sky-high from immense fountains. Sometimes one was in a garden, green and ebullient, bosoms of soft trees in gentle May colours, temples on islands in lakes, all calmness, energy and jollity.

Laura. Laura Cardew was here. The discomfort of the knowledge that he had hurt her had now in an interval come uppermost again. It was anathema to him to hurt anything, and he thought he had quite badly hurt a young girl.

When the war started and he knew that his eventual call-up was inevitable, the thought of having to fight and kill people had thrown this young scholar into a turmoil, which nearly overwhelmed him. As the time approached, he must find some reserved war-work suitable to his talents or be ready to volunteer. It was during the ensuing earthquake of feelings, of wondering where to turn, his wife totally engrossed with their first child and un-free for her husband's conflict and need, that he met Laura, sent to him for some special subject teaching in her third year. Eager, articulate, "spirituelle", with the cautious air of a young animal just let out of a cage and about to frisk (for her father's defection had taken the lid off for Laura) she touched him, interested him with the things she said, the ideas she put forward.

Laura's fault was that she fell in love with him, his mind, his wit, his quiet gentleness. Her days and nights were soon full of the vision of that charming smooth face, anguished in thought, the wide, generous mouth, eyebrows arching suddenly above greyish hazel eyes, the bright, errant gold hair, the encouraging kindness of his manner. She was in awe of him, as undergraduates very often are in awe of their tutors, even those relatively young. She did not therefore show her feelings save by becoming sometimes tongue-tied, shy, and unduly distressed by criticism. He was unaware of the depth of her feeling, though allowing the adoration in her eyes to warm as much as amuse him, until a day when she dissolved into tears, confessing herself unable to explain why when he patiently and kindly asked her. He should have rung up her tutor as soon as she had shuffled down his stairway, and suggested she would be better with someone else. But it was only for a few more weeks and he had not the heart.

By the end of the term, he was greeting her with an endearment, an arm about the shoulder, a joke as he helped her unwind her limitless scarf. Finally a rather loving kiss. She was bringing small tributes like a cat to its master; a flower, a piece of chocolate ration, a printed broadside dug out at Blackwell's, a slice of the cake from home. Her body bloomed, her brain sparkled, her eyes danced, her small teeth shone. It will finish with the term and the vacation in between. So he says to himself bitterly, the more since at the end of June he is to leave Oxford for the duration whatever it might be and disappear into the rigours or languors of the war effort. The thought makes his stomach turn. When he has to say: this is no good you know, little Laura, I am a happy married man with a son: by then it is too late. She is half-seas over in a devouring, consuming love (the way prepared by various calf-loves before) a whole and ordinary love, not just pupil adoring master. A yawning and demanding hollow ever-hungrier lives inside her, unfed and uncalmed. All the worse that by now she thinks she knows he is well roused also and for two pins would sport his oak, draw the curtains and lead his willing captive to the sofa. But Gavin thanks heaven for the close of term, and playfully, firmly refuses any plans for the future.

Next term Laura fails to get a first, eats her heart out for four months waiting for her country to need her and finally lands up with the unsuitable employment she now pursues. The fire still burns steadily inside her, there are times when simply to know it burns is enough. But she feels a consuming need to search for someone who will make her feel as he has done, who will eclipse that fire, one fire puts out another. She has felt the warmth of the beginning of a great mutual fire, she will never be the same again.

Almost as if her person sensed his presence, Laura found her mind had wandered from the music, from Prudence beside her, from the National Gallery itself. Slowly descending the steps from the reading room of the Bodleian library, rounding a corner by a window, she is suddenly confronted by Gavin himself, running up the stairs with an armful of books, reaching the small, stone landing, dropping with perfect precision on to one knee, his hand on his heart, then flung towards her, blowing a kiss; rising and hastening on, no word spoken, only delighted brief laughter, hers and his. Hers repeated itself now. Prudence looked sideways, alarmed, as Laura bit it back.

Gavin Kitto waited, his face hidden, watching the two girls go. He was working in London. Because of his facility with certain languages, there had been found a necessary niche in the world service of the BBC. He had rented an empty cottage cheaply in partial countryside, whence he could make the journey to town, and his family would be beyond the range of bombs.

Edwin looked across at Prudence after supper as they sat quietly waiting for Big Ben. (The Christians all had a minute of prayer for the country, he forgot who had suggested it. The Christians have not the monopoly of goodwill said Edwin Kyle.) Prudence looked very sad tonight. Hurt. But he had made her laugh this morning. As the chimes began, he caught her eye, winked. She laughed. Pop's eyes, the colour of a cold sea.

His diary was upon his lap. Edwin's entries into his diary were characterised by a general fury: a relatively quiet, shy man, much seethed beneath his apparent calm, and the diary, whether he knew it or not, acted as a safety valve. He was civilised enough to try to delete his crossness from his everyday life, but in his diary felt no such restraint. Sometimes he found himself wanting to swear with words he scarcely knew he knew. His supervisory self, still insistent, curbed this, even though he intended that no eyes but his should ever see the diary. When he turned to the family and in particular to Prudence, his words became gentled o'er with a rather bashful tenderness. But his tongue was feared in his department. After the news, he wrote his diary. (He did not write it every day.)

> Having relieved Leningrad those untrustworthy Russians are into the wretched Poland...

(Many people took Edwin's tone of voice about the Russians)...

It is said the Ukraine is swept of Germans. Prudence has a Pole at the office, he suffers for his country as if he were there, seldom smiles, seems to have lost touch with his family. Made Prudence laugh this morning with Lord Haw Haw. How young she looks, can't believe she has done her degree, won her research place, works for her living, my little golden girl. Allies can't seem to get to Rome, been at it weeks. What in hell's name is going on? Landing at Anzio a few days ago had to be re-inforced from the Gustav Line, where they are stuck. So they admit now. Why, what's gone wrong?

4

Not many steps from the office in an area which in London's earlier days had held a market was an exquisite licensed sandwich bar where all kinds of un-war-like delicacies were somehow available, at a price— smoked salmon and smoked roe, Parma ham, turkey, crab meat, even caviar. Here, to meet her second son Willy for lunch, toddled Imogen in pleasant anticipation. Heaven alone knew where Harry was, but he too would telephone her when he could: rather rarely, he being more secretly, more dangerously occupied. The place was crowded, but near the door, waiting for her, was dark, square William talking to a thin, pale young man in mufti with an anxiously sensitive face, a face and head quite noticeably too small for the rest of him.

"This is Matthew Tate, Ma," Willy said when he had kissed her. "One of Harry's friends, at Oxford. As you work at the same dump, I thought you might meet." Imogen was disappointed; she liked to have her sons to herself. But she greeted him with friendly charm, she had heard of him, writing away under his blotter when he had no work to do. He did not look a strong person, the small face exaggerated this; his thinness, his jerked movements, his tautness seemed to her like a bent wire twisted, requiring straightening. His whole person said anguish, anxiety, and struggle. He seemed at first very shy. They managed to find a place while William joined the queue at the bar.

"It is rather a dump, our place, isn't it?" she said. "What are you doing there?"

He thought he knew at once what she meant, she meant why are you not in uniform with Harry and Willy? (In fact she did not mean this at all, she meant what section of intelligence occupied him at the ministry.) He looked at her so uneasily, she said quickly, "Oh don't tell me if it's secret." This should have let Matthew out, but he did not want to escape. He wanted to talk to William's Ma, she was the kind of mother he had always dreamed about, she was ravishing, charming and full of compassion. (He decided this on seeing her, whether it was true or not: but it was.) To many people he would say, eyes, it was my eyes. But he could not lie to this person.

"I was in the air force a little," he said, "but they found me psychologically unfit."

She looked straight at him with sympathy and nodded.

"I was not asking that, but thank you for telling me," she said.

William returned with a piled tray, drinks, sandwiches. Fresh bread, real Irish butter.

"Peace," Willy said seizing a glass, "and an end of this coercion."

May you survive, may you simply survive the second front, his mother said in her heart.

"Whatever kind of a peace," muttered tortured Matthew, his mind wondering as it always did if Communism would not be the answer.

William had been at an art school in London, halfway through a course: William, so strong, large, and capable of driving tanks was learning the most delicate work, he was a glass engraver. He learnt to handle, to work upon glass, as frangible as eggshells, full of light. How could he, his mother thought, manipulate those juggernauts of destruction? He spoke of coercion, which of course it was: but he had chosen. Would it not destroy forever that delicate command of the hand?

The pile of delicious food melted away quickly, the two young men ate and talked with gusto. There was nothing wrong with Matthew's appetite Imogen noted, he might be starving.

"Harry," Matthew said between sandwiches, "wherever he may be," raising his glass.

"Well, has anyone any news?" William asked. "For I haven't."

"Just still training, when last I heard," his mother said quietly, looking doubtfully at Matthew.

"Ma, you must know he's utterly reliable. Dash it, you're all sworn, in your place, anyway!"

Imogen emptied her glass, before she threw her head back and giggled. Matthew smiled, in his enchantment. His face took on the look of a happy, comical puppet.

"Do you hear from Harry, Matthew?" she asked.

"No, no, I've no idea—don't tell me—ears all round—" Willy leaned to him, rather proudly, Imogen thought. (And how she could laugh she could not imagine, presumably it was nerves.)

"He'll be jumping," Willy said, so soft she could not hear, only see his lips. Matthew nodded, struck once more with their bravery, his inability. Suddenly he looked as stricken as a child, a puppet sad.

Lifting his head again William saw a khaki wrist, a large pale hand, removing his mac from the crowded coat stand near the door.

"Ho!" yelled Willy in a kind of belch, rising up, pushing round Matthew, people standing solid between them and the entrance, Willy's eyes upon the vanishing person causing him to disregard the bodies in between.

"Could you excuse me, my mac's being stolen."

"Hell, my drink's being spilt."

"My foot's being stood on."

"My arse's being bumped."

Imogen's horror dissolved into helpless, soft, whoops of laughter, even Matthew giggled. Willy's arms, raised aloft in a kind of swimming movement, and his repeated urgent pleas, got him a passage through the drinking throng, the laughter increasing with the tale of physical damage, increasing to drown the comical obscenities they thought of.

William reached the door, his mac long since gone, looked both ways, saw an officer walking sedately up towards Piccadilly, hared after him breathless and half-laughing: not at all stern, supposing it came to blows?

"Excuse me, but I think you're wearing my mac! By mistake no doubt. May we look? You were in the Cockerel just now?"

"Yes—I—?" Looking appalled, the officer allowed William to unbutton and pull it off. (He was feeling ill.)

"You are Lieutenant George Turnbull?" read William.

"By no means," said the astounded officer.

"Neither am I," confessed William Wicklow, feeling so foolish he could not even laugh. "I am most terribly sorry. What shall I do? Take it back, will you come back? You were wearing one, were you, you're sure you had one with you?"

"I'm never sure of anything these days," said the officer, bewildered and pale. He had just come out of hospital, the world was a strange nightmare to him, he still longed for soft-bosomed nurses and bedpans. Was he, on top of everything, stricken with amnesia?

George Turnbull?

"Let's assume I hadn't. I must get home." He smiled nervously and turned, evidently deciding to let this nice puppy sort out his own jumble, hailed an opportune taxi, and rather shakily got in, feeling very cold.

William walked back bearing his prize, roars of derisive approbation greeting him. He searched the stand, his mac was gone. He took the other straight to the proprietor, helping out at the crowded bar, who borrowed someone's cane and banged on the counter, roaring.

"Gentlemen. Lieutenant George Turnbull, is Lieutenant George Turnbull still here?"

The lieutenant elbowed his way to the bar.

"Your mac, sir. I'd look after it, this gentleman's lost his. I'm very sorry indeed, sir," he repeated to William.

"Rotten luck. What're we coming to? Decent of you to rescue mine. Who was it?"

"Another officer. Taken by mistake. Lost his, too, I expect."

Little trickles of dishonesty happening everywhere during the war, like gravel through the roots of a noble fallen tree, foretold the almost total landslide, the demise of reliable everyday goodness in England, over the next thirty years, bringing this puritan country down to the same level of general improbity as many another.

"It's greed," Willy said. "Sell for quite a lot on the black market, my mac."

"It's shortages," idealistic Matthew suggested.

"It's dishonesty," stated Imogen unequivocally, looking at her watch.

Through the throng as William had first parted them she had caught sight of Marie's fair head smiling up at a middle-aged city man in a dark suit, her painted face happier than it ever was at work. Both wore buttonholes, drank to each other. Marie, turning at the disturbance, looked quickly away, did not want to meet her eye. So. Some illicit love, she supposed. When they went out the couple had gone.

Matthew walked with Mrs Wicklow back to work.

"What are you aiming for when it's over, Matthew?" she said. She knew of him, he was ringed round with successful almost famous relations for two generations back. Why should he look hangdog unless it were the sense of oppression, the over-shadowing competition that this caused?

"Oh, I want to be a poet, an artist of some sort. I want to write novels most I think."

"Your family are all medical, scientific."

"Yes, you can't think how hard it is wanting to be, being, on the other side, they simply think I'm malingering. We'll meet again now, won't we?"

"I'm sure we will."

Laura was at a Board.

She sat rather nervously upright on the edge of her chair in some lofty eighteenth-century government room lying somewhere off Regent street. She had been asked about her family and her interests and her reading and her degree. She had been bold enough to confess that she could not find her present work of paramount interest; it was alien to what she was used to.

"The trained mind, Miss Cardew, can turn itself, should be able to turn itself, to any subject whatsoever, and upon that axiom our civil service is run," he said. "Now, your rank at the moment is temporary. You know of course that there are great opportunities for a permanent career here. (I don't mean in your wartime ministry.) There are very competitive exams. And we have a house-party system, where people are invited for a weekend so that all the other things about them can be assessed in an atmosphere away from work and offices."

Laura had heard of these official jamborees.

"Have you had any thoughts on the matter, any ideas as to becoming a permanent civil servant?" he asked.

There was a pause. Laura bit a lip. He studied her face. His pale eyes twinkled.

"Or wouldn't wild horses?" he suggested.

She let out her breath.

"Wild horses would not," she gratefully agreed.

Prudence hovered downstairs; she had had her interview first. It was late in the afternoon. It was not worth going back to the office. Should they go to the Wop shop, find some tea? The Italians could not make tea. They drank coffee, an unheard of habit at half-past four, soon to become quite usual, indulged in by the Americans. The Italian girl's hands were bloated and crinkled with washing up lunches.

They compared notes, deciding the head of the Board had really been a kind, patient, discerning man.

"For instance," Laura said, "did he say the thing about wild horses to you?"

Prudence laughed her amused laugh, and nodded.

"It's all very well for you, you haven't got to think of it yet, with your research studentship waiting. But what am I going to do? I certainly don't want to go on doing this afterwards. But I must earn my living. Will you be a don, do you suppose?"

"Yes, I think I should like teaching. People who really want to learn," Prudence decided.

"You are lucky, to know."

"But you know. You keep saying it, I've heard you say it often, the only thing you know you want to do is write."

"But I must earn my living. Do I say it as often as that? How boring. People say I can't possibly earn my living, writing."

There's journalism, my dear, the head of her college had said. Oh, I wouldn't be any good at that, Laura knew. Then you must find some job in the right direction and write in your spare time.

"…write in your spare time," Prudence was saying, as Laura came back.

By the door as they went out sat Daisy with somebody so round-faced and plump and blue-eyed that it must be her mother.

"My mother," said Daisy, who had left the office early to meet her.

Next day, Daisy hovered, putting down Laura's horrible coffee on her table.

"There's a novelist upstairs," Daisy offered, as if he were an animal in a cage. Daisy's position as a clerical assistant gave her the run of various departments, or perhaps it was her position as coffee and tea maker. When Laura or Prudence wanted to know who people were, when their names appeared on memos, they asked Daisy. Daisy usually could tell them but would often say, after proffering the information, in serious, moral and adenoidal tones, if the subject were male:

"He's married."

"I don't care if he keeps a harem," Laura protested once irritably, "I'm not looking here for a husband."

Now Daisy went on: "His name's Mr Tate, Matthew Tate. Would you like me to introduce you?"

This time Daisy did not say, solemnly, he's married.

Laura looked up at her.

"I know you're interested in writing, you see," Daisy said. "I've heard you say so. My mother and I couldn't help hearing yesterday," she admitted.

"Oh, Daisy. Yes. How nice of you. Now?"

"Coffee time's a good break. I know he's there."

Laura downed her cooling mug in a few gulps.

"All right," she said. Tall, she thought, shy but friendly, fair-haired, grey-eyed, amusing, she half-smiled realising that it was Gavin she thought of. And he falls for me, and I fall for him after a suitable interval. And when we marry, I have time to write, he does some job and earns the money and I have time to write, oh bliss I have time to write! Blue eyes might do, she added.

Following Daisy into the room, she saw Matthew.

Matthew half-rose, crouching over his table like a navy-blue crow, while Daisy explained who Laura was. Then he sank back, his very small white face wearing an anxious mask.

"Sit down," he said. "Oh, someone's pinched my spare chair."

"It doesn't matter, I mustn't stay long," Laura said eagerly. "Daisy says you write novels."

"Under my blotter," Matthew said, lifting it up, revealing sheets of fountain-pen writing, small, rather crabbed. "There's never enough to do, you see. Have you enough to do?"

"Usually, now," said Laura. "Have you published any?"

"Not yet."

"What kind of novels?"

"This is really a poetical novel, it's mainly people's thoughts."

"What, stream of consciousness, *The Waves*?" Laura said.

"Not *The Waves*, I'm afraid," Matthew said with a twisted smile. "I like her, though, don't you?"

At the moment, Laura adored her. She said so.

"I would love to write a novel," Laura said.

"Then do. Under your blotter. In your spare moments."

"Doesn't it need more than spare moments?"

"Maybe. But why waste even those?"

"Oh I don't waste them."

"What do you do with them?"

"I read. Poetry mostly. Sometimes short stories."

"Why don't you write short stories?"

"Yes, I do have a go, sometimes."

Matthew found her a pretty girl, "but rather intense," thought he. Laura thought going down the stairs, what an awful pity he is so unattractive. Her steps became slower and slower. Mr Watson, passing and greeting her, was surprised to get no reply. In a brown study, thought he, biting upon his empty, stained, cigarette holder, to give him courage as he stumped along to pursue a vendetta that went on with Mr Harvald.

"Come in, come in Miss Cardew," said the friendly, deep, almost furry voice, "I do hope I'm soon allowed to call you Laura, it does ease communication." (Such a kind voice, gentle, a deep bass, honey brown in colour.) "Sit down here, and I'll grill you!" Mr Kitto laughed a little, she laughed, relieved, at ease. How nice he was, how reassuring that voice. Thank goodness, he was not old and frightening and sarcastic.

O my beloved Gavin how I do long for you! Laura said, opening the door of her office.

Anyway, no pretty girl would want me, Matthew Tate was thinking, making a tattoo upon his wooden table with his Government Issue ruler.

❦

In the Brompton Oratory Imogen knelt, having called in on the way home, taking the Almighty to task for the relentless, useless (she was sure it would prove useless, wicked acts so often did) systematic destruction of Monte Cassino by the Allies' bombs. (She could not know that the Americans' false conviction that the place was a German stronghold was fed by perpetual sniping at them from in and around it, perhaps by Italian partisans, in defence of the Italian refugees inside.) It is one of the strongholds of the spiritual world, prayer goes up like flame, she pleaded.

The wicked stupidity of men is not always overruled said the Virgin Mary. Moreover, Monte Cassino has been destroyed four times already and risen again, she said. Neither is it any longer what you think it: though prayer did once rise up like flame.

The Virgin's voice was somewhat like her mother's. Imogen knelt in anguish, nevertheless, she knew not how long, just in case one stone might be left upon another because of her sorrow. When she got home she looked up Monte Cassino in her husband's encyclopaedia and found it to be true, what the Virgin said. She thought she had not known this before, but could not be sure. She must be extremely cautious, about hearing voices. She hoped she was not going to start on *that*. Besides, why should the BVM speak with an Irish accent? Inherently improbable, said Imogen aloud, and threw back her head laughing, and clapped the encyclopaedia to.

Shuttlecock," Mrs Wicklow muttered half under her breath as she sat looking flushed, patting, feeling, patting all over her table, her dimpled hands in their exquisite rings somewhat grubby.

"Shuttlecock indeed," she repeated slightly louder, pouting, still patting the deep layer of thin papers in little piles but overlapping which totally covered her table as she sorted them, and which consequently buried everything she needed.

"Shuttlecock!" she now spat, as if it were an expletive, a little louder, and suddenly turning into laughter.

Laura had just become aware of the patting and looked up to enjoy the laughter.

"You've lost your pencil." Mrs Wicklow was always doing it.

"I've lost my pencil, I've buried my rubber, I—ah!" She pounced. "I'll shuttlecock them. Why, anyway?" Her green eyes glinted over her half-spectacles, smiling at Laura.

"Some notion of flying back and forth? The messages?" Laura suggested. "Keep it going, your turn, don't drop it?"

"Ah."

For all reports had numbers, and before the numbers were the mystic letters S-C or sometimes the whole two words Shuttlecock. Code names after all had forever been used. Code names for desperate, audacious operations planned in secret, not known until years later. Code references or quotations for emergency messages, secret, between co-operating parties telegraphed or radioed from a distance. For these, people drew on Shakespeare, *Alice*, the Bible, the *Pilgrim's Progress*, Edward Lear, that abiding idiosyncratic pool of serious or humorous literature, allusion to which every English officer would be sure to recognise. As code name for a series of intelligence reports, Shuttlecock seemed poor in comparison and moreover led to obscene variants, which Mrs Wicklow would try to be deaf to, and then be seen to be giggling at.

To the great delight of Laura and to the chagrin and deprivation of Prudence, Mrs Wicklow had been translated to the top secret work, where if anything she was more at sea than Laura, where the Shuttlecock papers were full of things like heavy water, liquid nitrogen, launching sites for rockets, and radio parts for pilotless planes. When Laura took the easiest, most direct route of finding out about, say, heavy water, which was to ask Dewdrop, Dewdrop surveyed her with disapproval of a pitying nature and said she would find it hard to understand.

Mrs Wicklow had subsided, her pencil found. Laura, facing the door, saw it silently open, saw the deprecating, penny-sized, enquiring face of Matthew peer in, pretend not to notice her, quickly withdraw, and the door quietly to shut again.

"That was that novelist," she stated. "From upstairs. I wonder who he's looking for?"

Imogen, well knowing who he might be looking for, peered over her half-spectacles and sniffed. She would in that case sit tight, not go to lunch yet.

Matthew Tate had indeed come to see if Wicklow's fascinating Mamma would have lunch with him, on the spur of the moment, as he passed the door: but seeing the thin dark girl who had bearded him and questioned him so intensely, had hastily retreated. He did not want her to think he was pursuing her, for nothing was further from his thoughts. (He was afraid of her a little but did not admit the fact.) But Mrs Wicklow, Imogen was her unusual name (he did not remember how he knew this) which with its overtones of poetry and purity struck him as exactly right for her, she had become an object of excitement and longing to him. Such a mother, so beautiful, merry, sympathetic, interested: what lucky devils the Wicklow boys were, how he envied them. He thought of his own parents, pre-occupied always, for as long as he could remember, in their medical research, in different but overlapping spheres. Not his childish or schoolboy or undergraduate needs ever being first, but always their work. Once when he was a child his father told him as a laughable joke how he had carted him as a baby up to a London hospital at least once, sometimes twice a day, to be fed. Why didn't you just feed me at home, he had asked puzzled? Because she was a good mother, she was breast-feeding you, we had to get you to her. Thinking of his mother's nipples with shame and some distaste (he had lately learnt about breast-feeding from a boy at school) Matthew had joined in the laughter too loudly and always remembered the incident. He had been hatefully aware how relieved his parents were when he went off, first to his prep school, then to his public school. Even more when he was at the university, deemed to be on his own feet, grown-up. Duty they had always paid him. He knew he was a disappointment to them in that his mind did not go on their lines.

He would have to ring her up about lunch, since that girl was in the same room. Had he known how largely that girl shared his view of Imogen Wicklow he might have been sardonically amused.

Laura's admiration of Mrs Wicklow was tinged with envy too. Partly on her own account: what a pleasure it would be to belong in rich, privileged, foreign-travelling circles, so far from her own small town origins, to be as beautiful, as worldly-wise as she. But even as she grew fonder of her, drank in her Indian stories, laughed at her amused but usually loving reactions, noted her apparently joyous faith, Laura envied her more on her mother's account. That she should have all this, and the happiness of a romantic marriage too! The sort of relationship which Laura knew (by the way Imogen glowed when she talked of her husband) that her own mother set higher than anything else in the world. That Mamma should have been so cruelly cheated of it was a constant sorrow to Laura, she had accepted it less, perhaps, than Kitty herself. One paid, Laura early decided, out of all proportion for blindness. Why had not her mother seen, realised, the insoluble difficulty in marrying her father? Always, everywhere, everyone learnt too late. Why should Mrs Wicklow, then, be so blessedly fortunate?

Laura and Marie sat suddenly and unexpectedly engrossed in a deep and personal conversation, all their defences knocked for six within two minutes, both flushed and intense, striving to see each other's life and point of view as if they had been bosom friends for years, instead of acquaintances for a few months. How had it happened? One of Marie's electrifying phone calls had come into a room empty of all but Laura; she had taken it in radiant relief (it was later than usual and thought to be not coming). Replacing the receiver she turned to Laura, saying challengingly, "You must wonder who it is rings me up."

"Anyone could guess it's someone special," Laura said. Antennae from her own heart, her own sadness probed towards Marie. "Is he married, or something awful?" Laura said.

"How did you know?" Marie replied, tumbling out with the whole tale, so commonplace, yet to her its anguish as fresh as if such a wound had never happened before.

"It's the people we live with. A friend and I share a flat in this house. A lovely house. They're quite rich; he's in the city somewhere. They made a fuss of us from the start, asking us down. But Sadie doesn't often go. I like it, I've lost my parents. Then he began asking me to meet for drinks. And asking me down when she was out at bridge. We've been awfully careful, I'm sure she doesn't know. She'd kill him if she knew. Worse than that, we'd lose the flat, and it suits us, so Sadie would be furious."

"Doesn't Sadie know?" Laura asked in astonishment.

"Not how much we feel." She paused, sitting on the table near the phone, watching Laura's face. "You think I'm behaving wrongly, don't you," she stated. Marie greatly minded that she should be proper, perhaps even genteel was the word.

"It happens, Marie. It's happened to me," Laura confessed.

"That's why you knew."

"But mine got finished, by him. He was older than I, and strong-minded."

"Not as much older as Charles than me, I'll bet. He could be my father. But even if he were free he's above me, he's different, I don't know if he'd marry me, though I think he loves me. People's friends mind about your background, your education."

"Do you mind about not being able to marry? Or would he divorce her?"

"She wouldn't let him. What I mind about is not giving birth," Marie stated formally. "It's every woman's right," she added in the tones of the agony columns she doubtless read. "I mind dreadfully."

"But Marie, haven't you got lots of friends of your own age and kind?" said Laura. "You must have."

"It's very difficult when you're Jewish," Marie stated.

"Why?" Laura was astounded.

"Well if I meet men who are practising Jews they don't want to know me, because I'm not, we weren't ever. To tell the truth, it's not Jewish men I like. Best. I'm English first, being Jewish doesn't mean much to me."

"What about the Jewish state, what about Palestine?" (Laura had once done a paper about Palestine under British mandate, at school.) "Wouldn't you like to go and live with your people?"

"*Last* thing I'd like," said Marie. "But we know lots of people would like us to go, want to be rid of us."

"Marie! That can't be true, not in England?"

"*Can't* it just. It's always been true. Don't you know I often get taken advantage of, being Jewish? This is one reason nice boyfriends are so hard to find. It's easier for you, I expect, your kind of person, educated and all that, Oxford. I'm only a typist. Someone here was very rude to me the other day, they wouldn't do it to you." For one thing, she added to herself, you wouldn't grasp it. The sexual innuendoes I must put up with would be double-dutch to you—in your middle class circles.

Laura was bewildered. Marie disliked her Jewishness, it seemed, regretted her social class, wished to rise higher, wanted to give birth, was transfigured by this love for a married man. Marie wanted her sex passionate all right, but genteel. Marie wanted to be accorded consideration, gentleness, romantic ardour, not crude, vulgar innuendo and assault. Marie read women's magazines, no doubt, Marie probably read some of the tales of gentle romantic love Laura's Mamma wrote, nice, decent, touching, never crude. Plenty of love and no sex her mother would say smiling.

"This is why I like Charles so much, you see," Marie sighed. Laura saw perfectly why she did.

Laura had read, while still a schoolgirl, her first newspaper account of an early pogrom, how Jews had been made to run the gauntlet of savage warders, who had hit them with anything they had to hand, spades, forks, poles; heads had been cracked, eyes struck out, limbs broken, stomachs rent, it had been made a game of. Your people, schoolgirl Laura said to God (for in those days she spoke to God direct). These are supposed to be your people, Jesus was one of these, how can you let these things happen to them? She had felt sick with horror, had tried to exorcise it in a poem, which Kitty had fondly kept.

"The awful things that they do to the Jews, to your people," she said now, expecting Marie to mourn with her. But Marie did not see them as her people. "They're Germans. Or Poles, to me. I don't feel them as 'my people'. I never read those things," Marie added firmly. "It's better not to. I'll have to go, he'll be waiting."

As she waited for Prudence, Laura brooded upon Marie's luck. How wonderful, how exciting, to be going to meet your lover for a lunchtime drink! She supposed they were lovers (where did they safely meet?). She supposed Marie found it worth it, despite the lies, pretences and anxiety (how did Marie remain open friends with his wife, she must needs do so, to allay suspicion). But the joy, the joy of it! Were she going now, today, to meet Gavin, would she be wild with joy or sick with apprehension? An occasion when Gavin was as hungry as a hunter floated into her memory: she had arrived a little early for the tutorial. Please forgive me, my dear Laura, greeting you with my mouth full, I was starving, didn't leave time for a proper breakfast, we were late, the babe was fractious.... Please, please finish it, you must be hungry she said. Within minutes the coffee and the unprepossessing wartime bun were gone. Do you feel better? A deep breath as he patted his stomach. Better, rapidly turning to worse. Come along; let's get to it. Read your essay. Read away.

"Laura, here I am," Prudence said at the door.

Prudence and Laura joined a queue on the top floor of an Oxford Street store where the food was excellent, for wartime. The queue was long: but at last they were served and found a place.

"Look who's over here," Laura observed, as they began to eat.

At a table within their view sat Mr Watson, Irene Wainewright, and a flushed over-smart middle-aged woman whom Laura soon knew to be Mrs Watson. A silent drama was being enacted, electric emotion emanated from the little group. Ted Watson, Laura noted, was nervous, furious and beaten; Irene was defensive, but casually, loudly charming, her drawl carried; Mrs Watson was triumphantly angry but hiding it under a gush of talk.

"Do you see what's happened?" she asked Prudence. "Look!"

Irene rose, collected her things, said her farewells, swayed self-consciously away.

"Mr Watson's asked Irene to meet his wife?" Prudence suggested.

"*Mrs* Watson's surprised them," Laura countered.

But Prudence was immune to the passions arising from the group. Prudence perhaps had not even noticed how helplessly in love with Irene was poor Mr Watson, how not in the least in love with him was she.

I seem to be surrounded, Laura thought, with images of illicit love and its attendant miseries.

Ted Watson glowered. How did she know we came to this place he asked himself? Hamstrung, he knew he would be hereafter. Anyway what did he really want of Irene?—He would not hurt a hair of her head, he double-talked himself, he loved and respected her. The while his fantasies tormented him and he wished they would not.

The appalling, terrifying switch-back throat of the air-raid siren, (to which one would never get used, striking at the pit of one's stomach as it did) dragged Laura back to consciousness just as she had fallen into her deepest sleep. She groaned. She knew she would have to go down.

Kitty had bought a large three-storied house in this suburb south of London, on a mortgage, and helped by Uncle Miles and various kind relations. London was a danger area so houses were cheap. The lower flat had in earlier days been made self-contained. Kitty lived in the middle and upper ones, sunny and pleasant. Laura's eyrie was right at the top.

"Lolly!" Kitty called softly. "I think you should come down!"

"Coming," Laura said gruffly, struggling with her gown. It was cold, too.

Part of the original stairs of the house now led up, from an outer garden door, to Kitty's front door. Solid outer wall flanked it one side, the whole width of the downstairs flat flanked it on the other. It was thought to be the safest place since they had no shelter. Kitty opened the front door, keeping the key in her hand, they descended halfway and sat on the carpeted stairs, Laura leaning on the inner wall. Before they were properly settled, they heard the menacing, throbbing hum of the bomber engines, getting louder and louder, not much flak against them. Somehow one, or two perhaps, had got through. Laura listened intently. It was an ordinary bomber, not the secret thing; it was the usual old throbbing ordinary bomber. It was a good many months since they had experienced a bomber raid.

"Going right over."

"The high street, the railway perhaps."

Shrieks dimmed by distance followed, shrieks of the bombs falling, enormous thuds and blast noises following them. Laura's thighs turned to quaking, trembling disobedient flesh, no thought or will could control them.

"Sorry, I can't stop shivering," she said.

"Nor can I," Kitty agreed. They laughed slightly, holding on to each other, absurdly and uncontrollably frightened. "Thank goodness we're together." My mother, Laura thought, suddenly remembering Mrs Wicklow, and how she had lately come to consider her as the most desirable mother there could be. This is my mother, my flesh and my blood, whom I love. Deserted by Papa, disappointed of romance, let down by life, but always grateful, always loving, bravely calm and humorous under most circumstances, even air raids, even being followed by a V1 in her morning train. For Kitty had secured some time ago a job as one of a bevy of underlings working for a famous agony aunt on an evening paper. She did a day or two a week in Fleet Street, but also worked at home. Large packets of letters arrived by post, or she would bring her ration back with her. It suited her exactly. Her old-fashioned standards of right and wrong, her sympathetic warm heart, her quickening to the comic, her good common sense, her unassailable belief in romantic love which could happen as suddenly as a shooting star, but must be preserved with continual effort: all these were just what was needed. The silliest effusion commanded Kitty's loving study. Kitty had been heard to say wryly that she, having made such a stunning success of her own marriage, was well qualified to help others.

They sat compulsively shivering side by side until warmth and the gradual diminishment of noise produced calm. At the all-clear, they rose, walked up the stairs, made hot drinks, giggled, touched cheeks and went to their beds.

How can I bear my mother's death mourned Laura day after day, month after month, rocking with grief, realising ever more bleakly how greatly she loved her. I want nothing so much as to creep back into her womb, to be there, curled and safe, to be part of her again. To be protected from the atrocious enmity of the world, from all the slings and arrows. There. I am there, I can do it, I can enact this fantasy quite consciously and reap its comfort, I can do it each night till the pain stills. It is only a simulated safety, an imaginary shelter from this grief, from all grief, but it lulls me. And I can go over all the scenes when we were together, that come back sharply and sweetly: how clearly I feel and smell the womb-like shelter of those dark stairs, in that shabby suburban house rocked with bombs, where we sat side by side shivering with terror, giving each other comfort. I have not finished, oh I have not finished with my loved mother.

"Ber-ee Per-ee Cer-ee," said the girl glottally on the switchboard where Tom Turner worked. (Good cockney, Tom said mimicking this, was fine to say but impossible to spell.)

Laura was ringing for lunch: a habit they had formed since their one or two meetings in Oxford when he visited his cousin. Laura had not seen Rosamund since they all left Oxford but Tom, somehow, had stuck. Working in London, as she was, he had pursued the acquaintance with spasmodic eagerness and complete objectivity. He liked Laura, but he could not think why. He was puzzled or affronted or critical of nearly every attitude she showed, and by which she appeared to run her life. Perhaps his interest in her was that of the observer of some hitherto unexplored species brought up, he gathered, in some repressive religion, in a society arranged in layers, the lucky at the top, the squashed at the bottom, Laura and her like conscious of their place in the middle; everything tight, ordered and authoritarian: she nonetheless had a bright enough mind to attract him, a certain candle-like, serious, homogeneity.

Laura liked Tom, though little about him was what she was used to. She thought Tom was the first totally classless person she had ever met and quite unconscious of it. Tom was without religion, seemed amazed at its being used as a set of rules, but was passionately interested in philosophy and mankind. Tom had done a degree at Toronto, and was working as a chemist, while he devoured what he really loved, philosophy and psychology, in an external degree from the University of London.

They talked about writing, especially mad experimental plays, and poetry and music. He prodded Laura in a brotherly way, over her desire to be a creative artist. He was a kind tease, an ironic thinker, a good listener. He was the good New World, a humanist, a socialist, yet not a materialist, caring little for appearances or possessions. Their acquaintance had never taken any personal turn and remained platonic, for which Laura, still love-lorn, had been grateful.

"We were nearly bombed last night," Laura stated, as they sat after lunch later. "Mamma and I."

Tom regarded her kindly through the square-topped steel spectacles, his centurion's face amused. "A miss is as good as a mile, I believe you say."

Acerbic, unsympathetic. She raised her eyebrows slightly, smiling. "Why, did it shock you?"

"Oh not really I suppose, we're used to it."

"Then why do you want sympathy?"

"Oh, Tom, do I? It was just for something to say. I couldn't stop shaking at the time."

"Are you afraid of dying?"

"I never think of it. I'm afraid of being buried alive. Are you afraid of dying?"

"I think dying, pri—mary–ly, would be a disappointment. For anyone young. Not doing all the things we've planned. But since we shouldn't know anything about it that perhaps is a senseless remark."

"How do you know we shouldn't know anything about it?"

"On the face of it, squashed flat or blown to pieces, it doesn't seem likely we'd be self-conscious."

"What about our mind, soul, spirit?"

"Ah, well. The great question. To be or not to be."

"I was brought up believing the souls of the righteous are in the hands of God."

"It depends what you mean by God, as my worthy professor would say," said Tom in the precise, spindly, shallow accents of C E M Joad discussing the deity on the *Brains Trust*. "Ros now, Ros declares—"

"Oh, how *is* Rose?"

"All right. She declares we're all little sparklers off some Great Spirit like a Roman candle and we'll all flame back again."

"Yes, I remember someone nicknaming Rose the Great Spirit! Does reading philosophy help you to *master* anything?"

"It makes you think out the alternatives. Anyway, girl, you aren't dead. What are you writing? Are you DOING any?"

"A short story."

"What about?"

"A ghost I imagined in an eighteenth-century chair in an antiques window, in a square."

Tom groaned.

"Probably a Parker Knoll. What happens?"

"It hasn't yet."

Tom neighed.

"You're not very attracted by *now*, are you?"

"No," agreed Laura, after thought.

6

"Anny wants to bring Keith on Saturday. Can you get off?" Kitty said.

"Probably. If I work late all the evenings."

"It would be nice if you could be here, Lolly."

Laura looked up from her plate.

"Why, is it something special, do you think? Is Anny going to marry Keith, for instance? What did she sound like?"

"Commanding," her mother smiled, "secretive, a little pompous. You know," Kitty described her elder daughter Marian. "She said she hoped you could be here too. They've both got weekend leave."

"Lucky old Marry-Anny," Laura said later as they sat looking out at the greening garden. April was more than at its full, but it was that awkward time of year, chilly though quite light after supper, showery by day, when one could not decide whether to face the fire or the garden.

"If they're sure, I mean," she added.

"Well, we don't know it's that yet," Kitty said: and a long silence of uncertainty settled upon them. Kitty Cardew never ceased to be surprised that she had brought forth two such different daughters. Marian, shy, dour, inarticulate, her long, pallid face so often solemn, had got by in the classroom, but came alive on the sports field. She seemed to be an athlete, was in all the teams, lacrosse, tennis, cricket, did daring and beautiful things in the gymnasium, walked on her hands along the ribbed sea sand in summer. Of the various trainings open to her at the end of her schooldays, she chose domestic science, she liked sewing and cooking, she was determined to have six children. By the time the war started, she had done several varying jobs, and joining up promptly in the women's army, quickly became an officer using her own skills. But in every other respect, Kitty reflected, the army totally transformed her. Marian took over whole the hearty, school girlish army jargon, whether flippant or solemn: it gave her a way to talk. Inarticulacy gave way to a general, bossy expression of received officer opinion, often loud-mouthed and overbearing. A confidence, a kind of confidence she had never had, and which might be spurious, took over Marian. She loved the social life, having been (as she complained) starved of it in their restricted girlhood, and had many friends. Then, about two years ago, there was Keith.

"He's *regular* army, isn't he?" Lolly said suddenly.

"Yes, I gather so."

"Surprising how she's taken so completely to the army."

Keith arose in Laura's imagination. Keith, at a first meeting, gave the impression of being totally square, Henry VIII square. The slightest shade shorter than Marian, he was muscularly tough, a rugger body, his square face, set on a solid, an almost fluted pillar of a neck, was dominated by his crooked nose broken in some early scrum encounter. Thin, light-coloured fair hair tried in vain to conceal the nobbles of his cranium from which his ears stood out like projected wings, begun but stunted. He seemed unable to keep still, his frame juddered as his hands were rubbed together, his weight went from one massive leg to the other perpetually, and when he sat down, crossing them, the upper foot in its twinkling brown shoe jerked like a puppet, arbitrarily, in some theatre of the absurd.

Well, I don't know I'm sure, Laura could remember her mother saying. But now of course they knew him, they could even conceive that a person so totally different, so strange to their own family interests and behaviour, might be right for the new, the army Marian. The Marian who needed to be "in" something, a part of something.

Keith and Marian evidently thought so as they arrived quite early. Keith masterfully cornered Kitty in the drawing-room, ordering the girls to make the coffee: and with a quake of laughter claimed Marian as his with her mother's consent, and a loud, acted kiss on each cheek. Marian clicked her heels and saluted. Laura felt faint.

"Let's all go to Kew," Kitty said after lunch. "Let's go to Kew, to celebrate your engagement."

"Kew?" said Keith, in astonishment.

Marian flushed to the roots of her dark auburn hair, the colour, Laura always thought, of wet beech leaves lying in a wood.

"Haven't you ever been?"

"Never."

But he was, none the less, very good with a few hints from Kitty at working out the journey, ringing up the station, rounding them all up. There was no petrol, even for officers on leave.

It was, perhaps, bold of Kitty to suggest Kew, yet in a sense inevitable. Kew was part of Kitty's romantic girlhood, she had even sung a song about going down to Kew in lilac-time: which she and her brother and their widowed mother invariably did, from the house in suburban London (bought for its hollyhocks more than its convenience) in which she passed her widowhood. Their love of the trees, flowers, follies, waters and secrecies of Kew was adoring and breathless, a sense which Kitty soon passed on to her daughters. Her brother Miles on the other hand was more knowledgeable albeit equally worshipful: he was himself a botanist. Going to Kew was therefore a regular treat for Marian and Laura when staying with Uncle Miles. Papa liked Kew, too. That crazy pagoda, he would say, creaking with laughter, I could just push it over. Laura could call up in memory the surprising heat, smell and damp of the earliest visit to the palm house, the hairy trunks, the slowly flickering leaf patterns so far, far above the head of a gazing child. Kew was a kind of touchstone to the Cardews.

Keith marched into the hollow of the Rhododendron Dell as if he were one of the six hundred into the jaws of death. Kitty scampered politely to keep up with him, her neck turning wildly from side to side, not to miss the few bushes that were out.

Laura and Marian lingered behind, they hardly realised why.

"There's that pale pearly pink nearly out."

"There are some azaleas blazing, in there."

"Always earlier. Look at the crimson with yellow speckles!"

"Do you remember the fairy's skirts?"

In late May, the ground had always been covered with crisp, waxen, fallen flowers, barely faded: Laura had a tiny celluloid fairy doll, who fitted them.

"We hid them in our knickers," Marian laughed.

"But they made me drop my dandelions. Even dandelions, pernicious weeds, you mustn't pick."

"Perhaps he'll like the temples. Or the pagoda," Marian said, looking after the vanishing Keith.

"Poor Mamma," she giggled.

"Or the palm house," added Laura with a snort.

"I'll have to educate him about flowers," Marian ruminatively said.

Laura felt very close to her dear sister: who being five years older had often mothered, even if she had bossed her.

Would things from now be different? Without saying so, both wondered.

Prudence Kyle put her gold head round the secret room door and spoke almost in a whisper, as if she feared to be there.

"We think this must be yours," she said, holding out an S-C intelligence slip to Laura.

"Well, come in, come in," said Imogen Wicklow, pleased so see her. Prudence was quietly approaching them when a sudden, immense, echoing roar from an adjoining room stopped her dead, changed her expression to horror, she almost paled. It was presumably a roar of rage, open-ended, for it made no recognisable word. Mrs Wicklow's black brows went up as her spectacles slid down. Laura's smile faded. Mrs Tripp clicked her tongue, and shook her head at Miss Richardson who had clapped her hand on her mouth. Marie scuttled in at the door, one hand clutching typing to her chest, and quickly closed it. Nevertheless words had been heard at her entry, the more clearly.

"…Conceit…bloody ignorance…mySELF…stupid…at ONCE…"

A sound like a chair falling, a shaking of partition glass as a door was uncontrollably slammed.

Prudence looked from one to the other with consternation.

"Our superiors," sniffed Mrs Tripp. "Not seeing eye-to-eye. We suppose."

"Does this often happen?" Prudence asked.

"Not infrequently," remarked Mrs Wicklow, her face comical.

"We don't know why," Laura said. "We never can hear it *all*. Besides, they aren't our section."

"Mr Harvald's very haughty," put in Marie, who suffered from it.

"Mr Watson's too meek," said Mrs Tripp. "By half."

"If you ask me, Mr Harvald's a very strange young man. Very strange indeed," said Miss Richardson with mysterious emphasis.

A particularly loud crash followed, sounding like the drawer of a steel cabinet rushing home, or even falling to the floor, having rushed out too far. Imogen Wicklow's restraint melted into quiet infectious laughter. Daisy arrived with tea, looking most disapproving. Prudence made good her escape.

Laura doodled over her blotter, with her tea. Mr Harvald, of course, was much younger, his Cambridge engineering degree quite recent. She supposed he not only despised poor Mr Watson for being from a lesser university, or perhaps from no university at all, but when asked for co-operation, opinion, or a deadline report, made it his pleasure not to comply.

Some such account of it Prudence gave her father.

"Disgracefully unprofessional behaviour. They'd be better apart. In different sections," said Edwin at once, with the common-sense pragmatism of the established civil servant. "Why doesn't someone see to it? Can't someone approach the head?"

"Well, *I* can't, Pop."

"What about that older, Irish lady?"

"She'd die if we suggested it, I think."

Edwin hissed through his teeth like one of the Large Cats in a rage, an expression of impatience that had always made his daughter laugh, which she would ever remember.

Reaching for his diary (there being more important things afoot than quarrelling temporaries) Edwin wrote:

The bombing is terrible, devastating, accurate at last, so they boast, and not before time. The US fighters and our Mustangs go with the bombers, they raid in *daylight* every day, they can see what they're doing, so even these blundering Americans can't miss too often. They've got on to the German synthetic oil plants, destroyed numbers of them. And the French railways and bridges, smashed and crippled, awful pictures. Where are the French resistance? This is just when they should be most active, where have they vanished to? I suppose we are not being told. We all know what we are working up for. Death and damnation: I daren't think what Donald will be doing. Margery won't talk about him. She's like a bruised bag of wild, festering fears, and I cannot help her, if she won't talk.

"I thought I'd go up to Oxford for the weekend," Laura announced. Kitty was wary, her policy of non-interference vying with her sense of moral rectitude. Still, it was a full year.

"That's a nice idea," she said. "You're due for a break."

"Godfrey's going to be up, we thought we might meet."

Kitty was reassured.

"Good. You'll enjoy it. What's he doing, still ambulance stuff?"

"Yes, in London. Awful incidents, as they call them, from time to time."

Kitty regretted Godfrey, a dear young man whose mother she had known slightly for years, and who had loved Laura with devotion in their second year. Laura had quite obviously returned his love, they had been very happy, until Godfrey's mother had made the fatal mistake of trying to dissect and confirm Laura's feelings, when she stayed there once, with a view to tying her down, to commitment, even to marriage within a foreseeable time. Perhaps Laura had been already falling out of love, perhaps that disastrous thing with the tutor had already begun. In any event, it had finished the affair, which like several others had turned into a pleasant friendship. Kitty still vaguely hoped: they had been so suited in background. Was Lolly getting back with the one, being unable to have the other? Was she feeling jealous of Marian? Her first thought occurred to her again and made her break her non-interference rule.

"You're not going to try to see Gavin Kitto I hope," she said firmly but reasonably.

Laura was evasive.

"Well, I shall enquire. I must know what's happened to him, he may be fighting," she said, glumly urgent.

She has evidently made all her arrangements before telling me, Kitty thought. Never unloving to Laura, she was grieved to the heart at the sadness this mischance had brought. Nevertheless:

"You know you can't have him," she said implacably. Her mother was pretty implacable about right, thought Laura, though not to the degree her father was. If circumstances made right bend, she had been known to bend with it, or at least accept it as inevitable.

"You know you wouldn't break up someone else's marriage. But I suppose if you could meet normally and be friends it might help."

Laura said nothing. Prudence's verdict had been implacable too, though she knew none of the details, nor even who Laura's man was. How long since you heard? A year, after schools? He doesn't want to keep in touch. If you make him, he'll either be cruel to you, or you'll unsettle him. Either way, it's appalling! But I must know if he still feels anything, I feel paralysed till I know, Laura heard herself wailing. You do know, you know you wouldn't do it. From her standpoint of intellectual sagacity and ethical sternness, and no emotional understanding, Prudence had made clear what she thought.

Walking up from Oxford station, Laura saw the hoarding still there, which had always carried the slogans. *Dig for Victory* said a very early one, causing ribaldries about the savaged college lawns where eager dons coaxed meagre vegetables. *Housewives, we want your Bones*, they had next read out, jeering. Simple, someone had cried, boil us down, do. (She had just discovered this was what they did to medieval kings killed in battle far from home.) Or again: *What do you do with your old clothes?* Wear them, they shouted in ironic chorus. Laura read *Careless Talk Costs Lives*. There was no ready riposte to this, the current one, which confronted you everywhere with Fougasse's funnily sinister drawing.

At the porter's lodge in a sort of frozen dream Laura enquired timidly, "Is Dr Kitto ever here these days?"

What would she do, if he were?

"Occasionally, miss. Not for a long while, as resident."

"Can you tell me where he is, what he's doing?"

"I can't, miss. There's an address near London. Shall I look that up for you?"

"Oh no, thank you," she said, as if the idea burnt her fingers.

After all, it would not have been credible, it could not have happened. She was mercifully jolted out of that state of dumb, unreasoning, over-riding desire, which belonged to last year, another era, into which she had foolishly let herself slide. She walked through to view the two famous chestnuts, to cast a cold glance towards the staircase she had mounted with such excited joy.

All the flowering trees of North Oxford vibrated with bees and bloom. Laura was a country girl and could not like suburbs. But if we must have suburbs, she thought, this is their season. Every garden had its rare, brief coronal, its aching cry of mutability. From the palest papery white to the richest magenta pink, from prunus petals frail and modest, to the candy pink, overdone bundles of the ornamental cherries, from wine-coloured leaves to gold and green. Petals snowed the pavements near the Dragon School. Why do people come back, Laura wondered? Do we come back simply to the beauty of the place? That can't apply to everywhere. Do we come back to pretend (vainly) we're still young? Do we come to savour our lost irresponsibility? Do we want to poach, vicariously, on the happiness (or grief) of the current lot? Some only return, she had heard it said, in the first few years and rarely thereafter; some obsessively and frequently all their lives; some, particularly men, when they reach the forty-years-on vein. Why have Godfrey and I come back, I wonder?

At the ferry was Godfrey, his foot proprietorily upon a punt. His pale ascetic face lit into a smile.

"Hullo! I have the punt."

"I have the supper. Lovely to see you."

When they were settled, he poling, she looked at him laughing.

"What's funny? Am I out of practice?"

"No, no. I suddenly remembered how our friendship was forced upon us."

He looked puzzled, then nodded smiling.

"My goodness. It ought to have put us off for good. I practically lost consciousness."

"So did I. Your skull, forehead, so hard."

"Yours, too. Exactly the same height. Crack!"

In their first year in the blackout after a meeting, on a pavement totally dark, a head-on collision: both pretending they were unhurt. They only discovered the connection with their mothers later. To collide with Godfrey Harris was an inappropriate way to meet him: tentative, retiring, saintly, a flute player, a singer, she was lucky to have got to know him at all. They had had most of his four terms around together at times rapturously happy. A Quaker, Godfrey went before a tribunal as a conscientious objector and asked for alternative service. Now he drove an ambulance and carried stretchers to the wounded and dying in bomb incidents. He talked of it.

Laura considered him.

"Practical. Active, you have to be. Could you have been a monk, Godfrey?"

"You mean a contemplative? No-oo," he said slowly. "Why do you ask?"

"Only that I sometimes think you look like a monk."

"I just had to prove it wasn't actual physical danger I was objecting to," he said.

"I think it's wonderfully brave of you," Laura said, meaning no flattery. But he took it as such, and it displeased him. He went dumb, sulky, in the way she remembered so well. She grew flustered.

"I mean to say, you meet danger much more regularly than most people fighting?"

He shrugged his shoulders. She relapsed into silence too.

"Laura, I've something to tell you," he said presently, in a special voice; as if her earlier question had precipitated his decision. Laura watched the drops fly off the pole as he flung it up. He is going to tell me about some girl, his girl, she thought. What a pity I did not go on loving Godfrey, and why did I not, she asked herself, preparing now to be glad with him?

❦

Monday was May morning. (Godfrey had gone, late on Sunday night, kissing her cheek rather sadly from the train.) Laura went to Magdalen Bridge alone, watched some huddled, sleepy-looking punters jostling for position in the dark green water below the tower. At least it was not as cold as usual; they might even have their river breakfast in comfort. It was a fairer May Day than most she could remember. As the clocks struck seven, silence fell. The Latin carol arose from brave treble throats on top of the tower. The police had halted the traffic, so that listeners could hear the clear music even if not the words. She counted the verses, holding her breath. After the third, engines roared, gears changed, hooters blared, the officious wartime traffic surged forward, over-ruling the policemen, setting at naught the tradition of hundreds of years. Mammon deafened the listeners, drowned God's boys on the tower. The industrial juggernauts roared on towards the motor-works, whose ill-judged position so close to the city was shaking its ancient stones apart and had already destroyed its illusion of isolated peace. The Beast conquered, white surplices fluttered high up in the wind while Beauty's servants sang on, unheard.

When she was waiting in the London train, somebody thumped on the carriage window, dashing past.

"Keep me a seat," mouthed Tom.

He appeared breathless a moment later, and squeezed his long thin frame into the exiguous space she had claimed with her handbag, the non-existent fifth seat. Laura, pretty thin, gave him as much room as she could.

"What fun, how nice to see you! Been up for the weekend, like me?"

"Yes," he said gustily, patting her knee. "Thought I'd missed it. Lord. Given myself a sore throat running."

"Where do you stay, Tom, now Rose isn't here to arrange it?"

"I've got friends in Summertown with a newsagents' shop, they have a spare room. I always go there."

"That's lucky."

"Yes. A bit far out, though. I came up for a lecture on Friday night and stayed. Nothing till this evening's class in London. What've you been at, girl? Maydaying?"

"I went along, yes. Mainly I came to see friends. Went on the river with Godfrey, one of my best friends up here, he was having a break from the fires of London. And I was asking after a man who used to teach me a bit."

Tom looked at her curiously; the upheaval of his breath now subsided. He looked so long down his thin Roman nose that she eventually looked at him.

"Was that the one you lost your heart to?" Very quietly, so that the passengers could not hear.

"How on earth did you know about it?"

"Tomfool knows more than you think."

"How?"

"Ros mentioned it."

"Rose, did Rose know?"

"Everyone knew, I think. That something was wrong. You looked ill, she said you looked like death. Anyway, it got about. They all thought how ill you looked. And sad. And washed up. From time to time."

"Lots of us did. Finals. I remember Gwyneth Heal totally collapsed one day. Lying on the floor in the JCR. I said, Asleep or Fainted? And she groaned. So I handed her my nice mug of hot chocolate I'd just made with powdered baby milk. She recovered at once." He laughed, aware that she had turned the subject. Yet in Laura's heart a chasm had opened, the retrospective view of herself had flooded her again with that hopeless ache like warmth returning to frozen hands. The pangs of love, the pangs of love, not one word any poet ever said was a half of it, she mused.

"And is you heart still lost?" whispered Tom, teasingly.

"Afraid so," said Laura, laughing.

They rattled into Didcot, less dreary than usual in the green of May, and slowed down. As the train dallied through the station, Laura looked from the window: and saw Gavin Kitto, Gavin, across the line, on the opposite platform, waiting for the next to Oxford! Gavin, the sun brilliantly lighting his serious, sweet face, his burnished hair, his spare, tall frame, his slightly crooked stance, his anxious movement from foot to foot, his nervous toss of the head. Laura gasped, sat forward, her eyes suddenly misted, the colour rushing to her cheeks, and as suddenly draining away, as she suffered the blows of the breathless heart on the sight of its beloved. Gavin, said her silent lips.

As the train moved she flung herself back with a great gasp, his figure gone. She had forgotten Tom. Tom observed the sudden movement, the signs of shock, the lips, and now the tears squeezing below closed eyes.

"See someone you know?" whispered Tom.

"Yes. Talk of angels." Her eyes remained closed, she disregarded the tears.

"How extraordinary." He took her hand, and held it on his knee. She did not withdraw it and the touch was a comfort. But she herself withdrew. Tom noted that she spoke barely a word as she floated away from him. A look of calm, glowing joy took over her face. When they reached London, she said goodbye to him as if in a dream, not noticing the concern in his manner, the new interest in his eyes. He shook her shoulders slightly. "Goodbye, girl…I'm sorry…. See you soon?" She nodded. "Please. You are kind, Tom. Thank you."

She was enveloped in a glow, an exaltation, of the sublimest, purest, single-hearted love, love like a singing shaft of golden light, such as she had never, she thought, experienced before. It mattered not at all that he was not hers, would never be, it mattered only that he existed, he was well, they inhabited the same earth, the same incomprehensible glory illuminated them both, held and enfolded them both. The warm light lasted all the day and had a calming, peaceful effect. It made her happy.

O h dear," Laura sighed, her head in her hands, her elbows upon a red-checked Wopshop tablecloth stained with coffee.

"I know," responded Prudence miserably. "Isn't it terrible? I feel just the same today. Perhaps it's the weather."

Prudence and Laura, ridiculous girls, deep in gloom, pulling each other in deeper at every moment; no Mrs Wicklow at hand to dispel it, the Italian girl glummer than usual, the cold May day a traitor to its season. Like all despondency, their despair appeared formless, inchoate and reasonless. In fact, various causes provided footholds in the mud, if they had had the sense to look. (Give despair a reason and it is half dead.) Laura, for one thing, should have been used by now to the sleeplessness, which from time to time, according to the secrets of her body, she suffered. *Une nuit blanche* had afflicted her last night. It would come to be called pre-menstrual tension: how increasingly public the whole of life was to be, as it entered the age of the national health, the man in the street, the sensational press. Acts of sex in every film, buggery upon the stage, girls discussing techniques of love on the radio, babies born upon the television screen; reporters bursting into hospitals, photographing dying men; waiting round at violent executions; making the victims of hideous catastrophes talk as their faces flowed with tears. All that should be private, a person's own, or his family's, exploded into publicity: one of the cynical aims of some sections of the media becoming the total destruction of personal privacy for the delectation of other people.

Quite right too, many people would say, as permissiveness broke the last dams of puritanism. Blow away the cobwebs, the prudishness that causes ignorance and fear. Good riddance to hypocrisy! (But what of the warm cheeks of shyness, what of her? What of reticence and proper modesty and justifiable shame? All sweet virgins gone to the wall. So Imogen Wicklow was to say, an old lady, her merriment more frequently silenced at the last by horrid astonishment.)

So, Laura had not slept. Prudence at this time was suffering mute, dread apprehension on account of her younger brother in the army, with parents who (suffering the same, indeed more) spoke never a word.

And, day after day, the bombers droned overhead in their hundreds to destroy the communications of northern France, preparing for her eventual liberation. For, finally, over the whole sentient country, brooded that shadow with its certainty of tragedy, savagery and horrible hardship, the coming Second Front. Gloom was difficult to avoid. Prudence made an effort.

"You haven't told me about Oxford," she said. Laura looked back to the sober joys, the immemorial places, the blossoming trees and the memory led straight to the sight of Gavin, standing upon the platform in the sun. The sudden joy of it lit up her face again.

"Did you find out how your heart-throb is?" The jocular expression made them both smile. Laura had never mentioned Gavin's name, though she had once confessed her feelings to her friend.

"Prudence, you'll never believe it, it was glorious. I *saw* him! Looking perfectly all right, just as I remember him."

"What did he *say?*"

"Oh, we didn't meet, he was waiting at Didcot on the up-line platform, we were in the train coming back to London, Tom got on to my train, my Canadian friend. There he was, standing there in the sun, waiting for a train, it was heaven," her voice almost broke, "it made me feel so happy!" There was a kind of surprise in her voice at the memory. Tears stood in her eyes. Prudence studied her with tenderness: thinking I wish Laura could have this man, whoever he is. How she does love this man. She does really worship him. It is real, it's a real love, I think. A distant envy plucked at her.

"Did he see you?"

"Oh, no. The train was moving, he couldn't have seen me. It was lovely though, such a treat. I'd asked at the college, they say he's working in London, some war job."

"He probably knows best about not keeping in touch," said Prudence sadly.

"I expect he does," said Laura, a flurry of tears suddenly dropping into her plate. "Anyway, what does it matter, what do my affairs matter, how can I be so selfish, with all this?" Was Prudence luckier than she, to be so heart-free still?

"What matters to us is Donald. Mum and Pop are terrified sick about Donald, I can tell."

"Of course."

"But they never say a word."

Laura could imagine the tight-lipped, cheerful, shuddering trio. Nobody was lucky: nobody with brother or boyfriend at this moment could be counted lucky. Nobody of their age, here, in France, in Germany, in Italy or any other fighting country, with five years of their lives distorted or wasted by the exigencies of war. They were much luckier than most, simply to have got through their education.

Laura said so. Prudence agreed.

"I'm going to Cambridge next weekend," she divulged, smiling.

"Good, I hope you'll enjoy it. It's a kind of anchor, feeling it all still there."

"Perhaps if it has to be one, it would be better if it were Willy," Imogen Wicklow prayed, or at least thought, in her fearful heart. (For who was she, to suggest alternatives to the Almighty?) "Willy, at least, has no girl, no attachment, that I know of. It would be he, alone, and us, Jane and Victoria, Harry and I, who suffer." Oh, but not dark, square, gentle Willy! Loving beauty, delicately handling glass! How could she sacrifice Willy? Her youngest, her merry, loving baby, who had been so close to her all his life. His face came vividly up in her mind, a burning wave of sorrow followed it, arising from deep inside her, and issued in tears. She felt her hands wet over her eyes: Holy Mother, no, not William.

She remembered, which one always tended to forget thinking of her as Queen of Heaven, that Mary, thus Mary, an ordinary mother, suffered before and after the crucifixion. Perhaps if she let herself contemplate for a little the hill and the crosses...?

Imogen Wicklow knelt at the very back of the pews in Westminster Cathedral, where she was in the shadows, far off from the altar, hidden from the sightseers and other people praying.

Her fears, like those of the Kyles but doubled, had brought her to such a state of exhaustion that she had decided she must prepare to lose the boys in advance. Would that not help her to be calm, and make it easier, if it came to the worst? Unlike the Kyles, she and Victoria could speak of it: even more, she could pour it all out, knife the abscess, to God (perhaps): certainly to the Holy Mother. Perhaps simply to her own heart, the unbelieving would say.

What about dear Harry? She asked next. Why should I long to keep William at the expense of brilliant Harry, who loved his life, as theatre critic, journalist, broadcaster. And already married, his wayward heart attached with passion to Monique. Why should Harry whom she admired so much and who brought her husband so vividly back, why should he be the one?

The fact is I cannot bear to lose either, any of my children, she confided, and I know I have to be ready to lose all. (Even Victoria, she supposed, might be killed driving Red Cross trucks in France.) I have to be ready to lose all three: at least Jane is safe.

She returned to the hill and the three crosses. Three crosses. Three. She was there. In the darkness she forgot all else. Death shall have no dominion, said Harry's voice gladly, reading Dylan Thomas. Eventually the whole landscape of the crosses seemed illumined after that darkness. There she stayed, held in warm light. An apologetic shake, tentative but urgent, on her shoulder. She looked round, her eyes blank.

"Mrs Wicklow, ma'am," whispered Paddy, a sub-verger, an extra, whom she knew well, who came voluntarily to help do chores.

"What is it?"

"Your handbag, ma'am. Don't leave it behind you, on the pew, I beg, looking for trouble it is."

"Paddy! In the church?" she whispered, scandalised.

"It's not only Christians come in this church. And it's walking round I must be, not hovering, guarding your handbag, pardon me ma'am," he protested.

"How long have you been here?"

"A full hour and more, Mrs Wicklow, ma'am. Here." He thrust the bag at her; she put it before her knees.

The landscape with the crosses was gone. Later, considering the incident, she remembered with some dejection about Willy's mac.

Prudence went to the Whithorns, whom she loved, as home from home.

Arriving just before seven on the May evening, and forgetting to walk down the train, since she was near the front, she was swept on to the top of that inordinately long station, and smiled to herself walking back. Quickly, one forgot the tricks.

There were still cherries and prunus in Hills Road, too: Laura had talked of them in north Oxford. She arrived in Long Road quite breathless, having forgotten how far it was, but pink and cheerfully full of anticipation. The infrequent bus had not passed her.

They hailed her in with joyful cries and embraces, Mary Whithorn first, the professor hovering behind his wife, Justin their younger son lurking in the shadows, looking as if he were in the air force.

"He is, he is," Mary said. "Isn't it good luck, he's home this weekend?"

"Oh, but you won't *want* me," Prudence protested, thinking of families and serving sons and sorrows and farewells.

"Nonsense," said Professor Whithorn. "Anyway, he just turned up, too late to put you off."

Secretly they had been rather pleased. Of all the professor's recent girl pupils, they had liked her best, had even gone so far as to say how she would suit Justin.

Justin grinned at her; they had met once or twice before. Prudence greeted him as if he had been Donald, with unaffected pleasure and no feminine consciousness. Throughout the two days, she was exactly the same, friendly, serious, sympathetic, sisterly. In a sense, Mary Whithorn thought, it is perhaps our fault: we always treated this one as the daughter we never had; lodging with us like that, her last year.

Justin put her on to her London train after Sunday supper, earlier than he was to leave himself. She gravely wished him good luck, her honey hazel eyes full upon his, and said how nice it had been to see him. Then she turned and entered a carriage with only one seat amongst a hot, khaki crowd of cheerful boys jabbering. Justin imagined their remarks, caught a brief view of her, giggling, flushed, like a child almost. He hoped she would not be bothered. *Integer vitae*, he supposed: her candour would repel interference.

"She hasn't grown up much, has she?" he said smiling to his parents.

"Mentally," said his father, "she has."

"I think you mean she has no feminine wiles," said his mother with what he called her crooked smile.

"Perhaps I do," Justin said, used to service girls.

"That's what we like about her," said Professor Whithorn.

The boys in the train did not know what to make of her. They had moved up to make room for her gladly, several of them closing their knees together. They had offered her cigarettes, sweeties, even drinks. Not wanting it, she accepted a boiled sweet. To their barrage of well-meant kindly questions she gave kindly answers.

"You're not married, then." A statement, looking for her ring.

She shook her head.

"What's your boyfriend, army?"

"Air force! Fighter pilot! I guess."

"I haven't any special boyfriend," Prudence admitted.

"No boyfriend! Hey, miss, you join the ATS, you'll soon get one."

"What do you do then?"

"Intelligence," Prudence admitted.

"There. See. She's clever."

Prudence giggled, sucking the sweet, looking round them all, shy and not shy.

"She's nice when she giggles, clever or not."

Prudence giggled more.

"Where are you all going? Oh, I mustn't ask."

"No, hush hush. Don't ask. Just guess."

They all looked very young, Donald's age perhaps. They all observed her, interested, attracted, rather reverential.

"What's your name, then?" said one, as if this might reveal all. Perhaps it did.

"Prudence," she said. "What's yours?"

"That's a nice old-fashioned sort of a name," said he. "Mine's Dick."

"I like Dick. I hope you've got a Thomas and a Harry!"

"Ay, sure. And a George, and a Bob, and a Bruce."

They all began shouting their good British names. An officer put his head in from next door.

"I hope no one's bothering you," he said pleasantly.

"Certainly not," Prudence replied. "I've got a brother in the army," she added sweetly.

He smiled.

At Liverpool Street, Dick handed her grip out to her.

"Goodbye," she said, "good luck. Good luck to you all."

"Goodbye, Prudence," said Dick. They all shouted goodbye, unloading their packs. One did not say it, even to oneself, one thought it only in a corner of one's mind: that some of them would not make the journey home.

It was overcast by now, the sky heavy. When she reached the common, it was almost dusk on a deserted Sunday evening in wartime. She changed hands with the grip, hitched her shoulder bag on, and walked briskly over the grass.

A little more than halfway over she saw that she was being approached, diagonally, by a thin man intent upon catching her up. She hastened her steps, she was tall and vigorous, but her weekend bag somewhat impeded her. She did not look at him as he approached (those jolly soldiers were all very well, but she had no wish to hold isolated conversations on the common at this hour) but she was aware of a figure shorter than she, of an overall grey colour, pale faced.

"Good evening," he said, catching her up with a rush.

"*Good* evening," said Prudence briskly, in what she hoped was a tone of finality but ever polite.

"A nice warm evening." It was by now cool and grey.

"Will you come and have a drink? I know a place still open."

"Sorry, no, I can't possibly, I've been away for the weekend and I must get back," she said with decision.

"Aw, come on. I've been alone all day, I just want a bit of talk and cheer. You live near here?"

"Very near."

"All the better. We could go to your place. You live alone?"

"Certainly not. I live with my family." She had not meant to converse at all.

"Look, I've got these, it'd be quite safe. Let's go and get a few drinks and then go off somewhere, it's quite warm."

He produced a packet of what Prudence saw as small white balloons, he actually waggled one at her. She was totally at sea and beginning to be frightened. She did not show it. She took longer strides, hastening her step. She could see their gate, home was not far.

He touched her, he put a grip on her arm, almost running to keep pace with her. She flung him off, clutching her handbag (she supposed it was her handbag he really wanted, but could it be a sexual attack?) and began to run. Wretched shoes, she could have run better in sandals. She could hear him following, something rattling in his pockets, and a breath getting heavier. She put on an enormous sprint as if for sports' day and a plan evolved. When she thought the distance between them sufficient, she turned suddenly, and using the grip as a kind of battering ram in both arms, ran at him, hard in his stomach. He fell clean over with a harsh grunt.

Hardening her heart against helping him up, she fled for home, where she arrived both breathless and pale. Edwin had the door open as he heard her key.

"Well! Here you are!" A few tears, in the light of the sitting room. "What's wrong?"

"Oh, just tired. I hurried from the station," was all their daughter said, recovering her breath.

They thought that memories of Cambridge had upset her usual calm cheer.

But secretly in her room she relived the affair. Why that sudden, involuntary upsurge of angry physical strength? She should have "talked him along" until they reached the gate. She half-smiled, thinking of his falling like a ninepin. Perhaps he would track her down and sue her for assault? But no, it was clearly self-defence. He might well have tried to assault her or snatched her handbag if she hadn't knocked him down. She did not understand that childish play with the balloons.

On to a glowing account of her two days with the Whithorns, she appended to Laura a brief sentence or two.

"He kept wagging this packet of white balloons, little white balloons, at me?"

"Those are contraceptives," Laura said with deadpan casualness. "They call them 'French letters'. It wasn't your handbag he was after, my dearest P. What did you do?"

Prudence, half abject, half laughing, confessed what she had done.

"Hurrah. Serve him right. Good for you," Laura said, aghast with admiration and horror. Supposing he had been taller, stronger, beefier? What might not have happened?

"So what did your Mum and Pop say?"

"About what?"

"About this attack, these little white balloons?"

"Oh, I didn't tell them. I didn't want to frighten them, about the handbag. And they wouldn't have known about 'little white balloons'," she laughed at herself.

"Prudence! They are married people! What do you suppose *they* do?"

Prudence fell quiet, became reserved, even perhaps a little huffy, Laura wondered, looking sideways at her.

"We never talk about it, we never talk about things like that, you see. I mean they wouldn't talk about their marriage affairs to me!" Her tone was astounded.

"No, but what about your marriage affairs?" Laura was otherwise amazed. Were her parents so shy or such prudes that she could not talk to her mother even, of all this? And what about Donald, a rough initiation the army must have given *him*! But then, she reflected, neither could I talk, of course, to Papa. And even her mother had been pretty concise and minimal over the facts of life long ago: and tended to issue mild warnings about low necks, and short skirts, and legs apart; and held the view that the safeguarding of "holy sexuality" was, in the last resort and rather unfairly (Laura considered) always in the woman's hands.

"Och, all in good time," Prudence said laughing. Laura, with her aching heart, did not know whether to envy her friend this unconcern or not. To be so free of the nagging restlessness, the demands of the body, the longing for love, the need for the womb's satisfaction! Fortunate Prudence, Laura thought, who was single-mindedly in search of knowledge, not of a mate.

J une. It must be," people assumed.

Of course when you came to think of it, it must be June. Since February, in ever increasing numbers the American troops had poured in. Then there was presumably the collecting-together of all manner of equipment in vast quantities. Those who lived near the south coast saw it accumulating. The practising of the operation, in comprehensive variety, upon beaches inaccessible to the general public. And also, at no time before June was the weather in the Channel likely to be long enough trustworthy for the carrying out of so enormous, hazardous and detailed a scheme, and June itself, all knew, could be as spiteful as a changeable mistress. Besides, June left all the rest of the summer to consolidate things: leave it later, and an early autumn might pose unnecessary troubles. The fact of its imminence brooded over them all. Everyone, Edwin surmised, must be thinking of it: like drums in the distance it lurked, menacing them, but coming hourly nearer.

Few, it seem to Laura, talked of it. Distracted as they always were by all the other theatres of war, General Mark Clark at long last approaching Rome, General Slim enjungled in Burma, the Americans preparing to wipe out the Japanese in the Philippines; there nevertheless seemed a throbbing, gathering, immediate horror right above the head like some vast growth causing pain, which must soon explode. Possibly the not talking of it, (the inhibition expressed by Fougasse's picture of Hitler's moustache inside Charles II's wig listening to two wagging tongues in a club) was the reason for its nightmare quality to the ordinary person. So the verdict that it must be June was not bandied about in public places: but came to be taken for granted.

The other great question was where.

At what point along the opposing coasts would the combined forces leave, the combined forces land? Laura on the whole did not think, did not ask. Perhaps men asked their sons, home on leave, privately? She could not imagine Prudence's father asking Donald. Obediently, for the most part, the silence held. It held even over people living near enough to coasts to observe with their own eyes, where it was a vast open secret. Once, when four of them sat silent at work in the Shuttlecock room, Laura was aware of Mrs Tripp enunciating in a whisper to herself, as she stared at a map:

"Normandy."

Daisy, raising her eyes, slowly shook her head, her round face complacent, contained. Laura waited, watched Daisy. Mrs Wicklow, aware of communication, glanced from one to the other, blushed and looked a little accusing. Daisy said nothing, with a very great effort. Daisy had cousins in Kent, opposite Calais, who had been guilty in her view of careless talk, which should go no further so far as she was concerned she vowed, folding her lips with a sense of unrewarded virtue.

A few doors away, Mr Harvald threw the telephone at Mr Watson. (Marie found it next day, its guts torn out, standing neatly in a corner as if atoning for its own fault.)

Meanwhile, it was typical June weather. There are two kinds of typical June weather in England, as is well known. The first is the kind meant by "flaming June" and "the glorious fourth of June". It was the third of June this year when the second kind, the kind which will be found by statistics to be more typical in our age, struck. Cold, sulky, squally, then wild; in London rain lashed the buses and blinded the office windows and turned the shop fronts liquid, those that were not boarded up anyway.

On the coast, the storm was harsh: "such summer season saw I never the like" as someone wrote in Armada year (when it was also remarked that you could not tell summer from winter). It raged for two days.

Then, as if breath were let out, suddenly all knew from wireless and newspaper the fact of the accomplishment of "overlord", a massive joint landing in Normandy; the fact, but not yet the detail, the failures, triumphs, agonies. It was Tuesday the sixth of June when there had been a full moon. People sighed rather than talked, Laura noticed. What was there, after all, to say? Many, of the mind of Imogen Wicklow and Kitty Cardew, prayed.

An echoing crash, followed by a kind of subsiding lengthy rumble, awoke Laura who was deeply asleep. Also an unusual heaviness upon her chest.

In the green dawn light she blinked at the ceiling, seeing an unknown, dark, strange-shaped patch, like a country outlined, like those maps they had all been shown of Germany swallowing Czechoslovakia, Poland... .

She pulled her arm from beneath the sheet and felt. Plaster lay like a jigsaw over the middle of her body. Presumably, a pilotless aircraft, a V1, a doodlebug, a buzz bomb. Jeering Londoners had begun to make the nicknames in advance, with the warnings. The first of the secret weapons, upon which she had laboured for months, and one with her name on. It did not feel particularly funny as she came to, yet she supposed it was. They had begun almost as soon as the Normandy landings, but this was Laura's first near-at-hand experience. In fact, it was among the very first attacks.

Why were they in bed and not sheltering? She had been to meet Marian for a meal and cinema after work: Marian did not turn up, one had to be prepared for such things. So she had gone alone. She had reached home just as the siren went. Nothing happened, and they had very soon retired to bed, where her mother had already been. She now heard Kitty's door open below.

"Lolly?" she said, up the stairs.

"It's all right," Laura called, "but I'm plastered."

Kitty came up, her face long with concern and sleepiness, and looked from bed to ceiling.

"Don't move till I get something to put it in."

They did not say, they did not even think, we might be dead or even worse buried in rubble and suffocating, as some people in fact are. They simply knew that they would have to clear up the mess, and went into action. Practical action deflected people from their fears constantly. Kitty fetched a dustsheet for Laura's plaster and let her out. They walked from room to room surveying the damage. Maps of strange countries on every ceiling, dust in everything, ornaments dimmed with dust-film, crunching plaster on carpets and lino, pictures fallen, cold unexpected dawn draughts from broken windows. Glass, mind the glass, where's the General, under your bed, don't blame him. Wallpaper doing weird balancing acts like a grotesque ballet. Of course Kitty had known that the house had a good many cracks, had not been decorated for some time: she had acquired it cheaply, and wartime was not when you set about that kind of thing.

They sighed. It grew lighter.

"What's the time?"

"Nearly five. Wonder who got it, I didn't even hear it cut out."

"I heard it coming. Let's make some tea. Then get dressed, we'll never sleep again."

"No. Then get weaving." Laura yawned.

All round them yawning neighbours prepared to do the same: but you did not think of it, you bore your own burden until someone else's seemed too heavy for him. Tramping up and downstairs with dustsheets of crumbling jigsaw, dust-pans of tinkling glass, hoovers roaring while the bins bulged in every yard, and the piles of plaster grew. Dusters seemed no use, wet cloths were better.

At first Laura wondered if she should try to go to work. (It was Friday, the sixteenth of June.) Perspiration stood like a heavy dew upon her mother's face. She was flushed with effort. Laura could not leave her, she would work all tomorrow instead. She telephoned.

By mid-morning, people were telephoning them, Marian (anxious and explaining), Uncle Miles, neighbours, a person or two from Suffolk. Papa did not telephone. Laura wondered if he had even noticed where the bombs fell, what he would think if he had, whether he would worry.

Turning her attention at last to the spare room next to her own,

Laura was met by a vivid memory, which seemed so long ago yet was only within the war. Why, even the war had developed epochs, the war had been going nearly six years. It must be three or more years ago that she worked here, at a table in the window, carefully blacked out. She was working her eyes blind with a low volt wartime bulb of horrid blue in a Christmas vacation, she supposed: she had been marched in upon by a short, determined, aggressive air-raid warden in a tin hat too big for him which he did not trouble to remove, her mother hovering unhappily behind him. (For he had pushed his way in, as she opened the front door.) A crack of light had appeared, it seemed, in the window where the black-out did not fit. He was convinced that this girl, secluded at the top here, was signalling to enemy aircraft and it was no good pointing out to him Stubbs' *Constitutional History* spread upon the table. The preposterous suggestion had struck both Laura and Kitty into open-mouthed silence, which to him was the more suspicious. He took a lot of convincing, he was so disappointed: he had a consuming ambition to uncover a spy.

"Footling little rat," Laura had said, in a rage, almost stamping her foot. "You should have knocked him downstairs." (The whole family, tall and reasonably slender, had an unconscious propensity to despise those of lesser height, it was one of their commonest, corporate failings.) "Have they got a *right* to walk in?"

"Well, I suppose they have, he thought he was doing his duty," Kitty had said mildly, always slow to anger, used to seeing the other's point of view.

What a long, long time ago it seemed. The tunnel lightened, the armies were in Normandy at last. Laura came down the stairs carrying plaster, with tears streaming over her dusty cheeks.

"Oh, Lolly. It's the early waking, the effort. I'll make some coffee. In fact, we'd better stop for lunch," said her mother. "Have you seen the stairs to the garden door, by the way?"

Laura opened the flat door, surveyed the plaster in horrid piles all down, and quickly closed it.

"We were better where we were," she said. "That would have been quite heavy on the head."

Kind old Mr Heaton, who lived round the corner, came in the

afternoon: just, it happened, as they cleared those stairs, thought to be their safest place. He threw up his grimy hands.

"Not safe at all, we thought not. How are you getting on? Elsie says, please do come tonight, we have room for you, and cushions, and blankets…"

Laura tried not to look dismayed. The Heatons had had a concrete re-enforcement made, a bunker really, around their conservatory, in which they slept when necessary. The conservatory led off the drawing room. The width of their own and the next house sandwiched the bunker in what was hoped was protective safety.

Thereafter began the miserable deprivation of one's own bed, the embarrassment of sleeping in public. (Millions of people had endured it for long stretches of the war.) Mr & Mrs Heaton at one end, Laura and her mother at the other, the General (to whom the Heatons had been welcoming) leaning against Laura. Blankets, their own to be sure, but camping ones, smelling sour, reminding Laura of happier days in Suffolk sleeping in the paddock. Everything feeling airless, subterranean, except for her own dear pillow, like a friend in a crowd.

"Amongst the first! That it should be almost the first of them! And you working here on them!" Mrs Wicklow marvelled. "What *did* your mother say?" She had grown to expect Laura to quote her mother's remarks, mildly tart, or gloriously sentimental, or sweetly charitable. She looked forward to them.

"But I've never told her," Laura admitted, smiling palely. Imogen was astonished.

"Well, of course, you're quite right, my child," she acknowledged. "But how amazingly scrupulous of you. Don't you suppose she's guessed?"

Laura considered her dear mother, with a ruminative smile.

"No, I don't," she said with decision. Imogen nodded, noticing the detail like a stroke to a portrait.

"It'll be the beginning of the end of us, anyway," she said. "This section."

"Will it?"

"Surely. Now they're actually coming. All heads now are on how to intercept them, stop them. Not where they're making them, we must know that."

"I wonder we haven't bombed them all."

"We have some, no doubt. But they're going to get through for a bit, as you know to your cost."

"All those floating silver elephants," Laura said, remembering the early barrage balloons in shining, straining cohorts, over and around London, at charmingly different heights like some fantasy, some children's game. In a few weeks, thousands were to be replaced, south of London, to catch the V1s.

"I can't believe they're not a joke," Laura said.

Daisy was full of concern, studying Laura.

"You do look so tired," she said kindly.

"I feel dead. And there's plaster in my hair, must wash it."

"Brush it, brush it hard first. Or it'll turn to a species of glue," Mrs Wicklow said, with a peal of laughter.

By Monday, June had played its worst trick. A terrible storm arose, worsened, pretended to abate, returned in force, and became a part of history. For more than three days, it raged over the coasts of northern Europe and the Channel, defying anyone to do anything. Supply ships were kept in port, air force pilots (Justin amongst them) swore and champed and cursed, unable to fly, to give air cover, or the bombers to bomb. One of the clever Mulberry harbours used for the landings was destroyed. Many of the installations still needed, the landing craft still in use, were scattered like toys by a bullying sea. The Americans, fighting inch by inch for Cherbourg, were held up for supplies.

The Kyles thought of Donald. Donald, wet, hungry and fearful, with feet that were a misery and a cold in the head, was fighting for Caen, along with the rest under Monty, who announced that all was going "according to plan", but made no remark of the weather. Prudence thought of Dick, too, and all that cheerful crew in the train. Dick was dead, by great ill luck, hit by one of the German bullets that strafed the landing beaches as they were digging themselves in.

Imogen Wicklow thought of William: William's tanks were at a standstill, in mud somewhere, as stolid as their crews' courage. And of Harry: at least Harry could not jump in this. Harry was consumed with impatience, an exuberant character who needed to do all he did quickly, for his enthusiasm not to leak. His body was ready, his mind too; he exulted in being ready for dangerous, exciting action. He was so excited he could not even write a poem. God damn this blasted, treacherous weather, Harry said.

This, Edwin Kyle noted in his diary, will teach those fools who think there is a God who controls the weather. Prudence saw his sardonic smile one night, and wondered.

It was several weeks after their bomb that Laura walked up to the Hurst with the General, on a fair evening of early summer, which heightened the waste, terror, hindrance and futility of this endless war. The dear General was snuffing, pottering, going from side to side, and taking the steep slope of the road a little lazily. It was his favourite walk, the wood at the top full of freedom, trees, and smells of squirrel. The General was getting old, Laura thought sadly.

There were houses on only one side of the road. A great stretch of the hedge on the opposite side she suddenly saw to be burned bright brown, just as with a bad frost: the sudden gash of devastation, between the fresh green hawthorn leaves either side, was shocking. The grass and weeds below were also burned. Twisted metal remains lay in the field and the ditch: a piece, the engine perhaps, of one of the pilotless planes, the searing effect of the explosion and the fuel hideously evident. Perhaps it was their very one, it was quite near. There had been many others, none quite so near, it was clear they were on one of the lanes, they were getting used to it. Supposing I had been killed, Laura thought for the first time and objectively. Would my death have reconciled Papa and Mamma? But if I were dead, Mamma would be dead too, she realised, dismissing the situation as a non-starter.

The General was now ahead, near the top, quickening his pace in anticipatory delight. Laura followed him into the trees, the sweet, lacy birches of early summer, all silvered and quivering, and out into the sunlight.

In a patch of warm sun, in a small hollow, sat a pair of lovers. Why, they were not young at all, but middle-aged, an aura of glorious joy around them. In a mutual gesture like a dance, perfectly timed, exquisitely natural yet with the eternal grace of art, they turned where they sat to embrace each other, she lower than he, stretching up, he gathering her in.

Into this bright idyll blundered the General, panting and smiling, ever confident of his welcome. They laughed sweetly, separating, as Laura apologised for his tactlessness, but they said no word. She walked on, wondering if they were man and wife, almost deciding they were not, for there was a flavour of secret romance around them. Whether or no, it mattered not at all in comparison with their joy in their re-union. She envied them from the deepest recesses of her heart.

That, said Laura, that is what I seek. I would be sorry to be dead with that unfound. I wish that were Gavin and me twenty years on. I'll ring up Tom for lunch tomorrow, she thought. Though whether it was thoughts of love or of death which turned her mind towards him she did not consider.

"I was nearly killed again a few weeks back," said Laura to Tom, "but I'd better not talk about it or I'll be accused of angling for sympathy. The funny thing is when I didn't ask for any you gave it, in quarts." He looked at her, solemn, blinking, ruminative, remembering all too well the time in the train, and trying to remember the earlier occasion. "Yes," he said, "I remember thinking you did seem to need it, that time in the train."

"I did, I did. In a way. But it made me happy, seeing him. I've always meant to thank you."

"You did thank me. But you weren't *there*, you weren't with me. When we got to London, you were kind of...sort of...not so much absent...as transported."

"Was I? Well, after the shock, of seeing him, it made me so happy, I just felt floating on joy."

"That's exactly what you looked like, floating on joy," Tom said sombrely, recalling a sense of being shut out of paradise. "So what about this bomb? Was it a bomb? Come on, tell all, tell every detail, good for your psyche, never bury anything. All this burying of people, all this digging out, wonderfully symbolical. Come on, what happened?"

"A V1."

"A doodle-bug—it deserves an absurd name."

"One of the very first to come. There's a comical irony in that, if you did but know it." She paused. He stared.

"I do but guess it," he said, nodding. "What happened?"

"It wasn't too close, we were lucky, I was just half-buried in plaster from the ceiling in my top room. But the mess! The mess was frightful!"

"Never mind the mess, were you *frightened*? That other time, you said you couldn't stop shaking."

"I didn't have time to be frightened, it woke me up falling on me, the plaster, I never heard the thing coming."

"The time before, but the time before, you were shaking—Why?" Tom was interested in the psychology of fear.

"That was while we waited for it, we could hear them roaring over, approaching, *that* was an ordinary old bomber with a load of bricks."

"Yes, so you had time to imagine the bombs falling, the house falling on you, burying you alive."

"Yes, I suppose so."

"So it was your imagination, the shaking fear was your imagining what could happen."

"I suppose so."

"Imagination of what might happen caused the fear, helpless physical fear you couldn't control."

"Why all this?"

"Just interested in fear. Right now. Thought you'd like some kindly interest."

"I do." She smiled.

"Sure. What else are you afraid of, Laura?" Tom for some reason he had not yet discerned, felt urgently interested in her, in what she was really like, behind her quick mind.

"Good heavens, Tom, millions of things."

"Name a few."

"Um. Um. Very high mountains, steep, slippery paths."

"Switzerland, et cetera. Yes?"

"Rough people breaking me up."

"Fights, you mean? Do girls fight?"

"We did as sisters, sometimes. Dark corners. Sometimes. Men lurking to jump out. People following me in the street. Rows. People shouting at people."

"Your father."

"Perhaps, yes. And there was a game he played, being a giant, when I was tiny, I couldn't bear it, he didn't know, I had to rush at him and bury my head in his black stomach."

"*Black* stomach?"

"Well, he always seemed to wear dark suits."

"You had to rush at the terror and be part of it. It's called identifying with the aggressor. All very interesting. All quite ordinary, no phobias as yet."

"Oh Tom, you psychological caterpillar," said she.

"It was religious caterpillars," said he, delightedly picking up the allusion. "Two or three of them."

"Yes. Context?" She liked his knowledge of even fairly obscure plays.

But he could not remember, his mind these days filled to the brim with Plato and Locke, Jung and Freud.

9

Oh damn the rain," Marie said.

It had been a wet, rather dreary Sunday, though not cold. Marie had employed herself cleaning the flat (the two girls were both scrupulous in keeping it, but Sadie had gone home this weekend, to Essex, and would not be back till late at night) doing her washing, cooking her small lunch. When it was poor weather, one minded less. For four years now, Marie had had to accustom herself to being (virtually) alone, though her flat-mate was an agreeable friend. Her parents had died, one quickly after the other, she could not afford to keep the small railwayman's house that had been home and anyway thought a move further into London would bring her near good jobs. She was thirty, the war had made a better-paid typing job more easily available. She and Sadie had jumped at the flat near Chiswick, even if it was at the top of the house and might be bombed. It had held also the unforeseeable, undreamed-of gift of Charles, which had become the greatest comfort in life Marie had had since the loss of her parents.

There seemed to be little going on downstairs today, though she had heard the usual, quiet, rippling, music from the study where Charles often sat. If his wife were out he would sometimes ask her down. She supposed Mrs Best was in. When it cleared up a little in the afternoon, she went for a walk down to the river, enjoying the people, the greenness and the water. She indulged in sweet nostalgia, recalling the years her father brought them up to the boat race, here, at this very reach. She found (most unusually) a place for a cup of tea, and a seat where she could see the river. It was a poor cup of tea, being laced with powdered milk, and the Madeira cake was dry as sand: but it was pleasant to be out.

She reached home after six and could tell the Bests were out for the evening, since the house held its breath as deserted houses do. Perhaps after supper she would go to a film, as she had told Sadie she might. And perhaps she would not. She was well into a good story, of privileged people and romantic love. The sun shone into their sitting room, it was nice, it was home here. She cut some sandwiches and allowed herself a modest helping of poor sherry.

When the siren went at ten (it was still light) she said, "Blast." But something about being in the house alone made her lose her nerve for staying up here at the top. ("Come down, come down, you girls," Charles would call. Or Eileen would shriek, "Come on down, don't argue, it's our responsibility!") If they were out, though, she and Sadie would often ignore it. It went so regularly. They were pestered more and more with flying bombs; since Miss Cardew's bomb (as Marie called it) things had got worse and worse. Soon, the papers said, soon they would get the measure of them, keep them out, or destroy more on the wing. They had had nearly three weeks of them now. You could go and look at one, face the menace, sitting smugly in a bombed site in central London.

Down I go then, one, two, three, Marie said, the book under her arm, placing her sandaled feet precisely on the soft carpet of the main flight of stairs. Don't loiter, Charles would tease, come on, you're keeping us all in danger fiddling about! Over to the cellar door, which led off the pleasantly spacious hall, turn on the light, you're supposed to bar this door behind you, last man bar the door, Charles explained. Two metal bars had to be lifted across, to reinforce it. Marie disliked barring herself in alone and failed to do it when she shut the door. Down the steps, into this funny domestic dungeon, where in one far corner was the re-enforced part, the proper shelter, with deck chairs, cushions, blankets and so on.

A foundation wall about three feet high divided the cellar roughly into two, the lower half containing the stairs, the coal store, the air-raid shelter. Above this wall there was a catacomb of space where air could circulate beneath the house. Between the interstices of the timbers, in the series of small cubbyholes thus made, Charles kept his wine racks. He fancied himself as knowing about wine, Marie thought with affection. He would pronounce the names, French or German, with studied perfection, he would stroke the shoulders of the bottles with a loving hand, and he would give her corks for keepsakes. He would rage against the present lack of decent wines, none to be had. The overhead light filled the whole cellar. She wandered over to look at the racks, she pulled out a bottle. She could not read it, let alone pronounce it. Oh, if she were educated, if she could speak French and German! How it would please Charles! (Not that there was very much point in her pleasing Charles, save that it gave purpose to life.) She turned towards the shelter corner. Being below ground, she had not heard the throbbing buzz of the approaching pilotless brute, so the sudden silence and the enormous crash and the blast that took her breath and knocked her flat came as a total, unexpected horror. Rubble down the stairs overtook her, she fell sideways, her poor head, head, head poor head. Complete and horrible darkness into which she sank.

There was always this ghastly problem of where to begin. It had fallen two doors away from Charles's house: three houses were totally wrecked, several on either side partly damaged. Usually, one assumed the people under the direct hit to be dead: but if they had a shelter, if they were in it.... The men, mostly redundant building workers, directed by a leader who must use on-the-spot common-sense and judgement, and a kind of terrible imagination born of experience, set to work. Ambulances arrived. Unhurt but shocked neighbours sat or stood, dazed or weeping. At midnight the all-clear went. Shortly afterwards the Bests arrived home on their feet and saw that some of the lower side wall of their house, nearest to what was commonly called the "incident", had fallen in with the blast. Charles could not get along their side passage, which led to the back door.

"It's on to the cellar steps. She'll be all right if she's in the shelter."

"She's probably upstairs, little monkey—go in and call."

"Is it safe to go in?" The front door was open. "Anyway, she'd be down here by now." He went in to explore.

"Can she get down?"

"Yes, stairs still here. But the cellar door's burst open, the wall's fallen in on the cellar steps, I can't get down, I don't know what to do."

"I feel safer outside, don't you?" Eileen said, sitting down on the front step. Charles walked along, still stunned, to see what had happened. (They had come home from the other direction, and been refused entry. Nonsense, we live here, Charles said.)

It was the poor Norrises. And their two neighbours. It would be hours before the men would be able to help him. He would not begin moving rubble himself, it might fall in and make matters worse. Feeling suddenly came back to him, he realised that Marie, who had re-awoken his flesh and warmed his heart, was either dead, or trapped in darkness and terrified, possibly hurt and in agony. Charles turned back towards their own house, put his arms round a lamp-post in a cold embrace and his forehead against it, and began to shake. Eileen surveyed him from the steps. The ambulances came and went. Covered stretchers were borne away. The sound of picks and shovels on masonry went on and on. Marie would, he reflected with some irony, probably have been better upstairs today: though the window glass might have cut her badly. Most of the panes that side had gone.

"Hadn't we better go in? I'll make you a drink if I can," called Eileen's brittle voice, brittle as glass itself. Charles had long since slid his arms down the lamp-post and was collapsed on the pavement leaning against it. He could not go in, he could not bear the sight of the blocked cellar door.

"Now then, sir, your house?" A weary workman spoke. "Anyone inside, sir, do you think?"

"We think there may be a girl in the cellar shelter."

"Your daughter, sir?"

"Our lodger!" Eileen had joined them. "There should be two."

"I'm here, Mrs Best," Sadie called, sitting upon her weekend bag, leaning against a wall. She had been so tired, six hours in a held-up train, she did not know how she could stay awake. The sight of the house had awoken her.

"Oh, thank heavens, why didn't you speak to us, dear? Now, is Marie in or out, do you know?"

"If she were out, she'd be back by now," the warden remarked, collecting his men.

"Funny. Just that piece of wall."

"The hollow. Of the cellar. The blast—Don't go up your main stairs, sir, keep the other side if you're going in."

"Safe as houses," Eileen shrugged with a thin laugh. "We're not going in. Yet."

The men set to work.

An auxiliary ambulance came back, one of the Friends' unit, and waited.

Marie had regained consciousness quite soon and realised she could not be dead, she was thinking and feeling. Her legs were pinned, she could not move. She was very cold. Her eyes stung with plaster, they felt better when she wept, for it washed them a little. Her teeth bit upon grit. She spat it into her hand. Oh, the dark, the dark and the headache. This was her other hand, lying against her forehead, this was still she, waiting to be dug out, to be rescued, like all the other people. She could not feel the lower part of her, it was numb. She prayed that she was not crippled for life. After hours and hours and hours, coming back to consciousness and dozing and weeping at intervals, she heard the right noises of rubble being moved quite near, and was so grateful that her heart seemed to burst with relief and she fainted.

When she came to herself there was a shaft of heavenly light coming from the direction of the blocked cellar steps and within it a head, the head of a saint, outlined with a halo, curled dark hair, a fine thin nose, piercing black suffering eyes, open lips: why, it was her grandmother's icon: much loved, she had been taught when she was little to kiss it in secret by her grandma who was Greek and a Christian. Where had it gone, when her grandma died, where was it now? Up there, it seemed. Marie wondered if she were dead after all.

The icon spoke, pushing back its tin hat.

"I see you, we're nearly there. Can you see me? What's your name?" Godfrey called softly, finding out if she were conscious.

"Marie."

"Hang on, Marie. You sound all right. We've got a stretcher."

Her face was yellowish white with plaster except where tears had washed runnels in it, her fair hair was whitened too. Her eyes, red-edged with dust and weeping were very dark in all the white. She looked like a frightened little clown, the sexless essence of all clown hood, of absurd pitiable humanity, Godfrey thought. He had a wet rag in his pocket, he wiped the face as best he could and stroked it; and was surprised and delighted that she smiled.

As they carried her bumpily over the rubble she lay inert, still numb, profoundly thankful, not in pain. In the hall, someone sat on the oak chair sobbing. It is me sobbing, Marie thought.

"She's all right, sir, I don't believe she's hurt very much. Concussion probably, but her limbs seem all right. Your daughter?"

"Our lodger. Charles, do pull yourself together, she's all right."

"Is anybody coming with her?" Godfrey asked. "She's all right, but she might like a friend, someone to answer for her."

Sadie surveyed their landlord and his lady who gave no sign. Poor Mr Best was in no state to do so. She was very tired again.

"OK, I'll come," she said sighing, rising off the hall floor.

"Thanks," said the stretcher-bearer with a grateful smile, "follow us."

By now it was nearly daylight upon July the third.

Kitty and Laura exhausted with terror and with little sleep (for their beds were not safe and sleeping communally did not suit them), moved out of London. Day after day, leaving in different trains from their station at about eight-fifteen, each had sat screwed up and listening for the following flying bomb chasing them to Victoria or London Bridge. Laura would wonder which line it would hit, hers or her mother's. She never precisely imagined the loss of her mother, nor Kitty of her daughter: the actual, present fear absorbed them.

When this had gone on until both were pale and irritable they accepted Uncle Miles's suggestion that they go down into

Buckinghamshire, which seemed to be out of range of the weapon. They hoped (as he assured them) that Aunt Sibyl really seconded the invitation. They were still within reach of their jobs, but they must leave much earlier, the journey was long and the day was longer. But a bed, a bed alone, in a house unmenaced! Laura was anxious the first morning, having to get herself off (it was not one of Kitty's days) to a train well before seven, unwillingly swallowing cereal too early. Aunt Sibyl, trying her hardest, had offered to make her a small packet of food to eat in the train lest she be unable to eat breakfast. There it sat, by her plate, Laura noticed gratefully. And forgot it. Her aunt's reply to her apologies was inaudible through compressed lips. It was never proffered again: Laura sadly concluded Aunt Sibyl to be mortally offended.

There was a concert on the Saturday night.

"Let's get off then," said Uncle Miles, after an early meal for the occasion. "If we leave now we can walk, there's a field path some of the way, it's so pleasant. Sibyl, my dear, are you ready?" he called up the stairs.

"You go, you all go, I'll not come, Miles," she said in clipped tones from above.

"But why not, my dear, it is all arranged, I have the tickets."

"Why not, because for why I have more than plenty to do here."

"Oh, Sibyl," Kitty wailed, "let me stay and help you!"

"Certainly not, be gone, all of you." A door slammed.

"Best go, then," Uncle Miles said, looking crest-fallen. "Sylvia's coming tomorrow," he remembered, "she feels pressed. I'd no idea she'd gone against it."

The concert was in the great barn at Old Jordans. The peace of the beautiful building, the July glory of the evening fields all besprinkled with gently shuddering pollen, lifted them up, all three. The place seemed like a lake of pure spirit from a past that was part of eternity. Why was this? Do centuries of meditation distil thus? Laura was excited too, though a little dubious. It was the young musician Benjamin Britten, back from the States, in partnership with the singer who shared his exile, Peter Pears. Her doubts were due to her total bafflement, one day several years ago in Oxford town hall, at Britten's first violin concerto. They were soon scattered. Lovely English folk songs, with new, crisp, piquant settings, dear songs she had loved and sung all her life, in a light, springy, steely, humorous tenor, rippled over the tired audience like breezes over the still green corn outside. They sighed, they laughed, they longed for more. England, our England, many thought in their war-worn hearts. Miles even forgot about Sibyl.

Poor Marian telephoned, in distress about her wedding amongst all the bombs. They had fixed a date early in August, for Keith was expecting very soon to be off abroad. Kitty had pointed out that her home, from which her daughter naturally wished to be wed, was in the direct flight of these monsters, roaring over regularly, in increasing numbers. Surely, surely, it would be best to postpone this wedding?

"They won't, Mamma, they won't let me put it off," Marian almost sobbed down the line. "They say it's unlucky!"

"Foolish people," said Kitty in exasperation, "it's pure superstition. Then we'll just have to go ahead, darling. I'll speak to Uncle Miles, as I'm here." Uncle Miles was to give her away: failing Laurence. Marian had not even told her father.

"Let's just not *invite* anyone on our side!" Laura said, grinding her teeth. "Supposing the guests get killed? That'll be more unlucky!"

But to administer such an insult was to Kitty too uncharitable.

"I shall certainly warn everyone," she said.

And Marie was back. They all flocked round her, welcoming, wishing her well, adjuring her not to do too much. She was thin, pale, altered, even the attention scarcely moved her, attention which she would have found warmly comforting and flattering before. They were still in the house, she said, but she and Sadie must look for somewhere else, when the repairs began.

"She's very far from well," Prudence said in worried tones, to Mrs Wicklow.

"It is an awful shock, that kind of thing," Imogen replied. "She'll take months to be over it."

Laura kept her counsel. Marie pined, Marie bled inwardly, with a wound Laura recognised.

"Marie," she said, at last catching her alone. "How are things—your friend, your landlord?"

"Treats me like a stranger," Marie said thinly. "Hardly spoken since I got back from hospital."

"Why, Marie, why?"

"Must've given himself away I suppose. Sadie said he was sobbing when they brought me out. She must have rumbled it, you see."

Laura was speechless.

The traps, the traps life laid.

10

"But a slow hanging," Laura said under her breath, dropping her frowning face into her hands.

"The medievals did it," observed Prudence, looking into space, alleviating the imagination by a piece of exactitude.

"Perhaps the Roman crucifixion is one degree worse?" Mrs Wicklow questioned with pursed lips, saying crucifixion with a small "c" who must always visualise it with a capital.

There had been a bomb attempt upon Hitler's life, which was reported in the papers of the twentieth of July. Its main begetter, Colonel von Stauffenburg, was executed at once. He was fortunate. Atrocious details had now begun to circulate about Hitler's revenge, which mentioned piano wire, meat hooks and a Führer observing all with glee.

When people talked of the Nazi horror as bestial, which they often did, Imogen demurred: this is an insult, she would think, to the endearing beasts. The subhuman, she would call it—the inexplicable cruelty which perverts us. Its concentration presented it as being on a larger scale than at any time since decaying Rome and the dark ages, but such a generalisation, Imogen realised, is incapable of proof. There had been for several years now unbelievable rumours about the torture and destruction of Jews and others, in camps. In the autumn of 1942, Anthony Eden had put to the Commons, who had passed it with many protestations of anger and disgust, a resolution publicly deploring what had come to be known. It was all they could do.

The immediate effect of this latest news was not only shocked regret that the plot had failed, but an inescapable increase in people's feelings of hatred. Hatred for Hitler became like a palpable fog, a poison gas, a choking fume. Laura, a girl of deep feelings, thought often with her heart more than with her mind. The welling up of loathing and fury at the antics of this monster frightened her. She said so.

Imogen nodded.

"From the purely practical point of view, for the good of our digestions as well as our souls, we are bidden to forgive our enemies."

"But how! Such men!"

"It happens. Recall the Crucifixion."

"And Socrates," put in Prudence.

"No doubt. And countless others. Have proved it possible."

Edwin Kyle was if anything more concerned with the blindness of chance, which yet appeared so often so deliberately cruel. He said as much to his diary, in a frenzy of disgust.

> If only they'd pulled off that plot, it would have saved thousands, probably millions of lives! Why must it turn into disaster when it should have been a great good! Yet some wicked circumstance, something the wretched conspirators did not know or did not think of, poor fools, has foiled it.

"What are you prepared to bet that that poor Colonel called upon Providence to aid him?" said Edwin, raising angry grey eyes to his daughter.

"Whether he did or not," Prudence replied, deliberating, "it can only be chance, unlucky chance or human error, made them fail."

"Chance. That's it. Chance is blind and cruel," he threw out.

"Pop, you cannot personify chance! *You* will not even personify Providence. Chance is simply what falls out. Chance isn't the opposite of what Christians call Providence, is it?"

He laughed with affection. Her thinking things through was one of his great pleasures.

"What then *is* Providence?" he angled. "What was it doing on July the twentieth?"

"Oh Pop, you know I do not know."

"Supper," Margery said with an unusual glint of wit, overhearing at the door. "Supper. That is Providence."

All through July, the Russians had advanced across Poland. Hordes of their infantry, peasants the depths of whose deprivation was beyond the ken of most moderately privileged west Europeans, swept through town, village, and countryside. All across Poland, therefore, they stole. (The oddity of the things they stole! From kitchen knives and cheap mugs up a scale of increasing value to the virginity of farmers' daughters.) As the rumour of their coming spread, all manner of secret places were devised for the hiding of property and of daughters: girls were bundled halfway down wells, into shallow graves beneath yards, on to shelves in barn roofs.

On Tuesday August the first, when the vast Russian army was halted outside Warsaw, the Poles inside arose with heroic faith against their German oppressors. As the news reached the world, most people assumed that the Russians would enter the city and deliver the Poles.

Imogen Wicklow met Mr Gorzinska in church on the morning of Friday the fourth. Like a man with a cancer, Mr Gorzinska, growing ever thinner and paler, accompanied her on to a bus from Kensington to the office, biting his lips and saying little. She invited him to supper.

"You are eating your heart out for your country," she said, when he came. She had hurried home and prepared borsch, the garnet red in the hyacinth blue soup bowls caused him to exclaim.

"Tinned, I'm afraid, the beet. And there is no cream to put in, only the top of the miserable bottle. Your anxiety is making you ill."

"Yes, yes. It is my country. But I am selfish as we all are. It is much more that I have lost touch with my family."

She had suspected this, but always felt she did not know him well enough to ask. "Tell me."

"I came over in '37, I am naturalised, as I expect you know. I visited my family in '38, there was a kind of coolness at my decision, which hurt me. Because of this, I suppose we wrote rather rarely, I wrote most to my sister. My mother and my sister visited England early in '39, I saw them briefly and heard from them soon after. I have not heard since." He almost choked on his soup.

"You are consumed with sorrow and guilt to have left them to that fate," she supplied.

"Yes, yes," he said seizing her soft hand, as she crumbled some bread. "It is exactly so, exactly that, how can you know?"

Not in the least difficult, Imogen thought, my poor young man. Though he was not exactly young. Early thirties perhaps.

"They live in Warsaw?"

"Yes. My father is in broadcasting; he is an economist, journalism too. My sister is an artist, a fine etcher, engraver. My mother, my mother is all manner of things of good intent. And suffers much from pain in her bones, her limbs."

"Arthritis?"

"That is it. I should be there, there to help them."

"You would be fighting or imprisoned." Or dead, she thought.

"Just so, I tell myself. And now, our country being ravaged, our capital will fall to a far worse enemy than those who have crushed it so far."

"Can that possibly be true? You're assuming the worst too quickly."

"You will see what will happen. They will sit outside our city and they will let the Germans kill our people like rats in the sewers and they will afford no help. And where my people are, and whether they have more to suffer, I cannot know, I only ceaselessly imagine."

"You have written?"

"Not since September '39, the fall of Warsaw, I cannot decide what to do, I fear to compromise them."

"And no word from any of them?"

"None."

"There is the Red Cross," she said.

A great full moon was up when she, much later, bid him good night. It was fair weather.

"I hope it keeps so, for Laura's sister's wedding," she said, presenting a warm human event as a compassionate sop, an anaesthetic, to his vast sorrow. How one longed these days for the ordinary, for small domestic minutiae, the dear routine of life.

"Ah! Yes. I had forgotten."

"Go quickly, before the siren. I shall pray. And think."

He bowed over her hand, kissing it. She loved his courtly manners.

❧

But to Marian, at the centre of this particular domestic hubbub, her marriage seemed not small, not ordinary, but cataclysmic, looming much larger than the fate of Poland.

Keith's mother had produced a goodly list of guests for Kitty, avowing airily over the telephone that none of them would be in the least dismayed by the possibility of the robots landing near. Kitty, with a slight sense of grievance, which tickled her (did Keith's mother think that she and her daughters were afraid?) made out at first a minimal list of relatives only.

"Lolly," she exclaimed, however, "how can I not ask the Priestmans?" Laura shrugged, since she could easily have not.

"What do you think about the Coads, darling, surely we must ask the dear Coads?" was the next thing.

"Think of their journey," Laura pointed out.

"Well, they don't have to come."

Or: "Today I thought of course we have to invite the old Bradfords?"

And: "Isobel! We can't forget Isobel, when she hears, she'll be hurt!"

To these repeated afterthoughts Laura responded with a sniff, with a smile, with a laugh. Sometimes she even made her mother laugh. Yet:

"They are asking everybody they want to! What is the use of our holding out? Our plan of keeping folk out of danger has been foiled!" Thus Kitty rationalised the modification of her first resolution. Laura gave up. Laura invited Prudence. Prudence lived in another bomb-ridden suburb, which for some illogical reason made it seem no more of a risk than if she had stayed at home. At least Laura realised it was illogical.

That siren which Mrs Wicklow bid Mr Gorzinska evade duly went. In the middle of the night a flying bomb fell. It awoke Laura and her mother, but was at some distance. It filled the waiting wine glasses on their trays with dust from pulverised walls, so that Laura must polish them all again in the morning.

Kitty looked at her elder daughter with tears in her heart. Far from the confident officer, Marian had shed her self-possession with her uniform, and looked simple, lovely and vulnerable. Let my daughter be happy, her mother prayed. All my deprivations will be mitigated if my daughters, both my daughters, are happy in their marriage.

Uncle Miles, who had not long since given away Sylvia his own daughter, held Marian's arm in the vestry while they waited, calmly reciting to her the botanical name and habit of all the flowers in her bouquet, trying to quell the flutter of her heart by the concentration of her mind.

Kitty's large lawn with its pretty trees and flower beds, which Laura had spruced up for the occasion, was bright with guests, buzzed with chatter, popped with corks. Laura handed food and wine in a trance, responded to banter wanly, her ear cocked ever for the wailing warning. The minute the last guests were going, it came.

"Providential," said Kitty. Prudence, just departing, overheard her and smiled secretly, imagining her father's irascible reaction. Laura's mother was so simple, so warm-hearted, she could not help loving her.

"I'm away, Laura," she said. Laura, she thought, is involved with that best man: I wonder how much there is in *that*.

"Oh, dearest P, thank you for coming! Go quickly, mind the bombs!" Laura called.

It was true that part of Laura's dazed sense of dream, as Prudence's amused observation had recorded, was because she had been coerced and flattered by the attentions of the best man into imagining herself ready to love him. He had arrived yesterday, and quite unknown before, leapt right into the small family Kitty and Marian and Laura made as if he were one of them, helping in all kinds of ways, and hindering in as many others. He was a cousin of Keith (whose own brother was fighting in Normandy) a lean and sinuous Welshman in the Guards, with liquid roving eyes, and a twisting nose with a will of its own, quite a pretty wit and some perception. He took in at once Kitty's old-fashioned propriety, her romantic idea of love (which was evident when she spoke of the marriage) and was a perfect gentleman while she was there. But he had taken six days' leave for this wedding which fell at the Bank Holiday, he was far from his regular girlfriends, and here was a pretty, spirited creature with a slim body and a sad face who needed some fun, whose inhibitions, he suspected, needed breaking down. So he aimed below the belt, straight at the physical. On the evening of Marian's wedding, he came to take Laura for a drink, and returned her late, kissing her passionately for minutes on end beneath Kitty's lime tree in warm darkness, the kisses punctuated with charming talk and Laura's equally charming, half-amused replies. Laura, who had not so far wanted anyone but Gavin to kiss her thus, gave in for the hell of it, the fun of it, and for that Marian was married on a hot summer weekend.

There followed five days of trance-like pleasure. Everything, every pleasure Rees suggested, was animal. They ate, they drank; they dined, they danced; they swam, they sunbathed; they walked, they ran. Down hills holding hands in the country, through London after buses and non-existent taxis. Admittedly they talked, he was a great talker and so was she. What did they talk of? Laura could never remember. His hands, like his eyes and nose, were mobile, finding their way inside her clothes as if magnetised, the more so when the dim lights in railway carriages went off altogether on the way home (as they frequently did). If they go up too soon, she thought, I shall look pretty undressed. She was ashamed of herself for allowing it, for one thing it was vulgar, it was not how decently brought-up girls behaved. But it was as pleasurable as it was funny. The failing lights he could not have arranged: but he adroitly arranged the missing of last trains at night.

"Of course you can sleep here," Kitty said more than once, with shining innocence concealing the maternal gleam in her eye. "There's plenty of room. I'm sure Laura won't mind your flopping into her bed. Or there are two in the spare room. Here's all the linen, help yourself. We sleep in the neighbours' shelter, as Lolly's told you. It's high time we got over."

Ree's dark eyes took on that glazed, suffering look, which Laura had begun to know well.

The sixth day found Laura in a flat, tired, sad calm, stranded: and split. She looked back upon the frivolous creature who had had such fun in amazement. Her other self, her thinking self took over. The thought of Gavin made her suddenly conscious of the difference between that love and this: the difference between true and false. Is this at all the kind of person I ever dreamed of marrying? No. Do I trust this person? Not particularly. Is anything we have said to each other memorable? No. Has he any depths? Not as yet visible, he has a sort of Celtic melancholy bordering on poetry, but it is fairly inarticulate. But our bodies felt as alike as two peas. Why am I not like Nadia Trent at college, who gave herself to anyone she reasonably liked (especially from the services), and did not worry? Do I wish I were Nadia Trent? My flesh does.

But her father had implanted in Laura a deep mistrust of her flesh.

Ten days later, there followed a weekend. Rees's eyes were more melancholy, his hands more urgent. It rained. Wild rain lashed Laura as she hurried over the lawn from the shelter to breakfast him and get him off early on Sunday morning on a train he must catch. He stripped off the wet things and kissed her cold breasts. He stripped off his own things and held her against the huge hardening part. But I wasn't going to, Laura thought. This was her first uninhibited encounter with what her cousin Sylvia would call with exaggerated laughter the male organ. She had been far more moved by his head between her breasts. He laid her down on her own bed, she closed her eyes, conscious only of the weight, the hardness, calling up in her an immense, almost supernatural tenderness.

"How shy you are. Oh, goodness, oh Lolly," he groaned. Well might I be shy thought Laura with irreverence, confronted with this. Then her objective self was overwhelmed once more with ancient simple instinct which said don't mock, here is your due at last, have pity also, accept, accept and be grateful.

But she could not.

Why can't I simply succumb? Laura asked herself. Once her busy mind began to question, instinct was silenced for good. It will take ages, she thought, one knows it does the first time. Besides, it's not safe. Anyway, do I love him? Also, what *is* the time, is there time? She remembered the train. With a huge effort as if from under water, fighting his increasing excitement, she raised the thin brown arm, which wore the watch and squinted.

"Rees! Your train! You've twenty minutes flat!" she gasped. "Let me out!"

"Oh help, oh Lolly."

"Get in the bath. Quick! I'll get some coffee. *Hurry*!" Scalding coffee, pouring cold rain. Somehow they got ready. They ran to the station. They kissed they waved, almost unsmiling.

Perhaps I'm really a tart, thought Laura, during the rest of that long, wet Sunday. Enormous tiredness overcame her, a sense of standstill after battle.

Monday morning and it still rained.

Laura, somewhat leaden, was approaching the entrance to their offices through squally gloom. What was the matter? A crowd on the pavement, vehicles, shouting, piles of concrete, rubble, glass, twisted metal, police, air-raid wardens, filing cabinets queued up.

"A direct hit. I asked the warden. Clever of them, wasn't it?" said Miss Richardson with venom. "I just wonder how they knew? We're allowed in, to help clear up," she added, seeing Miss Cardew rooted to the spot.

Oh no, Laura thought with a sigh, I am so tired. But she proceeded like an automaton with the rest to pick up papers, sweep up dust, shovel up icicles of glass, piles of plaster. Wet plaster. While the men busied themselves with the files marked Top Secret. Their side of the place was blast-damaged but safe to enter. Raw wet rain and wind blew through jagged windows.

"That's three," Miss Richardson said, sipping Daisy's coffee. (By some miracle the electricity supply still worked.) "Three private bombs."

"*Private* bombs?"

"Three bombs we know about. Miss Cardew's, Marie's, and now the office. Perhaps that will stop it."

"Perhaps it will," Imogen said in kindly disbelief, catching Laura's eye and looking quickly away. Marie looked sick, fearful memories aroused, Daisy ordered her to sit quiet or go home. Mrs Tripp swore (immoderately) cutting herself, Mrs Wicklow secretly laughed at this, Prudence overhearing wore a twisted smile. Miss Wainewright flew to the aid of Mr Watson: Laura offered to help Alex Harvald. Though why on earth we should, she complained, I cannot imagine. Why should dustpan and brushing be considered women's work only? But it was. In the office. By Alex Harvald. Mrs Wicklow thought of Matthew: she picked her way through glass and wet plaster and pools of rain along the corridor and up the stairs and into the doorway of Matthew's room where the door hung unhinged.

Matthew knelt as far away from the window as he could get, in the only dryish corner of the room, crouching and rising, stooping and stretching like a busy spider, dozens of wet, handwritten pages spread out before him on the floor like a game of patience, forming little piles to which he added now and then, but untidy piles, for the pages were too damp to put neatly on top of each other, they had been blown about the room, rained on, stood on, people's boot soles had printed them back or front, unregarding, uncaring. Tears streamed down Matthew's oddly small face, or was it simply rain: he brushed them away with his hand, he read, he pored, he sought sequences, occasionally added a page to a pile. A great choke, really a sob, came forth: and Imogen, staring, realised his distress. She stood aghast, amazed. How could Matthew mind so much, about sheets of paper, about what he had written? When young Germans were being killed in hundreds in the Falaise gap, blown apart by the Allies' bombs? When Harry had jumped behind German lines as the Allies made for Paris? When Willy sat in his tank, in imminent danger of being blown to pieces, perhaps already blown to pieces?

The wind blew, pages flapped off their piles, Matthew snarled, pouncing, putting down thin pale hands here and there, blue with rain and cold, stained with smoking. And saw her.

"Oh, Imogen," he said, unthinking. (He always thought of her thus, talked to her thus, since knowing he adored her.) "My novel."

"Oh, poor Matthew."

It was Matthew's own, it was the motive force of his life, it was as important to him as their courage and sacrifice were to the others. This was, she suspected, all he had.

"It's all smudged, it's all wet," he choked.

"Blotting paper, you need blotting paper! Do the piles matter? Blot it, get it dry first! I'll go and get all I can borrow."

She hurried downstairs, into every room, begging, borrowing, stealing dry blotting paper, arriving back pink and breathless with armfuls. They dabbed and patted, scrambling about on the damp floor.

"Never mind the order, get it dry first, you wrote it, you can sort it."

Which is more than I can, she thought, glancing from time to time at a sentence here, a paragraph there. It was very modern and inconsequential, there seemed to be no reason why one order was better than another.

"I *do* mind the order," he snapped.

"Of course you do. You can do it when it's thoroughly dry. It needs taking home and putting in an airing cupboard. Have you got an airing cupboard? No? Well, let me take it home and put it in mine."

There it was, a huge fat pile, interleaved with roughly torn blotting paper, untidy but rescued, on his desk.

"Or can't you bear to part with it?"

Matthew choked, overcome with his love, with the faint expensive scent she exuded, her ivory skin so close. He turned awkwardly and clasped her in his arms, in a boy's bear hug, his cheeks still wet, oh God he loved her so much! "Imogen, you're so sweet, you're so kind, thank you for helping, and not laughing at me." He dropped his head on to her shoulder and shook; she rubbed his back with tender, motherly hands. It was like Willy, at ten years old. He hugged her tight.

"There. So," she said in her delightful Irish voice. "Now you can re-write it more or less from this."

"Or I can begin again," he mumbled into her neck.

"Yes, you said the other day you were stuck. You can begin again." Pause. "After all that."

He giggled sheepishly. She went into smothered peals of laughter. They rocked, laughing.

"Let go, Matthew. Let go," she ordered, giving him now a series of smart slaps on his thin buttocks. "Let me go, what are you thinking of?"

"You, I love you."

"Nonsense, now. Bring it down, put it in my basket, I'll dry it off for you. If you really need it, you wretched boy."

She was flushed and merry, he loved her helplessly.

Terrible things were happening to Laura, she walked about in a dream of despair and tiredness, wondering why, forgetting what toll an emotional battle takes of one's body as well as one's spirit. She sat absorbed in a tube, her face a mask of tragedy, becoming aware that three fat Americans and their shared girl were discussing her. That girl, she looks happy, holy crows doesn't she just look about the happiest girl there is. Hush, she's probably lost someone, she'll hear, shush.

She went to have a sheet of photos taken (for Rees had asked for one), which took you in twenty or more different attitudes, looking to the four points of the compass. (What am I doing this for, she wondered?) That's OK, dear, so far, but do smile now, I've nearly finished, and you haven't really smiled, he'll like one with a smile, the anxious photographer pleaded pansily, won't he? Will he? Laura made an immense effort, she tried really hard: but she could not smile, it was as if she had forgotten how to do it. She was like the girl in the Wop Shop.

Kitty noticed here daughter's tiredness and begged a weekend of Miles and Sibyl. Marian, bereft of Keith, was to join them. And Sylvia was home, also husbandless. Sylvia would make Laura laugh if anyone could. And the dear old General was always made welcome by Miles, if not by his wife.

Kitty sat next to Sibyl, in a basket chair that squeaked, on the gravel outside the drawing-room windows.

"C'n guess what they're talking about," sniffed Sibyl, clacking away at army socks on noisy needles, surveying the three young women sunbathing at the far end of the garden, Sylvia and Marian rolling about in giggles, Laura apparently sleeping, the General stretched beside them snapping at flies.

"Well, come on, how did you get on?" Sylvia was asking, pushing at Marian's bare shoulder, giggling immoderately.

"Couldn't get it near me," Marian replied, "simply couldn't get it near me, at first."

Laura smiled, secretly, thinking of Rees. Was Sylvia lucky, who considered sex one vast, various, utterly hilarious joke? She was at it now, egging Marian on, who until fairly recently had been as solemn as Laura, to impart more details, to add her own.

"By the way, Lolly!" Marian called, when the laughter had subsided. "There's a message for you. Via Keith. From that cousin the best man, Rees."

"Oh yes," Laura said.

"I gather you had quite a time with him? He says he's sorry if he led you to expect anything."

"He didn't. Or at least, not what you mean by anything," said Laura enigmatically.

"He's more or less engaged, Keith says."

"He didn't need to send a message," Laura said. "I never for a moment took him seriously." She realised at once how true this was.

"You won't take anyone seriously," Marian chided. This was so far from the truth as Laura saw it that she gasped, inwardly, and knew not whether to laugh or cry. She thought she was far from a tease. She thought she took most things much too seriously. Love she took so seriously, searched for so diligently, she was in danger of never finding it at all. (It had found her, once.)

"Poor old Laura," Sylvia giggled. "Is it still that don, that love of her life?"

Who told Sylvia? I could cheerfully strangle Sylvia, Laura thought.

Next week, in a daze, she stepped on to a descending escalator by mistake, leaping off with a backward twist at the frenzied yell of a man above. It was Tom, the man was Tom. Coming down. She started going up again, on the right staircase this time.

"Laura! Wait! Can you wait? I'm coming up!"

"Tom," she said, with no voice. "All right," she nodded, unsmiling.

He raced up with the moving stair, alarmed.

"Laura, what is it, what's the matter, you look dreadful, you're not thinking what you're doing! It's dangerous, to get absent-minded on the underground." He shook her slightly by the shoulders. She looked at him like a refugee, dazed.

"What's happened? You been raped or something?"

How near the mark was Tom, was often so. She shook her head, in a clamp of silence.

"Got time for a drink? Eh?"

"Thanks." A smile, very small at last.

"You're going to have strong black coffee, not talk," said he, in the nearest buffet. "Or you'll walk under a train." He put down a steaming cup, weak as water.

"What's up, anyway, now?"

"I think it's probably just tiredness." All of a sudden, she told him about not being able to smile. Laughing almost as if she were crying over the weak coffee that was too hot to drink.

"Well, you've broken that, but don't get hysterics. Why should you be so tired?"

"Oh, bombs and shelter-sleeping and all that lark."

"Don't believe it. It's a man, a lightning affair?"

It was uncanny. "How did you know?"

"Written all over you. Conflict. What happened?"

"Well, it was Keith's best man. We just had fun, you know, we roared about, we fell for each other a bit."

"But has it all ended? Why do you look like you do?"

"Oh, it wasn't serious, good heavens, he was engaged to someone else anyway."

"When did you find that out?"

"Not till afterwards," she admitted, with half a smile.

Laura, said Tom in his head, are you grown up at last? I wonder, I wonder. I wish I could have done it. He was overcome with a sudden rush of passionate jealousy. What is this, said Tom coolly, why do I care if some playboy took the cream off this dear girl? Is this girl getting dear to me?

Laura raised her eyes at Tom's silence, and saw his temples flushed. Tom never flushed.

He looked at her, very serious, considering. "Would it be too rude…too un-English…to ask…if…yes, it would," Tom said, folding his thin, straight lips together, nodding his head.

Some new gentleness in his manner warmed her, some new consciousness of another person minding about her cut through her self-absorption, she felt better for it.

"So. How much are you minding? You looked shaken to the core." I'd like to knock him down, thought Tom simply. But why has some flippant infatuation caused her such conflict; shaken her to her foundations, he asked? Is she so fearful of men? Of sex?

"I don't know why it upset me at all," she began honestly. "Because I think I knew he wasn't my kind of man, all the time. When I heard he was tied up anyway, I knew for sure."

"But no one likes a slap in the face?"

"Well, he was simply having a bit of fun, and I…let him." She said this with such deep gloom that Tom smiled.

"Come on, Laura, it is fun, it's meant to be fun, not frightening. You girls, oh my lord, you well brought-up English girls, you miss all the fun, the perfect, lovely joy of just giving in, when it happens, when you're young. What a pity, what a waste," said Tom, deviously. Hoping perhaps to draw her on, to get an answer to what he longed to know.

"To anyone?" said she, smiling.

"Better anyone than no one," he teased. "You look sane again, girl. Good."

Her cheeks held a faint pink. She laughed a natural, amused laugh.

"I feel better, just having it out with you," she realised. "I hadn't talked about it to anyone." What a good friend was Tom, she thought once again.

11

Swaying along on a bus one evening, on her way home much later than usual, Imogen Wicklow considered the unlikely expedition she had just made. Miss Richardson, poor soul: she wanted to feel affection, even pity, compassion, but was unable not to find Miss Richardson sometimes ridiculous. God help me, said Imogen Wicklow in perfect seriousness.

Miss Richardson had bearded her one lunch hour, the room empty: Miss Richardson, with a story of seeing Mr Harvald, time and time again from the window of her regular restaurant during this summer, meeting a dark foreign-looking young man, often walking away with him. She was convinced Mr Harvald was passing information, was a spy, that this was all to do with the office being bombed. Would Mrs Wicklow join her for supper, observe them, advise her what to do, who to tell? Imogen had summoned her patience and charity, had gone tonight, had watched what she suspected would be an obviously sexual assignation: and had enlightened Miss Richardson as casually as she could. A puff of laughter escaped her at the memory of Miss Richardson's exclamation, in a cringing whisper, of the word "sexual": Imogen guiltily condemned her amusement as most unworthy. The subject was not, to her, funny, but Miss Richardson's shocked amazement was. She did not suppose for one moment Harvald was a spy. From what she had observed of him, she thought him too self-satisfied, too ordinary, too dull to harbour the strength of conviction, or the fury of resentment that a traitor must have. Besides, what knowledge could he possibly have that would benefit the enemy? Now Matthew, though: she could imagine Matthew letting himself get into such a corner. She pondered the mentality of spies and collaborators. Since the last week in August when the French General LeClerc had entered Paris followed hot-foot by de Gaulle, and the German governor had surrendered, there had begun to be shocking accounts of collaborators hunted down and dealt with in their thousands. Pictures of women with shaved heads, or even shorn in public, bitterly sullen or horridly propitiatory. What a punishment! How it hardened the features, to be bald, how it shamed spirit and flesh together for a woman's hair to be raped. Physically abasing, it seemed an exact cruel symbol of their crime. Would they ever recover their self-esteem, did they deserve it? One must believe every human being of equal value, she chided herself. Were the men now receiving brutal rough justice, luckier to be put summarily out of it? She sighed with mixed relief and sorrow; she had heard from Harry, who now stood a better chance to live his life out. What was he doing? Re-discovering the tarnished capital, the corners he had loved now destroyed or obscenely defaced?

She wondered what the news would hold tonight. The buzz bombs still came; a day or two before de Gaulle entered Paris, one of them had killed two hundred people at Barnet. Nevertheless, at the end of August the papers were saying that something like ninety out of ninety-seven were being caught by the defences.

The other weapon had begun as well, a rocket commonly called the V2. A supersonic boom had been heard all over London when the first of them landed in Chiswick early in September. It only killed three. Last resort of a desperate enemy on the defensive (so the Ministry of Information was telling them) it would be used as a morale-shaker like the original 1940 Blitz. They would very probably send them in day-time, to crowded shopping centres in suburbs, full of people. In Shuttlecock days one of their permanent trials had been the inextricably muddled detail of the two weapons from sources more eager than technically informed. But Shuttlecock was disbanded now and they had returned to their own departments, since the weapons were no longer secret and destroying the factories and launching sites was all that mattered.

It had been someone Upstairs, pursuing painstaking photo-reconnaissance, who had originally pinpointed one of the main rocket-launching and experimental sites, at Peenemünde. (The RAF had bombed it severely in the August of 1943.) Rumour (knowingly confirmed by Daisy) had said it was a woman; Imogen gave a satisfied nod of approval, remembering this.

Meanwhile, getting across the Rhine seemed to be too much for the Allies. Eisenhower had taken command of the combined land forces from Montgomery, but no decisive advance had been made. Imogen wondered where Willy was, and prayed for both her sons.

Laura's feet, heavier than usual up the plaster-saturated carpet on the garden stairs, her key in the lock, the subdued hall light, and immediately she was aware of her mother's voice wavering in bewildered tragedy. Laura was very tired, she had worked rather late.

What now? she thought, in almost angry despair. Who's dead now?

"Oh, no—o—o, oh my dear…oh my poor Bruv…yes…yes…oh I am so grieved…for you all… ." Kitty sat by the phone leaning against the wall, her long face wearing an expression of wild, distraught, refusal. "Bruv" was Uncle Miles, an abbreviation from their extreme childhood. Eventually, after many half-sentences, enquiries, and expressions of anguish her mother rang off and looked at her.

"Gilbert. Killed." Laura nodded, having guessed.

"Where?"

"Holland. Some bridge. Trying to get over the Rhine. Some muddle about taking the bridge, paratroopers too far away, some unexpected Germans in between, Miles thinks. Infantry couldn't get through. Died leading his men, it says."

Laura sat down on the stairs leading up to her room. They looked at each other, dumb. They had not seen Gilbert for years, Gilbert was a stranger. But he was Uncle Miles's only son, brilliant, amusing, excoriating, rebellious. Laura could not pretend to feel deeply for Gilbert her cousin, save only for the rape of his promising life, but they all loved Uncle Miles. And Sylvia.

"How's poor Uncle Miles?"

Kitty looked bewildered.

"So calm, so philosophical, such equanimity, I couldn't believe it, you'd think he felt *nothing*."

"Men don't like to show it, do they? How's Sylvia?"

"Burst into sobs and never stopped. Crying still, he says."

"How's poor Aunt Sybil?"

"Numb, he thinks. Comforting Sylvia."

"He's married, isn't he, there's a wife, poor girl?"

"Yes, that Australian girl, he met her in Singapore, a rather beautiful girl. Oh dear, I forgot to ask."

They ate in silence, searching their memories for this suddenly exploded person, trying to collect him as a being you loved. For he had not been exactly easy to know or love, as a schoolboy and undergraduate. Aggressive, teasing, shifting youth, wildly funny often enough, scornful of them all, their religion, their standards, their politics. Uncle Miles always smiled at his cynical sarcasm. Not the real Gilbert, he would say. And the Cardews had seen the grown man so little.

"Waste! Such a waste," burst out Kitty, who was so seldom angry. "Such a clever fellow."

Laura sat for Sunday lunch round the table with the Kyles, Prudence had asked her some time ago. Kitty had gone over to see Miles. Laura could not pretend she was bowed down with grief, she need not even mention it. And she liked the Kyles so much; they were kind and salty people, happy together.

"Well, now, so how are you, my dear?" Margery said, pursed up always, but kind. She was a little nervous both of her daughter's and Laura's "brains". She, now, had been a nurse, ordinary, competent and practical, not clever in their and Edwin's way.

In Laura, lately, moods of almost stupid silence alternated with moods of excitable and frenzied loquacity. She found herself, with no warning, beginning to tell them about Gilbert. Her talk flowed like some chattering mountain stream rushing over or around any rocks of interruption, as she reported her cousin's death and poured out all the childhood memories of him. After a few sympathetic attempts to dam its flow, the good Kyles gave in to it. Margery, in dumb show and desperation, served on, plate by plate.

But it was not this unknown stranger about whom the Kyles at once began to think. It was their own victim, it was Donald, Donald who was also with an infantry division, somewhere in that hardly advancing front. Margery's face became tight and pale as she listened; Edwin's, observing her, expressed the inability of pity. Grave Prudence, with an anxious eye to both parents, assumed an unhappy, faint smile of apologetic affection that at last penetrated Laura's consciousness.

"Oh, I'm so sorry," she gasped. "I'm so sorry. All these memories. Someone you don't know at all! I can't think what possessed me!"

"It is much better to let them come," Edwin shyly said, and steered the conversation elsewhere.

Only in the train going home, in a hot rush of misery, did Laura fully realise her mistake. To talk of Gilbert's death, when they feared for Donald! How *could* she? And why should she?—she could not be said to love, hardly did she know Gilbert. What loathsome, gloating instinct, what ghoulish vulgarity, had caused her to make capital of tragedy, as if she wallowed in, got some reflected credit from the ill news! Horrified discomfort and shame flooded her. She would explain tomorrow, apologise again to Prudence.

"Och, it's no use their refusing to face the possibilities," said Prudence with affectionate kindness, "no good at all. You always feel things deeply, Laura, you sometimes have to blurt them out. I often wish *we* weren't so reserved. You see what Mum's like, paralysed with fright about Donald. And she won't talk about him, about it. Pop's more objective, I think."

Laura thought that Prudence was like her father. Prudence was cool and sensible and clever. Yet she was a warm-hearted, loving friend, as Laura had come to know. Laura loved and admired her increasingly. Oh, why could she not be cool and considered? What was she to do with all this splurging feeling? Why could she not be kind and objective and jolly? I hope you are all well and jolly, Prudence would often say: it was one of her most usual greetings.

Imogen Wicklow was preparing a kind of love feast at breakfast for the two young men, who sat politely talking about the news while she made their meal. The news had been so bad, the loss of thousands of infantry and paratroopers killed or captured after the Arnhem bridge failure: EPIC OF SKY MEN. THE AGONY OF ARNHEM, the headlines had wailed. Almost worse, tales of Warsaw, of the grinding out of Polish resistance after two months' terror, by angry Germans coldly savage: such bad news that she had thought, seeing them both leaving the Oratory, she must do something to reiterate against all apparent odds the love of God. In whom we live and move and have our being. (Mr Gorzinska was usually at Mass: but what was Matthew doing in church? She had seen him lurking in the shadows several times. She thought Matthew was a kind of Communist. Could he possibly be coming simply because she went?)

Somebody had brought eggs, real eggs from the country last week, her two visitors ate an enormous pile of scrambled egg each, with ravenous attention and few words; while she took the French rolls from the oven, rationed them, two each. (They must last her for days, baked by Louise, Victoria's exiled French girl, found in some Brompton basement kitchen.) The flat smelt of quite good coffee and there was black cherry jam from a tin, sent in a parcel from Canada. It was good to see pale, anguished Mr Gorzinska eat. Matthew's curious face looked pugnacious. How much did he realise that Mr Gorzinska, whose looks were so striking, whose manners so courtly made Matthew seem a clever, plain, bristly, surly schoolboy?

"It isn't likely to be Harry, is it?" Matthew said as she came in, laying claim to some knowledge of his hostess's family. "Captured at Arnhem, I mean?"

"Oh, no, thank God, I've heard from Harry. Bad infantry casualties, I believe. Laura's cousin was killed."

"Ah. Poor Laura," Mr Gorzinska said, looking up with genuine sympathy. He had every reason to follow the campaign: with the paratroopers was a Polish brigade. Matthew was not interested in Laura's cousin.

"We shall be better when the Russians get moving towards Germany. That'll occupy the Germans and help our push," he observed.

"The Russians!" Mr Gorzinska spat out, his cup rattling down in its saucer. "The Russians act with most base, lowest cynicism!"

"They know what they're doing," Matthew countered, "they're seeing to the two extremes. They've cleared the Baltic—now they're obviously going to clear the Balkans. They know very well what they're doing."

Imogen was surprised, Matthew evidently followed the war intently: many young people seemed not to.

"Ah, they know very well what they're doing," Mr Gorzinska's voice was savage with irony. "They are murdering my countrymen as surely as if they did it themselves. For *two months*, for two months the Germans torture and kill more and more Poles, the Russians allow, the Russians by stand, the Russians have no heart for persons, even their own persons, only the state."

The Soviet Government in a note to Britain had condemned the rising in Warsaw, two week after its start, as a reckless adventure from which their high command would dissociate itself. The effects of this statement had become quickly obvious.

"Now, rolls, Mr Gorzinska, butter, Matthew," Imogen said anxiously, pushing forward her two ounces to the angry young man.

"The Russians," shouted Matthew, "are helping us WIN the bloody war, they are a powerful ally. They have their reasons, to do with supplies and men no doubt, why they can't help Poland, or to do with strategy. Their ideas are much nearer to any sensible young English person than those filthy, capitalist Yanks, who blunder us into trouble and bomb the wrong targets and stay complacent and self-satisfied throughout."

"The Russians are atheists, atheist Communists, it is why they hate my country!" Outraged, Mr Gorzinska screamed too. He screamed of the atrocities in his country. "Millions, millions of my countrymen, they are starved, tortured and deported!"

At intervals Imogen fled to the kitchen, she must fetch more rolls, she must shut their mouths with good bread, the bread she had meant as a kind of prolongation of the Mass. They were going at it like tigers, both the food and the argument, it grew faster and faster, more and more venomous. Oh, Holy Mother, for Jesus sake, stop them, I never thought of it, I am so stupid, overrule my stupidity, she muttered, burning her trembling hand on the oven.

But things took their natural and inexorable course, her prayers proved helpless to annul the consequences of her ill-judged invitation. What was Matthew saying *now*? Oh no, Matthew could not be saying that! He could *not* so!

"How do you come to be *away* from your country, why have you left your country? I should be greatly interested to know how such a lover of his country ever came to *leave* it!" Mr Gorzinska almost choked upon his bread, spread with the tart and lovely jam. He pushed back his chair, his face stricken, his eyes darkly disbelieving.

"Oh come now, come, stop, do eat, I meant it for a loving breakfast amongst friends!" she pleaded.

"This young man dares, this young man, who also I note is not fighting for his country, this young man dares ask me," the Pole said hoarsely, standing up.

Any histrionics and I'll get in first, Matthew thought, leaping up from the table, his chair falling backwards, furious at a taunt which only equalled his own.

"There are reasons for my not fighting! And I'm going. Thank you, Imogen, I'm going!" He made for the door, in angry horror at the figure he was cutting in beloved Imogen's eyes.

"Oh, don't go, don't both desert me, I shall think it was my fault all day."

Mr Gorzinska seized her hand and kissed it ardently upon the burn, which hurt. Matthew turned from the door and saw the gesture. I have held her in my arms, he raged to himself as he slammed out, and now what will she think of me?

"Forgive us. You are so kind. And we have blackened your kindness, your love feast," the Pole said brokenly. "I have not heart to stay, I shall go, I am ashamed, I cannot stay."

"You must forgive Matthew, he seems so very young still, in so many ways."

"I find trouble to forgive *me*," said he, vanishing with a sad smile.

In the wreckage of the room, the debris of the table, Imogen went to the telephone.

"Victoria?"

"Ma?" Yawning.

"I've just had a fight to end all fights over my breakfast table."

"Who?"

"My Pole, my poor Pole. And Matthew."

"Of the novel?"

"Of the novel."

"What about?"

"The Russians."

"We can guess the Pole's views. What are Matthew's?"

"I suspect he is a Communist."

"Ma! Why ASK them together?"

"I know. They were both in church. I didn't think. I'm so stupid."

"You are that. And this is in the nature of a confession. What's a Communist doing in church? What happened?"

"They screamed, they tore the air, they taunted each other vilely, personally."

"What about?"

"Leaving their country. Or not fighting for it."

"Lord. What then?" Victoria experienced that vicarious excitement everyone feels over a scrap described.

"That finished it."

"It would."

"Matthew slammed out."

"And the Pole?"

"He was 'shamed' to have 'blackened' my kindness, my love feast, such colourful expressions he uses. And went. Leaving me forlorn."

"Poor Ma! I like the sound of your Pole. Let me meet him."

"You shall. They ate all the rolls."

"All your rolls! And the butter ration no doubt. Why put them all out?"

"I was trying to stop the quarrel." Victoria could see her mother's crestfallen face.

"I've no sympathy, you lunatic woman."

"Matthew behaved disgracefully."

"He would. He's jealous."

"Nonsense."

"Ma, don't be purblind."

Peals of laughter. Nothing purblind about her.

"You go back to sleep, my darling daughter."

"I will, you idiot Ma."

Some weeks later, as Matthew had foreseen, the Russians entered Belgrade and joined forces with Tito and his Yugoslavian partisans. Mr Churchill flew to Moscow so that he and Mr Stalin could define their spheres of influence in Europe. A few days after he had announced to the House that British relations with Russia were never more "close, intimate and cordial", Mrs Wicklow joined Mr Gorzinska in the lift going up to their offices. They said no word, she looked shyly at him, and laid her hand on his arm, knowing his feelings.

"My daughter has leave, next weekend. Come and meet her. On the Saturday evening," she said impulsively.

"I will be enchanted, thank you," said he, bowing with his usual charm, still vividly conscious of the last occasion and the more grateful for her kindness.

P rudence, so unassuming, was often secretly to be caught rejoicing in the tool of her thirsty intellect. This evening she was in a tube train having left the office earlier than usual, on the way to a palaeography class provided by London University. It made her feel excited as well as satisfied to be started upon something towards her future career. She knew she was lucky to have her next step so pleasurably defined, perhaps almost within reach: and found herself positively happy to be confronting the problems of reading ancient documents. She felt almost guilty at this happiness when she stopped to think of the mounting misery of millions of other people.

Even Laura was much less lucky, she thought, not knowing what she wanted to do when at last the war should end. Prudence giggled to herself, feeling the long nail on her right-hand index finger inside her glove, carefully guarded, growing well and not snapped yet.

"Prudence!" Laura had shrieked at lunch. "Your nail, your fingernail! What on earth!"

"Chinese!" Mrs Wicklow proclaimed, "Chinese, my child. An enamelled finger-guard, for sure, that's what you'll need!" With a delighted peal of laughter.

"It's a marvellous help," Prudence had told them. "You can keep your place, you run it along under the text, keep your eye on the right line."

"Well, for goodness' sake. It'll break if you let it come any longer. Don't paint it red, will you?" Laura had warned.

After the class, Prudence dashed to the university canteen feeling unbearably empty. She had cut lunch, to make up her time: and was concentrating upon scalding tea when a figure approached the table, tentatively.

"Do you mind if I join you? Haven't I just seen you in the palaeography class?"

"Yes, oh, please do!" Prudence swept dirty cups to one side of the table. She had noticed him too, with some surprise, for he seemed considerably older than the rest of them. She did not remember seeing him at the class before. He seemed nervous (his speech had a fluent ease about it at variance with his manner), he sat down opposite her, stirred his coffee wildly, and looked hesitantly across the table. Prudence, upon whom life had as yet left few stresses, smiled openly back.

"Are you finding it interesting? What you want?" he asked.

"Oh yes, it's the beginning of proper work again," she said eagerly.

"Proper work being?" His smile seemed an effort to him.

"I'm to do a research degree, back in Cambridge. In medieval history."

"Ah."

"And you?" she asked politely.

"I'm temporarily doing war work of one kind and another. But my life... ." He stopped, frowning. He had been going to say *my life has fallen apart*, how could he suddenly say such a thing to a strange girl? Yet the inclination, once more, was compulsive.

"And your subject?" Prudence asked, after waiting for the sentence to finish. She watched him collect himself, with a real effort, come back to the present moment.

"Also early history," he admitted, half-smiling.

"But you must know all about how to read documents!"

"I never did enough. I always just wrestled with things as they came. This seemed a good chance to get a better technique, get into training again, while I'm in London. Also...at the moment...I have to keep going...fill up every minute there is... . Who put you on to these classes?" he added quickly.

"My Cambridge supervisor. As I'm working in London still. At least now I feel I'm getting ready for what I want to do."

He smiled then, very sympathetically, a smile that strangely revealed all the more clearly an underlying burden of sadness. He seemed touched by her untarnished enthusiasm and evident thirst for knowledge.

"Which is to pursue historical truth. A will o' the wisp if ever there was one. Have you got any inkling of your subject yet?"

"Not precisely. I'm just reading and browsing in the period, mid-twelfth century. In a field my supervisor suggested."

"Mm. Church and state, pope and king. I envy you. One of the most exciting times in a scholar's life, that first time." Modest Prudence had not yet quite accepted herself as a scholar. "Like a first love affair. At the time, there's so much flux and so much choice. The wood and the trees. And so much nervous doubt as to whether one can do it, face it. So often feeling plumb lazy! And being afraid one isn't up to it. Then," he lifted his eyes, looked at her kindly, "after a while it crystallises. And glows, as if it's been there all the time, that light in your eye. Your own particular light…. You know what someone said to the Pilgrim? "Do you see yonder wicket gate…keep that light in your eye…"! Months, years away…. And off you go in pursuit!" he finished this reverie, waving a fine thin hand.

Prudence enjoyed this, she laughed in anticipation of the chase. He saw that he had charmed her. How could he still be, with all that had happened, as vain as that, why did he bother to charm her? Watching his face, she observed all the enthusiasm he had called up to encourage her (she supposed him to be a teacher himself) drain from his face: the interest, the joy, erased, as if a fountain were turned off and one saw the jets quietly subside to a bubble and disappear.

"You suddenly look so sad," said she, with natural and unselfconscious sympathy. She was not usually impulsive with strangers. He studied her. She seemed as innocent as a rosebud. How could a creature as unhurt as this understand hurt? She would understand nothing; to try her was as useless as it was impertinent. Yet.

"Are you in a great hurry?" he asked.

"Not particularly," said she, thinking of her parents at home faithfully awaiting her for supper.

"It is because my life has been blown apart…suddenly, arbitrarily, without reason. Six weeks ago, my life was blown apart…." His hands made the gesture. He saw her young and serious face flush with concern, her brow furrow with it.

"Something terrible has happened to you," she said.

"I seem to have to tell people…I seem to have—this compulsive need to keep going over it…it's quite useless, it's happened, it can't ever be any different…but…."

"You probably need to talk about it, if it still happens," she said sagely.

"But when will it stop, how can I stop living it over? I have lost my wife and my son in a flying bomb attack…she'd taken him to shop, into the town, into Barnet…I didn't even know she'd planned it," his voice rose in unreasonable protest, "it must have been a sudden idea, because there was a bus perhaps…. Why did she do it? I keep thinking if only she hadn't thought of it! I didn't know it was happening, I was in London, working…I suppose she thought it was a treat for him, he's nearly three…I just wasn't *there*, to look after them…I kiss them goodbye in the morning and when I come home they aren't there, they're gone, I still can't believe it…they are both completely gone…for ever."

Prudence remembered the bomb in a shopping centre, at the end of August. She felt dumb with distress: for there was no comfort, nothing to say. Yet sympathy she must somehow give.

"I am so sorry for you," she said. "Tell me the rest if you want to, it may be easier to a stranger."

"Why do I have to go over and over it? I keep going over and over it, as if I could make it not happen…." His voice rose in a plaint again. "I get home to our village about half past six, as a rule, it varies, I bike from the station…. The garden gate was shut, there weren't any toys on the lawn…it's a charming cottage on its own…I knew she'd be getting him to bed…or she'd be in the kitchen doing the supper… . But the *door* was locked!" He said this with a gasp as if it were an affront. "So I knew they were out…I went all through the house calling you know, as if they could be hiding, so stupid, but they did once, for fun…. And she hadn't left a note…which was unusual, if anything different is happening we always leave each other notes…." He paused:

caught in that terrible limbo of the vanished present where the bereaved person constantly finds himself floundering, willing it back. "Left each other notes," he enunciated clearly.

"Of course. What happened then?" Prudence urged, instinctively pressing him to the end.

"Oh, I went to our nearest neighbour, she said have you heard the six o'clock news, she'd heard it. She said she'd happened to see them get on the bus…she clutched my arm, she said shall I come with you to find the policeman… . But she's got two children… . So I said no, I'll just go back and ring up… . Someone in Barnet… . The police said come in, come in at once if you can, we may be able to tell you which hospital… . I still thought it's all right, they'll be shocked and hurt a bit…but they'll be all right, they can't be…dead…I'll bring them both home." Two most unwanted tears by now rolled down Prudence's flushed cheeks. He looked up, saw this, and countered his own tears with savagery.

"Isn't human hope the most derisory, pathetic thing?" he said, every syllable like an icicle.

"Yes," she agreed without hesitation.

"I went back in, on the train… . There was a great crowd, I couldn't find anyone in charge at first…I still wouldn't understand, even when someone took my name, and looked things up and began treating me kindly… . My two weren't damaged…I felt sorry for the people who's folk were damaged…they looked a little…discoloured…but not damaged… ." His voice was now very quiet and gentle as if he pictured them: once more he had plunged through the horror and reached its hopeless end. There was a silence.

"So are you in the cottage? Who is looking after you?" Prudence said at last, urgently.

"I tried, I couldn't stay there…I shall have to turn it out later, I expect my dear Ma may come and help me…I'm with a college friend and his wife near London…they're letting me lodge there. This class is one of my ways of swallowing up time…so I shall keep it up if I can…everyone says keep things going, keep work going…but at times I think I am going out of my mind…I don't know *what* will happen, I'm sure."

"I am so sorry for you," she said again. She did not insult him by saying he would feel better as time passed.

"Thank you. I feel ashamed, blurting it all out, I always do," he shrugged.

"Why, why? Please don't."

"Goodbye. See you next week." He rose with a sudden impelled movement and a painful smile, waved that rather fine, beautiful hand at her and hastily departed.

At home, she apologised for her lateness, was about to describe its shocking reason (which had occupied her mind all the way back), when she noticed her father's subdued excitement. Edwin sat with his hands folded over a packet on his knee, a quirky smile on his face, awaiting his daughter and his supper. They always waited.

"Well. How did you get on this time?" he said with good cheer. Hungry though he was. Prudence collected herself. Father and daughter loved each other dearly.

"Very nicely! It's fascinating, Pop, it's a great thrill when you find you're a few words ahead of him! We were actually reading something together, by the end, and I got several words ahead!" she laughed. "I think I'll have to take up penmanship, write my own alphabet. The way the pen goes, the way the letters are actually made, varies different ways, by different scribes. Then there are some letters that always get confused with each other. And letters in pairs! How they get joined together. Differently. In fact, the whole subject of linkage—"

He listened to her fondly, but broke in.

"Well, if you promise not to tease me with tittles—"

"Not one jot nor one tittle," put in Margery out of her distant bible-reading girlhood.

"Jot? Yes, jot, iota, I?—Or with virgules, or thorns, or ampersands—I have got a present for you."

"Oh, Pop. What?"

"Here. I know your eyes are excellent but you did say he'd suggested one. It's a really good one, second-hand though it be."

She unwrapped it.

"Oh, darling Pop, thank you! It's a super one, lend me the paper, let me read the small print."

"Read it after supper, come on now, do," Margery said smiling.

Prudence laid the magnifying glass down and kissed her father. But later, as they sat at table, she told them why she had been so late.

Afterwards, Edwin noticed her face cloud frequently as she played with the glass, while he talked to his diary.

13

"I get it when I look in the mirror," said Laura. To her new-old escort, Hubert, standing swaying beside her in the tube train: both their images shadowing them along in the darkness outside, aping their nods and becks so precisely, it surely must mean something.

They had been to *Peer Gynt*.

How old, yet how new, was Hubert Cox. He and Laura and Marian had trundled in from their Suffolk village on the same noisy bus to their schools in the town. Though the behaviour of schoolboys and girls had not reached that level of deafening, rude, total possession of a public vehicle which began to pertain in the 'fifties and prevails in the modern day, they were nonetheless sometimes noisy and wild. Caps flew, satchels were raided, plaits were pulled (Marian's) and Hubert, probably because he kept himself to himself, came in for spiteful teasing and occasional horseplay, which he treated with an irritated and contemptuous sarcasm. As if he were old, mature, already. As in some ways he was. Laura kept herself to herself, too; they had it in common, brainy children, too old for their age in some ways, not old enough in others. Hubert, an only child, came sometimes to tea also, and they played hours of Monopoly and Lexicon: Hubert would rather have played bridge and chess, but these feeble girls knew neither. Occasionally in summer they met upon the Deben, kindly invited by the Butts (it was that Mr Butt who then and still managed Laurence Cardew's printing business) to sail.

Hubert would scowl, not good at ropes, but adoring the river and still more the sea if they reached it; his thin, tender hairless legs like leeks protruding from knee-length flannel shorts, his large feet in once-white tennis shoes stained yellow. Older than either of the Cardews, he went off to Edinburgh a year or two before the war to pursue some intensely scientific discipline which Laura could never remember. The war swallowed him up at once into radar, he was seldom seen in Suffolk, his widowed mother (of whose eyes he was the apple) used to complain to Kitty about it. When Kitty and her daughters moved to London, he might as well have been dead. Had not Mrs Butt suggested to Kitty that Laura join them and their son and a friend for a few days on a boat on the Broads. Laura could not abide fat Stanley Butt (when last seen years ago) but being warned that if she did not take all the days of annual leave due to her within the year she would lose them, thought it no bad thing to accept this ready-made holiday in late September. The friend proved to be Hubert, the Butts having forgotten the girls ever knew him.

Hubert, civilised but still shy, scientific but now also musical and a poetry-quoter, philosophical in a political vein, raspy-voiced, pale-faced, gentle as a girl. But still extraordinary to look at: that round, large head, that hair in a flop, that thin reddish neck, those opaque, shallow, pale blue eyes. Laura had grown more fluent and spirited than ever he remembered, and really rather pretty. Yet she was comfortingly familiar. He had made few girlfriends at the university, he was too shy and worked too much. Her thin brown body, her golden midriff bared as she fished for an escaped hat over the side of the unwieldy sailing cruiser, went straight to his heart and guts. He fell instantly in love with her and she was still under siege.

"When I look in the mirror. Sometimes," she repeated. "Who on earth am I? Am I anything? What's behind the eyes?"

"I know, yes I know."

They had watched Ralph Richardson gloriously posturing, egotistically boastful, enchantingly foolish, despairing, nonsensical, wise, by turns: unworldly and caught in the trammels of the world. Tenderly playing his mother to her death. And in blank, exact disillusionment peeling his onion. The unsurpassed performance, the lilt of the telling voice, warm while so precise, would linger in their ears forever.

131

"Don't we get to the heart of it soon?" Hubert suddenly quoted, his large face approaching hers.

"No I'm damned if we do…nothing but layers," she replied.

"But you know what he's saying, Laura, you know what Ibsen's saying—Love's the only purpose in life, only love makes sense of the onion layers, we exist in so far as we love, love calls us into being, Solveig's love has made him."

Laura considered this dangerous ground and nodded without comment. Hubert must have known the play well, before. She had read it only once, a schoolgirl.

"He gets back to Solveig, back home, you see," she heard his husky voice, in a tone of deep nostalgia.

"Home being only where love is," she suggested.

"Yes. Look. Here. Out."

Crossing the wide night gloom of blue-lit Victoria, Hubert was suddenly consumed with hunger, as he saw a dim open door and food in the hand of a man emerging.

"I'm starving. I'll get us something. Get seats, leave the carriage open."

"You've only got about seven minutes," she called. She opened the first door, left it swinging, sat on the prickly seat and thought of Solveig, loving at once and loving forever.

"But are you certain? This is forever.

There's no way back on the road that I've come… .

Be patient, my love. Long or short you must wait.

I will wait."

It's me, I'm Solveig, Laura thought. Am I going to wait all my life, wait for Gavin? Who is unattainable? What am I going to do? Who am I? Why cannot I love anyone else? The whistle shrilly roused her, she gasped, she stood up, leaned out.

At the barrier, Hubert fought the ticket collector. She could just see, in the dim light, the minute drama enacted at the gate: the man barring

Hubert's way, Hubert's arms waving, clutching at the man's wrists. The train sidling insolently away with that humming, clanking sound electric trains made, was not loud enough to drown the sudden bellow of frustrated fury, which reached her, as Hubert flung down the hamburger bag and jumped upon it, again and again, roaring. (The ticket collector, a farmer's son from distant Norfolk, told him reprovingly it was just like a cow calving.)

Oh, oh, ought I to have got out, waited with him? Laura thought, slamming the door, and pulling the window up. Oh, poor Hubert, she wailed (she was alone). Yet so seldom was he roused in this kind of way, he was so quiet, so contained a person that she was aware of a tiny, mean satisfaction in seeing his defences breached.

She was still worrying about it as she tramped down the wooden stairs from the down-line to the road at their station, where the ancient round-bowl gas lamp with string attachments still flickered at nights. It was regarded locally as an amusing antique and much loved.

She would await the inevitable phone call next day.

"Laura?"

"Oh Hu, I'm so sorry about last night. What did you do? Was there another train?"

"Got a tube to Wimbledon, it was OK."

"You sounded fearfully angry."

"I *was* angry. I wanted to talk to you. After that lovely play," he said huskily.

"We only had two stations to talk in. You were getting out at Clapham Junction."

"Two stations would have been quite enough, it was all in my heart, what I wanted to talk about."

"Well, talk away," Laura said with some apprehension, feeling that at least she owed him this. She was used to the phone calls anyway. Long and often.

"Oh—oh," he sighed a long husky sigh. "You know what it is, you know I love you, Laura. I love the look of you, I love your dear little face."

"It isn't particularly little."

"It is, it is, I often see your face as you were on the school bus, with one of those awful dark green hats you all wore, squashed down over your hair."

"I didn't look at all dear in my school hat." Laura, amused.

"Well, you're much prettier now I agree. And I love your hands, they're so soft."

"My hands! They're nobbly and too large for my wrists."

"And I adore your legs."

"My legs aren't bad, I grant you."

"Laura, I want you so badly, it keeps me awake. I want to make love to you, I want to be inside you." Laura had never known shy, self-contained Hubert so un-prudishly voluble.

"You don't seem to feel anything, how much do you know about sex, Laura?" he asked sternly. "Don't you know that everybody needs sex, everybody needs it in frequent and copious doses, young adult males need a full orgasm several times a week at *least*—I suppose you know what I'm talking about. Perhaps you don't," he sniffed.

"You sound like a sex manual," said she, after a bleak pause.

"Well, *please*, Laura, can't we, won't you—I know I love you."

"But I don't love you," she sighed, unanswerably.

"Not at all? Not even a little beginning?"

"Not at all. That way. And never would."

"Why not? Why are you so sure, you probably might if only you'd try letting me make love to you."

"I can't. I can't do that with someone I don't love! It's impossible! And I don't love you, Hubert, though I do like you."

"Why not? Why don't you love me?"

"Hu, what a hopeless question. It's an impossible question. I suppose because you're not attractive to me in the way I am to you; I am awfully sorry, but it is not my fault."

"But we have lots in common, lots of things to do, music, plays, poetry—I thought you liked our outings? We've even got some of our childhood in common!"

"I know, and I do. This is what is such a puzzle. You are a nice, kind, sensitive, generous friend, I enjoy going out with you. But we shall have to give it up."

"No—o—o," he wailed. "Why, Laura?"

"Because I know I will never love you, so it's cheating. Taking all this on false pretences. And I don't think I want to sleep with anyone till I marry him. Suppose I got—"

"Pregnant? Then marry me, marry me, Laura! I'll get you pregnant in a trice! But there are lots of ways of *not* getting pregnant."

"Don't be daft, I've told you I don't love you."

"There's someone else," Hubert gloomily surmised.

"There's been someone else for some time."

"Then why aren't you married to him?"

"Not free to marry me. But I know I still love him. Which is how I know I don't love you."

"Well what's the good of that?" Hubert said with disgusted conviction.

What indeed? Laura thought. But it's no good, it isn't Hubert, it'll never be Hubert.

"Laura?"

"Yes."

"Why won't you just let me try? Let me make love to you? Why are you so stuffy about it?"

There was no deflecting him.

"I suppose it's the puritan way we were brought up," she brooded. "But quite apart from that I don't want to, I told you why."

"I think you're scared. You soon wouldn't be."

"Hubert. You've got to find some nice girl who loves you enough to let you. If you need it so much. If you're so keen on all these orgasms every week. Then you can marry her. That's all there is to it."

"But I love *you*!"

"Let's not go round in circles."

"Oh, let's go on a little longer!"

"Well, so long as you know how I feel. Thank you for *Peer Gynt* by the way, I really loved it."

"Me, too."

"I must go, I can hear something burning."

"You can't hear a thing burning."

Laura evidently could.

What a monster it was, what a problem. Was sex. She really liked Hubert. He was all the things she had told him. Yet she supposed sadly that she must forgo their interesting talks, their delightful Wigmore Hall concerts, their theatres and Sunday walks, for she knew quite surely that he would never be attractive to her, and the thought of his passion made her shiver. What was the matter with her, was she simply dead-scared, as he said? But when she had imagined with longing Gavin making love to her it had seemed not in the least frightening, but some seventh heaven. (She had discussed this with a girlfriend ages ago, who had replied that by all accounts it was difficult, painful, absurd and prone to grave disappointment, and that Laura was being over-romantic.) Men, said one of the young women housekeepers who had helped Kitty before the war, men think only of one thing. Laura had always remembered it, said with simple amusement. The chemistry of it was inexplicable and deceitful. Hubert was a man with interests much nearer to her own than Rees, yet she had felt no disgust at Ree's passion. But as to barefaced lust helping itself to satisfaction from a total stranger (like the man on the six-forty train who had once tried to kiss her, his bristly beard pricking her, his tongue forcing her mouth open) that she did find disgusting. "Natural" though it might be thought to be. ("Natural" indeed, what evidence was there that to be natural was necessarily a recommendation?) And whose French grandmother was it who used to say shrinkingly of sex, "Combien le bon Dieu a-t-il pensé de quel saleté?"

From the office the flaxen Mr Harvald now came and went to the Continent. (At least this mitigated the sudden roars, furious arguments and loud crashes, which had used to come from his room.) No one knew quite what he was doing, it seemed possible that he barely knew himself. But the satisfaction on his face when he first appeared in uniform was scarcely concealed. The battle-dress bolstered his sinuous slimness, his swagger was the more noticeable for the stiffness of the cloth. Laura had helped him clear his desk and wished him good luck with affection and no regret: her friendliness got little response from Mr Harvald.

Between those who wanted to eat her and those it was impossible to arouse, was there not someone, somewhere, like her, free for her, and full of the same yearning?

Imogen Wicklow sat in the theatre with Matthew on one side and Laura on the other, knowing already that she had made one of her mistakes. How many more mistakes am I going to perpetrate, dear my Lord, in the name of love and goodwill?

She had wished she could ask Prudence too of course, so that it didn't look so obvious, her embryo scheme to interest Matthew and Laura in each other: but she only had three tickets. For surely Matthew and Laura should be friends? No one who knew Laura even moderately well was unaware of this lurking, tiresome, insistent desire she had "to write": and Matthew was already doing so. They could go off to the country together once the war was over and write till they burst, to their hearts' content, encouraging each other, scribbling away all day. And night. If that's what they wanted. (And much good may it do them, she added, finding herself laughing at the image thus conjured.)

It had been difficult to get them talking over their drinks and sandwiches for Laura was spirited and sombre by turns, and tonight seemed over-awed, even shy, of Matthew. (Perhaps that was a good sign.) The awe was expressed as admiration that at least he was, against all odds, pressing on with his novel. In the theatre he had very carefully arranged that she, Imogen, sit between them, which was not what she had intended.

Since last September Laurence Olivier had become King Richard the Third, writing an indelible hieroglyph in theatre history with his sinuous, red-gloved, sexual hands. All the world wanted to see him, tickets were scarce, Imogen thought herself immensely lucky to be given three by a friend who could not use them. Laura had jumped at the invitation: Matthew was more guarded.

"Really!" he stated in an interval. "It is the most ridiculous play! I mean—don't think I'm not enjoying it, Imogen—but how can Shakespeare expect to get away with that scene, that wooing, that widow, whatever her name is?"

"Anne," said Laura, still shocked at anyone slighting Shakespeare.

"Anne, being deflected, flattered, going to give in, when he's killed her husband, and her husband's father, is it, Henry the Sixth?"

"Well he *does* get away with it, and Olivier has got away with it, he's a marvellous Richard!" burst out Laura with spirit.

"We—ell—doesn't convince me."

"That's your fault," snapped Laura, to Matthew's surprise and Imogen's unwilling joy.

"And all these people," he hastily went on, "all these relationships, how on earth can we follow it, who they all are, it's impossible material for a play, all called by their *titles* as well as their names."

"All the history plays have that difficulty, if you don't do your homework," Imogen put in.

"It doesn't matter, it's the impact that matters, the drama, stop worrying who they are, stop being so *cerebral*."

"*You're* just being emotional."

"Oh, come, come," laughed Imogen, between their crossfire, praying for the curtain to rise. She longed for them to talk, indeed, but here they were quarrelling.

Now, on the pavement, Mrs Wicklow desired a taxi, and Matthew was intent on getting her one. They were very few and far between and it was necessary to be an opportunist. If any kind of a bus came first, going in even partly the right direction, it was better to take it. Thus Laura thought, still in a rapt dream of evil, comical, pitiable Richard, with her eye on dim shapes in the distance. Then everything suddenly happened at once; a taxi, for which Matthew sprang forward, and at least two swaying shapes of buses looming along and pulling in. Matthew, gleeful, bundled Imogen in and appeared to be going to follow.

"Matthew! Surely you will see Laura to Victoria!" said Mrs Wicklow, scandalised.

"But I don't live near Victoria, I live near you!" he protested.

Seeing in advance what would happen Laura had not waited, but had run for the first bus, was already pushing down it for a seat.

"Where is she? What's happened to Laura? We could at least have dropped her off!"

"She's gone, she must be on one of those buses. It's all right, she's all right," Matthew announced, scrambling in himself and slamming the taxi door firmly.

"It is not all right. I am ashamed of you, Matthew," Mrs Wicklow said. "I took it for granted you would see her across London!"

"No need. She's all right. She wouldn't want me hanging round I'm quite sure," he said sulkily, in cross despair that he had displeased her again.

Laura, between buses and walking, had passed from her ecstatic re-living of the tragedy of Richard the Third to a scornful assessment of Matthew the more pointed because of her slight humiliation at his indifference to her (for which her eyes stung as she ran for the bus). What an obtuse, insensitive creature he must be, to be unmoved by that amazingly calculated yet spontaneously vivid performance, what a dolt! She cared not a rap for Matthew, save only as an older person pursuing what she herself wished to pursue: she had been interested in him solely for that reason. Meanwhile, there was poor dear Hubert who would no doubt have telephoned tonight suffering acutely his frustrated passion, as Kitty said, "Oh she's gone to the theatre with people at the office." Her emotions aroused, Laura's heart swung to the thought of Gavin, which lurked always too near: those greyish-hazel eyes, that shining smile, that gold head, an image now often irrecoverable, but sometimes to her bliss as clear for an instant as in life itself. Walking an empty pavement, she suddenly re-lived the astonishing, exultant joy that the sight of him on the Didcot platform had brought. People pursued you whom you could not love, the one you loved remain glowing, unattainable. Through the ages poets had wept over this, troubadours had sung it: there was a kind of inevitable, piercing beauty about it, it was the stuff of poetry.

Stars in a deep blue sky were peculiarly visible above the darkened city by benefit of blackout. Laura surveyed their brilliance with an aching delight, her heart bursting with a larger, more general and invasive love following the catharsis of the theatre: and the sudden memory of that glorious joy. Love was everywhere, love was God. Those everlasting arms: they were simply love, your own and other people's, buoying you up, rising again and again, giving always a fresh hope, always to be trusted, underneath you forever and for ever. There must be some purpose, or some person, to be the recipient of so much feeling. And if there was to be no person, how was she to use it, where could it flow?

❦

Laura had met Tom for a Christmas drink.

"You've been very elusive lately," he said. "This autumn, I mean. I've rung you several times at home where your ma says you're out: and several times at the office, where you've gone to lunch or left early."

"Ah."

"So what's going on?"

Laura, entirely in command of herself, replied at once.

"I'm being besieged by a quite nice chap, a very nice chap, from right back in our girlhood, that I'm not in love with."

"I can tell that. Why not?"

"Oh, don't you start. That's what he asks. Why *should* I be, if I'm not? Men seem to think if they fall for you, you must fall for them."

"What do you expect, with all this free floating libido you put out?"

"What an expression, where'd you get that from? I don't consciously put it out."

"All the worse if it's unconscious, you're not in control. You pull and pull and when he's hooked, you throw him back, you don't want him. Why not, I bloody wonder?"

"I didn't pull Hubert, we just happened to re-meet while I was with folk we knew in Suffolk. He appeared to fall in headfirst. And keeps wanting to take me out."

"So that's nice for you." Tom sounded quite sour.

"Yes. But I'll have to stop it, I think. Since all he thinks of now is wanting to make love to me."

"Does he want to marry you?"

"I think he does."

"Don't you?"

"I've told you, no. Don't find him attractive that way and never would. So really it's not fair to go on with it."

"Pity. I was going to say why don't you go ahead and have a proper affair with him." Tom sounded cross now.

"That's what he says."

"I'll bet."

"It's impossible…to me. If I'm not attracted to a person. But after all, I want friends."

Tom said after a pause:

"What do you want most, Laura, to marry, or do this creative career you're always dreaming about?"

"Of course I want to marry. I want both. But I don't want to marry the wrong person. If you'd seen my parents you'd know what I mean, how I feel."

"Ah. Yes." Tom appeared lost in thought. "Met Ros the other day."

"Did you! How's she? You meet pretty often?"

"No, quite rarely. She's in a real stew about it."

"About what?"

"Not being married."

"Is she? Then why doesn't she?"

"Same as you, can't find the right guy."

"And does she have lots of these 'proper' affairs as you paradoxically call them?"

Tom hissed a half-laugh.

"Shouldn't think so. She's like you, isn't she? A well-brought-up, middle-class, clever girl. Here you all are, you 'proper' girls, poured out on a waiting world, ripe for mating but far too fastidious for any old Tom, Dick or Harry. Over-intellectualised. Riddled with the embargoes of the British class system, have to have sods from the right drawer. All that stuff. Puritan with it. What on earth's going to happen to you all?" Tom looked down his Roman nose.

"I daresay we'll make out all right in the end," said Laura smiling. "Anyway, what do you suggest we do?"

"I've said, I suggest you pursue one of these friendships to its natural conclusion and have an affair. You might find it turned into a meaningful relationship. What's stopping you?"

Meaningful relationships. Was it the very first time Laura had heard the expression? Increasingly used by the advocates of extra-marital sexual friendships, it was to become a cliché as society proceeded towards permissiveness. You hoped, if you had sense and conscience, it would prove meaningful. How did you know without trying? Precisely so, said they.

"What's stopping you?" Tom repeated doggedly.

"Not loving anyone. Except someone in the past."

He uttered a rather noisy sigh, of some finality.

"Unanswerable. Here, girl, have another drink. Merry Christmas."

"Merry Christmas, Tom. Do you want to marry, I never asked you?"

"I'd hate to marry a virgin," Tom said darkly, out of the blue.

Laura could have felt unspeakably abashed, diminished and foolish to be a virgin. (One had to have not-being-a-virgin as a dowry in Tom's circle.) But she did not feel this, the bonds of upbringing were still too strong. She smiled at him rather mysteriously. He thought again of the man who caused her to walk up the down escalator. He felt baffled, was perhaps a little drunk, he realised: but he was a thoughtful, objective person, he was four or five years older than Laura, and had become increasingly aware of his mind dwelling upon her. The more difficult she had become to reach, the more he found himself thinking of her and wondering what had happened. There seemed to be an area in a friendship where one accepted it as static however pleasant; or where one pressed it further, adventuring, seeing if the ice would hold. So here goes, said Tom to himself, raising his eyes and his glass. First, we'll clear the area of unwanted frozen scrub.

"Laura."

"Yes."

"You do have to learn to admit your physical needs."

"So Hubert keeps telling me over the phone."

She was as bouncy as a ball today.

"I don't wonder. But you're not going to fall in love with Hubert (what a name)?"

"No." She looked quite sad. "Simply couldn't."

"And that best man, who made you walk up escalators the wrong way, is not coming after you any more?"

"No. Anyway, I told you, he wasn't really a man I...trusted."

"You were manifestly right. How about this odd chap at the office, writing novels in His Majesty's time? That you've mentioned?"

"Oh, him. Matthew. Mrs Wicklow took us both to *Richard* the other night. He didn't like the play, he didn't even like Larry!"

"Well, that ditches him for sure in the eyes of any English rose," Tom observed with a grave face.

Laura laughed. Tom was pleased.

"So, let's see, anyone else on the roll? Right now?"

She shook head, smiling. Then, suddenly serious, she said:

"You know there's only one person on the roll. As you call it. At the moment."

"Only your golden tutor. Standing on the platform at Didcot. The sight of whom transports you with joy. I wish I'd seen him. I might have learned his secret."

He gazed at her sombrely.

"Charlotte Brontë," he said.

She met the gaze, smiled at the allusion.

"Isn't it a funny thing?"

"What?"

"Love," she said. "The wind that bloweth where it listeth."

"Why don't you turn it in another direction? You've disposed of all the others, you don't seem to want any of them very much. And you can't have him, it appears. Why don't you dispose of him?" he suggested. "It strikes me as a waste of feeling. And I'd like to know why you don't. Give it some thought, Laura."

"Are you turning into my psychologist caterpillar?" she said with a questioning smile.

"Might be. Could do. Real live case," he laughed, making a face at her.

She became aware of the very reserved, tentative sweetness of the look in his eye.

❦

Prudence sat with her parents over Christmas glad of the rest and glad to talk to her father, who followed events with informed assiduity and would bring her up to date.

In Italy the eight-month struggle for liberation continued at fearful cost. Many of the partisans in the north were communists, with a double aim, and as much against their own monarchy as against the enemy upon their soil. The Allies meanwhile had reached Ravenna but were still fifty miles from the River Po. In Greece for the past year there had been internal struggle, with mutiny in the Greek army, which amounted to civil war, British troops taking the royalist part against Greek communist forces.

"Pop, what's happening in Greece, exactly?"

"Well, you must have noticed there's a struggle going on between the Communists and the old government, the people who want the king and the status quo. Now the Germans are out."

"But haven't the Resistance helped liberate the country?"

"Yes. But it seems they're preponderantly Communist. And we don't like it. It's the same old fear as in Italy and everywhere else, we're afraid of Communism getting in with liberation. So I suppose we'll curb it if we can. I'm not quite sure we have the right to...we shall see."

On Christmas Day, Mr Churchill and Mr Eden flew suddenly to Athens to mediate and by the end of the year Archbishop Damaskinos was to be appointed regent.

"What you ought to be watching, however," remarked Edwin to his daughter, "is what the Germans are up to. In France."

For Christmas that year was dominated neither by the Italian nor the Greek struggle, but by the "Bulge".

To the astonishment of the world, the Germans, retreating on all extremities from their wartime empire, had staged in mid-December a desperate last push in the Ardennes, taking the Allies by surprise. *Aus der Traum*, wrote a German tank crew jubilantly on their tank: and because a week of fog prevented air operations, they had broken through the American lines in a puppet-like echo of their 1940 assault and were making rapidly for the River Meuse, in a long, narrow spearhead soon referred to as the Bulge. On each side of it, the American forces held out. The Germans had to bypass Bastogne, still held by a US force behind them; they called upon General McAuliffe commanding Bastogne to surrender: he secured his immortality once and for all by answering "Nuts!" When the weather cleared on Christmas Eve, the Allied aircraft went into action to smash the rolling German tanks. The day after Christmas, General Patton moved his army up from the south and relieved Bastogne. Though defeat was certain, Hitler still mercilessly danced his puppets, until nearly every German tank was destroyed.

Arnhem: Avenge for countered an American tank crew upon theirs.

14

I think we've just got to decide, and to do it," Kitty said.

"Yet he doesn't seem very ill," said Laura.

"Well, he had that glorious wood walk on Sunday, and the huge meal. Even though the swelling was worse. It's worse still today. Do we want to wait till he's feeling ill?"

They surveyed the good old General with sorrow. His bright and eager face, dear to all the family, was swollen so that he might almost have been a dog they did not know. When the swellings, which came and went, were somewhere out of sight it was easier to bear. Kitty had noticed it three weeks ago, rubbing him after a wet walk and had gone to the vet. It had been diagnosed as Hodgkin's disease, in its canine form, and virtually incurable. For a season or two he had had winter rheumatism, miraculously helped by small doses of aspirin. But never an illness. They thought he was at least twelve years old.

"No," Laura agreed. "But I promised I'd try and take him to see Papa again."

Kitty shook her head helplessly. They had not left him alone since his illness, afraid that he might suddenly grow worse. When Kitty had an office day Laura had taken him up with her.

The old dog was perfectly at ease in Laura's office, perfectly self-effacing, no trouble at all. He would find a patch of sun under Laura's table and lie in it. At lunchtimes she and Prudence had walked him in

Hyde Park and beside the Serpentine, where he had greatly enjoyed the seagulls, pulling to chase them, memories of his Suffolk seaside days aroused.

"Good God," Alex Harvald had said, back on a rare visit and catching sight of the large tawny form, as he chanced to come in. Otherwise his presence went unremarked or warmly welcomed. Mrs Tripp in particular loved him and made much of him, which induced Laura to confess that he was ill. After the first week the treatment had appeared to be having effect.

But now.

"No," sighed Laura again.

A good deal of Kitty's anguish was for Laura, who over this crisis was suffering all the more for saying little. Though bludgeoned by years of outrageous fortune into a calmer acceptance of calamity, Kitty could vividly remember partings with old dogs when she was young. She lifted the telephone to speak to the vet.

In the morning, Laura stood up creditably to the familiar ordeal of bidding an animal farewell, fondling his velvet ears with nostalgia, as he lay dead. But once outside, announced her intention of going home. It was still early.

"I can't go straight up to the office," she said. "I simply can't. You go, I don't mind."

"We'll both go home for an hour or so and go later."

Laura went straight up to her room and wept with complete and childish abandonment, noisily, so that Kitty could hear her, for a quarter of an hour.

Kitty sat down at her drawing-room desk, pulled out a sheet and began to write.

My dear Laurence, Kitty wrote and stopped.

My dear Laurence, she said in her mind, here am I turning to you for comfort, when no such thing has been possible between us for years and years—You will mind about the General, he was particularly yours, Lolly minds so much she is up there sobbing like a little girl again, I suppose partly she's upset not to have brought him to see you once more. How absurd it is, dear old Laurence, why can't I just pick the phone up and speak to you and say please come and comfort us, we have had to part with the worthy General?

Then she wrote the real letter.

Laura came down the stairs, went into the bathroom, splashed water on her face. Kitty made coffee. They looked at his basket.

"I'll disband it tonight."

"Yes."

They departed once more to the station. In the office, kind Mrs Tripp enquired.

"How is he?"

"He's all right," said Laura, not looking up from her work. Mrs Tripp touched her shoulder and nodded.

The young conductor on the bus, having checked all the passengers below, swung himself round by the bright metal rail on to the stairs and clattered up again, his bag of change and his ticket puncher rattling noisily. As he went forward to the passenger at the front, he slowed down partly in uncertainty as to what to do and partly in deference. This was the second time of asking the gentleman, the whole thing was a puzzle, outside his experience. He was a thin pale youth with oily curls and grey eyes, reserved from military service because he had been tubercular. Illness had made him gentle and patient.

"Sir?" he asked, his fingers ready to issue the ticket. The gentleman, who had been staring out of the window, looked at him again with an expression of acute anxiety and bewildered fear. His piercingly blue eyes were so afraid, the young man wanted to touch, to comfort him, tell him it would be all right, as he again shrugged his shoulders helplessly, and shook his head.

"You haven't remembered where you're going, sir."

"I—no—who—no."

"Don't you worry, sir. It'll come back. We'll leave it a bit longer. You watch the road, it may remind you." For at the first asking, the gentleman had put his hand up to his forehead and simply said he couldn't remember. He was a well-dressed, elderly man, he was no layabout, or spiv as they called them now, trying to get a free ride. The conductor had decided at once he could not turn him off the bus.

Now he wondered what he could do instead, it being his duty to get the fare.

"I know what, sir, you give me a two shillings to be going on with. That'll take you right to the terminus from where you got on, anyway. When we get there, I'll get someone to help you."

He would find the inspector, ask him to telephone a hospital or a doctor or something.

The gentleman's face took on an expression of suspicion and affront.

"I must take the fare you see, sir."

The passenger produced the florin with no word and received his ticket, heard the young man sway off down the bus, clatter down the stairs; and resumed his horrified staring from the window. They were in a very poor and dreary district, there were rows of dingy, broken-down, narrow terraced houses with two storeys and a basement, and broken boarded windows, and yards full of junk and lean-to sheds. Then there would be a space covered with rubble; a torn, ashamed, colour-washed wall of a bedroom; and then the terrace would start again, the mean houses and the dirty yards, the discarded baths, sinks and ovens, the ruined bicycles, the tumble-down sheds. And the bus was now pulling up where he could see into the squalor of one of the yards. And there was a dog, a poor dog, standing pulling, on a too-short chain, a beautiful ragged tawny fellow, barking, tongue hanging out, almost smiling at him: visible for several seconds while the bus juddered.

Laurence gasped, leaned forward as the bus started, looked back, but the bus had moved on and they had passed the yard, a wall hid it from view, the beautiful dog had gone. With the sight of the dog, the jerk of the bus, he remembered all about everything. Who he was. Where he was going. He had suddenly decided to go to see his poor sister, to spend the day with her. He had left quite early, it was right across London. He took out the gold half-hunter, which had belonged to his uncle and looked at it. It was still quite early. That dog. It was just like the General, just like where he had first seen him, that yard they had rescued him from, he and Marian. It was most remarkable, it was like a photograph of the actual scene. He wondered if it had helped to bring him back from what had been a most unpleasant experience. He shuddered, then shook himself. Was it the General himself on the retina of his mind, was it some dog just like him? By and large, it did not perhaps much matter.

"Palmer's Green," he said smiling, to the young man who had come up yet again. Keeping an eye on him.

"Palmer's Green's where I want to be," he said.

"There! I said you would, I said you'd get it OK if we give it a chance. Ever 'appened to you before, sir?" The conductor was really pleased.

"Never. Horrible," the gentleman muttered.

"I'll say, real frightening. You go to the terminus and get another from there."

"I remember."

"OK, sir. Glad you're OK."

With the remembering of course came back all the despair. But he was going to try and cheer up Lilian, he had not to be too despairing. When he got off the bus, he thanked the conductor, who wished him a good morning and went off to impart the whole curious episode to a man in the office. There was still quite a distance to go in the second bus: Laurence remained what he and Kitty had always called "rattled" for the rest of the journey.

The next morning there was a letter from Kitty, who had managed a friendly note, though sad enough. The old dog was dead. Also, she told him all the details of the illness and its progress, which he was glad of, one hated not to know what had happened. They were feeling awful, she said, Lolly was weeping bitterly. She even harked back to the time before, oh years ago, old Whisky: said that he had been calm and comforting and sensible then, felt she must write a line now. As if she needed, depended on him still. Said how much he had loved the dog, how the dog adored him.

> I am grieved you had no chance to see him again. He has been
> so bound up with our lives for the last nine fateful years that
> his going seems to mark the end of a chapter...

She even suggested a meeting in town, though perhaps he would rather not. He *had* seen him, he had seen the loved dog again. Pondering how strange it was, the vision of the dog or possibly the fortuitous sight of a dog like him, at the time when the deed was being done, Laurence read the letter once more, suffering his share of sorrow.

He was touched deeply and in spite of himself that Kitty remembered and was grateful for his being calm and comforting. And poor little Lolly, weeping, oh poor little creature, his little girl he had loved so much. Still loved.

She still came, faithfully, to meet him quite often, did not apparently blame him for leaving, as she had once as a schoolgirl in terrible tearful despair blamed them both as they shouted at each other. (Not that Kitty often shouted: but she would sometimes, in her vibrant contralto, roar.) And there was noise and anger, and his own fury rising up to choke him as he bellowed at their inability to do what he said, what was right, what he decreed.

How are we expected to grow up? Straight? In this? Lolly's shrill agonised voice pierced his soul from long ago.

Yet there was nothing to be done. Kitty's intransigence, her inability to see that it was all her fault, were absolutely unconquerable. He had tried to point it out all the time. It was simply no *good* his complying with her crazy suggestion to meet. He could not for a moment expect her to come bearing apologies and understanding and that sweet meekness she had had as a girl.

He was sad about the good old dog but forever glad he had rescued him. Much, much had he given to them all. He rather liked to think that the General had come to his aid when he sorely needed it; but had not said as much to his sister to whom he had described the amnesia, in a highly dramatised version his voice going hushed with horror. He would not voice the suggestion to her, for he disapproved of the occult, the inexplicable and the spiritualistic and his sister knew it. He had simply let her assume it was a dog just like the General. Yet now he wondered if he would ever tell them, tell Laura, of the strange vision, of how it had seemed at the time like a vision of the real dog, the first sight of him in that yard years ago?

He folded the letter and kept it.

Laura asked herself why the General's death was so much more than his death and sensed an answer. He was a catalyst, she thought, an obsessive, devoted uniter and releaser of the family feelings. Even his behaviour on walks when we separated was symbolic of it: he would rush between one group and the other, rounding us up, true to his ancient sheep-rounding instinct, which made us laugh. He loved them both, us all. He was the symbol of the family together, of the long, painful attempt at happiness, the effort to be a whole, a battle lost before ever I was born. With his death it is bared, shown up for what it is, impossible; his death has cracked it permanently apart, one can no longer pretend to hope.

But there is more than that. I have always grieved, she thought, immoderately for the deaths of creatures, sweet kittens, frail old cats, other ancient loved dogs, fluttering, broken, or frozen birds, even for moths, and mummified bees. She remembered heartbroken, angry tears to her mother, in adolescence, against the hatefulness, the obscenity, of death. Oh, but when you get there it can seem like a friend, Kitty had said. Have I still not begun to come to terms with death in general, the deaths of others, the death of all, she now asked herself sternly? How do I set about facing, accepting my own death in particular, in advance, before I am there? I wish somebody would tell me how, Laura reflected, it surely must be possible? But had soon forgotten the proposition, her own death being so far in the future as to be still impossible.

P rudence watched Edwin's hand move rapidly and impatiently across the page.

> The frantic Germans, animals sensing the cage close, dashed first for the Ardennes in that putsch nicknamed the Bulge, and also for Strasbourg, only just retaken. Rumour is that Ike ordered Strasbourg to be abandoned, the men to be thrown into Ardennes defence but that de Gaulle fiercely countermanded this, so the place holds on.

"One cannot help admiring de Gaulle," Edwin said, lifting his head from his diary. The general's very awkwardness, intransigence, was bound to appeal to Edwin.

"Och, yes," Prudence agreed. "Laura remembers seeing a daughter, once."

"Really? What like?"

"I was trying to remember an exact expression. 'Looking determinedly unassailable'," she said with her little amused laugh.

Edwin liked this, wrote it down, Laura had a splendid turn of phrase. Prudence wondered if she would ever read the diaries and remember, as she read, the occasions when they sat here, the family waiting for Donald to be with them again, Pop writing in the diary.

Looking into a future where you now almost could look, where they were all beginning to peer with furtive hope once more, Prudence did wonder. Knowing Pop, she thought it most probable he would burn his diaries. The vision arose of her father feeding diaries into some smoking garden incinerator of the future, as he now fed unwanted bank statements in. A pity, it would be.

As January wore on into its second week, its third, it became apparent that the vast, long-awaited Russian offensive from the east had begun. In the bleakest of mid-winters hundreds of thousands of short-statured, dumb, patient, frozen Russian soldiers stumbled slid and skidaddled, transported across the icy plains, through the shrieking winds of Poland in the north, of Silesia in the centre and of Hungary in the south: the lucky ones amongst them fur-hatted, fur-booted and gloved, the witless or unlucky suffering agonies of frost bite. Before them retreated the equally luckless Germans, abandoning entrenchments for the cruel air and blinding snow above. Snow-covered vehicles swayed and skidded along, for once totally and effectively camouflaged. Animals, donkeys, mules, horses (what were left) were inflicted by man's antics with abominable sufferings. Sometimes the sufferings endured in the aggregate overwhelmed Prudence and Laura.

"Only," said Laura, tracing squares in a gloom on the red checked Wopshop tablecloth, "you have not to add it all up. Each poor chap, or beast, bears, only his own: as C S Lewis says. Intolerable otherwise."

"Intolerable any wise," Prudence said in baffled anger at the stupidity of the war. "Who *can* endure it?"

"Agnus Dei," said Imogen, "qui tollis peccata mundi."

They regarded her with their usual polite incomprehension.

"But how does that help?"

"It is a symbol of a mystery…which can only be felt and not explained…. Those of us who feel it seem to be helped." She sounded abashed, apologetic.

Prudence wanted to point out that it was not Mrs Wicklow at this moment who needed helping, but out of respect and affection forbore. Respect and affection for one's wiser, longer-suffering elders was due and pertained: had they not borne it all, "tolerated" it, for three or four times as long as oneself? Could they not be expected to be wiser?

In five days from the beginning of the offensive, on the seventeenth of January, Marshal Zhukov was in Warsaw. The news was not long in bursting upon the Allied countries.

Too late, too late, too late, too late ran Franciszek Gorzinska's sombre thoughts, to the smooth rattle of the electric train carrying him down the southern railway to a place called Woking in the countryside of Surrey of which till lately he had never heard.

It was two and a half months since he had first met Victoria Wicklow (he was charmed by her having his sister's name) and they had become friends. He had been bidden several times to her mother's flat when the girl had leave. He had even, once or twice, taken her out alone. He had been grateful to Mrs Wicklow for acquainting her daughter with his story, no man wants a new friendship entangled at its beginnings with the brambles of distress: and Victoria's sympathy was discreet though lively. So charming and amusing a young woman must have many admirers and he thought of himself still as her mother's friend. Imogen had already asked Victoria, who drove ambulances for the Red Cross, about the vast organisation, which tried to trace the millions of wartime rootless lost. Of this Victoria knew little but thought she could find someone who did. Then one night over her mother's supper table, when he was talking with sorrowful affection and some pride of his family and his sister, an artist, a memory from the early days of the war suddenly awoke in her.

Down in what she called the wilds of Surrey, in the warm summer nights after Dunkerque, in her very early days in the service: meeting trainloads of badly wounded, lying in discomfort on slats; VADs making them more comfortable, giving hot drinks, transferring them to ambulances, driving them to hospitals.

Amongst all this, Celia Berkeley, a commandant from the Surrey division, a beautiful woman much older than herself, working as hard as she, with whom there had been an evanescent friendship in that dreadful and crowded summer. Victoria had been to her house, her father's house, several times. She had seen some of her work, she was a painter and aquatinter. Upon the wall of the studio was an aquatint, some animal, thought Victoria. She remembered only the quick disclaimer, "Oh that's not mine, that's the work of a Polish friend I have not heard of since the war, and I fear I never may." The words came back whole, never recalled before. She said nothing at the time, but later, scrabbling through an old address book, rang Miss Berkeley up.

"How odd, it's the same name! Perhaps you subconsciously remembered," said she. "But it's a common name. Send him down, I can possibly help him about the search."

So Mr Gorzinska, warned not to expect any revelation and needing no such warning, got off his train at Woking and was met by a taxi with a uniformed driver.

It was a large house standing in a large and sheltered garden, handsome but not old. (Had Mr Gorzinska been a native rather than naturalised, he would have classified it as stockbroker's Tudor.) On the south-facing front was a terrace looking over a wide grass lawn, and against the house wall the bare, thick, silvery, serpentine trunk of an old wisteria. What caught his eye, as he looked along from the front door in the south-west corner, were the birds, little, pretty bright coloured cocks, tails like miniature fountains, perching upon the bare trunk, enjoying the winter sunlight against the wall.

"Mr Gorzinska!"

"Miss Berkeley?" His arm was extended, pointing, his face broken in a delighted smile. "The birds!"

"Bantams, do you have them? Come in."

Her talk was general as she poured coffee for him, general, but excited, effusive, appreciative, telling him with a speed and enthusiasm which seemed sometimes almost to choke her, of her visit to his country, of the people she had met, of the organisation of professional and business women in England who had put her in touch with her counterparts there. She spoke so fast, so spiritedly, he was hard put to it to follow, he listened with concentration but even so lost a phrase here, a word there. While called upon to say very little, he had leisure to study her. She was a small, slim, elegantly made woman in very early middle age, he supposed her to be perhaps five years or so older than he. He thought she had the most beautiful face that he had ever seen, and longed to study it in repose. Now it flashed with smiles and gushed with words, and was networked with lines of emphasis, exuberance and delight. Oval and olive, the forehead was high, the nose delicate, (though broken, he noted) the lips naturally red, pursed, and curled as she spoke and smiled, the chin tiny and determined. Her eyes were a lively reptilian green, her hair dark but already silvered, her beautiful hands, tiny and expressive, were those of a craftswoman, but reddened and swollen in places with winter chilblains. He thought the effusiveness covered a kind of shyness, but also was due to an immense effort to put him at his ease, to proffer her sympathy.

Coffee done: "Mr Gorzinska," said she. "Victoria Wicklow spoke of your family."

"Ah," said he in a long sigh.

"What part of Warsaw, what address, Mr Gorzinska?"

"Zoliborz," he said from his burning memory. How young he had been, a schoolboy only, when they moved there, perhaps fifteen or so. "Thirty-two was the district."

"And the street?"

"Tucholska."

"And the number?" Her face mesmerised him. She seemed deeply excited.

"Why—ten."

She sprang quickly to her feet.

"Follow me, if you will, come into my studio."

He followed from the small morning room, across the large central hall, into a sun-filled room, full of the appurtenances of her art, easels, canvases, jars of brushes, shelves of paper, the walls hung with prints and paintings.

"Oh!" said Mr Gorzinska standing stock-still in the doorway.

"Used to be the billiard room. No one plays billiards any longer." She returned to shut the door behind him, took his arm, led him to a far wall beyond the fireplace.

"This. Look."

She dropped her arm from his and stood quietly waiting, the tension like a time charge. Upon the wall in a thin wooden frame and within a cream coloured mount, a print, an aquatint such as his sister did, he knew at once it was such, taught early to admire his older sister's craft. Upon the suggestion of a cushion, a couch, lay stretched in somnolence an old, old cat, the eyes in the velvet dark face barely visible slits of pale emerald as he dozed, the nose and chest pale tawny, the right front paw extended to balance him, turned outwards, its five faint pads visible: the right back paw tucked between the belly and groin, of such dark, short, velvet smoothness below the pads, you could feel it; the back left paw extended, pushing in a luxurious stretch, a position of self-satisfied easeful feline comfort, the great tabby tail flaunted in an upward curve upon the couch behind, the flakes of fur on its underside almost spiny: likewise the outline of his charcoal-soft, black back, the short curls within his ears, and outlining his sensuously peaceful face: the fur of a very old cat. A much loved, totally trusting cat.

What medium is better to portray the textured velvet graduations of the fur of a cat, particularly a dark tabby cat, than the aquatint? Thought Celia Berkeley studying the print again, awaiting the Polish gentleman's words. For two minutes Mr Gorzinska stood transfixed, wanting to touch those velvet pads, remembering the spiny black whiskers in the grizzled cheeks: unable to believe the miracle of his sister's signature below: Wiktorja J Gorzinska, (the signature was flourished); No 2. And on the left-hand side, the date, 1937.

"Victoria's cat. The old cat. My sister's cat," he said, gruffly and chokily. "How long—when did you get this? My sister gave you this? 1937, the year I came to England."

"When they came, when they visited, early in 1939, she brought it. Look here."

She turned him with difficulty from the old cat, to a long wall-bench where letters lay. A long one, typed, (the well-known address of his home at the top), two pages of it, dated Warsaw, eleventh July 1939. A shorter one, his mother's writing, three pages of small blue letter paper, and a note in Victoria's clear, neat artist's hand on the last page, signed with that great spidery sprawling W he remembered so well. Warsaw 4/7 1939 his mother had written. He stood in pale, shocked silence. She waited for him to recover.

"Miss Berkeley, you have seen them, the visit that spring, you saw my mother and my sister?"

"It was here, it was here they stayed. Some of the visit. Your mother addressed the Club I belong to."

"I saw them too."

"You were already living here, Miss Wicklow said this. They didn't speak of you, I wish they had given me your address, we would have been in touch long before this. Why did they not speak of you?"

He lifted his shoulders and dropped them in a great sigh.

"A sad, foolish difference, a kind of—what is the word—they felt perhaps hurt when I chose to become British—But I did it for my job, for my career. Within the British firm, you see."

"An estrangement, a coolness."

"Just it," he floundered.

"Just so," she gave him. "Your English is remarkable, but so is your family's. They did not tell you they were to come on here, you saw them in London?"

"I did. They said they were staying longer, out of London. They did not say where." He paused, not knowing how to ask the next question. "These are the last letters, you hear no more?"

"I've heard no more," she said quietly.

"Nor I" he said. "Yours are later than Victoria's last to me. Miss Berkeley, may I, will you allow me that I read these?"

"You shall have them, they are yours. So read them when you are home, not now. Also, the dear cat goes with you," she said impulsively. "No, no, not a word, no thanks are needed, they are so much more yours than mine, ours was a brief friendship, I met your family in 1933, never shall I forget the signs of the rise of Hitler in Germany as I passed through, screaming rallies of youths. But how did I not remember your existence, I had quite forgotten. They spoke of you then at the university."

"Yes. I cannot remember hearing of your visit."

"Very probably you did not. I think you should be fortified with a drink and some lunch. Very wartime lunch, not worthy the name of luncheon, Mr Gorzinska, I'm afraid. Come now, come and meet my father, and my aunt. Our good taxi man comes at two-thirty for you, he will put you on the London train. We keep no car of our own now."

All of them talked, kindly, quietly, even the old gentleman: assuring him that no news was not inevitably bad news, they talked him kindly through his abstraction during this memorable lunch not worthy of the name of luncheon: carrot soup, cold bird, mince pies. His abstraction kept returning, for he thought within every brief silence *they sat here, they sat at this table with these kind people, Victoria and Mamma sat here. Where are they now?*

She stood on a chair (she was so small yet so sprightly) and unhooked the cat from the picture rail, wrapped it in an old *Times*, put it into a brown carrier. He had the letters in his breast pocket, and also the address that he must apply to in his search. His farewells were heartfelt but almost speechless. From the taxi he turned to wave as she stood at the door, smiling.

It was by now pouring with cold rain. The little birds, he thought, perhaps have some dry place somewhere to go to. At the station he thanked the taxi driver with a bow and a smile (such as the man was not used to), tilted the black homburg (that so-London hat, he called it) over his eyes, clutched the picture to his bosom to keep it dry, and turning for the platform, wept at last. He was glad of the rain. Tears hot and freely flowing mingled with the sharp coldness of the rain upon his cheeks. The kindness for the moment melted the terrible ice of the certainty of her death, of all their deaths, that bleak, irrevocable knowledge. For dead he felt they must be, he would not let his mind dwell on what way. I should know, he said, if my people were alive, should I not feel it?

How wonderful, but how wonderful are letters, Mr Gorzinska thought, who could not wait until he got home. For he was alone, few folk travelled that wet, early afternoon in late January from Woking to London, he was in his carriage alone. In the letters they are alive, they are alive, said Mr Gorzinska, reading them again and again and again lest some detail, some meaning had escaped him.

We have now in Warsaw [he read in his mother's ordinary, spidery hand] a very lively Anglo-Polish Society and the

British Council is successful in its efforts to spread knowledge of the English language.... . I don't know what sort of Polish magazine is sent to you. Is it Poland edited by the YMCA, or La Femme Polonaise or the Warsaw Weekly? I write for the two last ones. My work now is mostly connected with our WAS. I am lecturing on the defence of the home, provisions and about all duties either of the housewife or a guardian in poorer quarters, also on the part Co-operation will have to play as a distributory factor of food. I have already spoken about twenty times...and you know; the first time I spoke in public was that faltering and clumsy speech at your monthly luncheon in London. And now I am thought a good speaker. Never say die!

(She was shy, his mother was shy and delicate, but how good, how fluent was her English, no wonder he wanted to come here, their very knowledge and love of England had pushed him!)

Victoria and myself are also taking different courses trying to learn things which might prove useful in case of war...all our women old and young are training now, but even if Poland is really a great training camp this additional work does not interfere with the usual business of life. You would wonder how quiet the country is, not at all as if we stood at the eve of a possible war.... . I hope that we shall hear from you sooner than it took you last time.

(He smiled, catching her small sniff, the glint in her eye.)

Because very soon it might happen that everybody won't be able to spend time on letter writing.... .

He turned again to his sister's letter.

...I have caught a bad cold—heaven knows where, in this heat.

(Wrote his sister, in the July of 1939, his living, breathing, complaining sister.)

> —And I feel like nothing on earth. I made a mess of my car-driving exam yesterday.... Can you tell me where the Royal Society of Etchers and Engravers hold their exhibitions?...How did you like the Polish Exhibition at the New Burlington Gallery?...I must stay up every day till midnight, as I am taking the place of a broadcast-controller who is away on leave and the nightly "American" broadcasts from midnight till three a.m. are my province. Nemesis, and no mistake, on one who detests the wireless as I do.... .

(He turned to her long, typed letter dated a week later full of news, full of detail, lists of wood blocks she had made that year, lists of the work she had promised to do, diatribes against some of her colleagues in her temporary broadcasting job. Her tone of voice, amused, querulous, was alive in his ears as he read.)

> ...the New Burlington Gallery...returned three pictures belonging to the State Art Collections wrongly addressed, so that the case was returned from Warsaw to Gdynia, and now I have to look after the whole business of setting matters right.... . My window is open and a big white moth is making a nuisance of itself—crawling into the typewriter and all over my neck.... . Mother is suffering very badly from arthritis again...our cook is going away to Austria to be married and we are all much attached to her as she has been with us for over twenty years.... .

(The Christmas sweetmeat, the delectable, sugary, heavily fruited sweetmeat she made! In his mind Mr Gorzinska suddenly saw her face beneath the cap, he hoped she got to Austria and was married.)

> ...It will be difficult to run the house without her and Mother is thinking of taking a flat, but that means all the upheaval

of moving... . Two nights ago...I came across a Spanish broadcast from Daventry/ 3 a.m. It puzzled me greatly at first...

Now I must get ready to go downstairs, so good night and best love...

W.

Did they move, did they go, where are they? he asked, their living voices for a lightning flash of time causing the illusion that they live. Ah no, sobbed Mr Gorzinska, shaking the tears from his eyes, clutching the carrier-bag, and emerging not in beloved Warsaw, but into Waterloo Station in London.

T he irony is," Franciszek Gorzinska, pronounced the word with some hesitation, "you say, I think, irony? That this lady has not news of my family, has no news of my people, after Warsaw fell: which gives no hope, but even more despair. Yet these letters brought my people back to me alive, and have so given me great comfort. This is the irony."

"You mean, you think she would have heard if they were...alive? Even if you haven't?" Victoria Wicklow almost whispered. "I'm glad you've got the letters and the old cat: but in a sense I wish I had never sent you to Miss Berkeley. So that you could hang on to your hope, Francis."

Imogen glanced across at her daughter, who was looking particularly beautiful, but had been noticeably quiet.

"But isn't it always better to know the truth, whatever it is, however terrible?" she said.

A silence followed, in which Victoria idly stirred the coffee in her cup. Imogen sipped hers, Franciszek drained his.

A silence that lengthened into an electrifying tension, seeming to spread out from her daughter, to enmesh or rather to enchant them all, to stop their talk, to impose stillness. It had now reached Francis, unaware of it at first. He was magnetised by Victoria. I ought not to be here, Imogen thought; in a moment I will make an excuse and go. I think I know quite well what is happening. Is it a good thing that this happen? There is apt to be great confusion between pity and love. Victoria sits there realising, I think, that she is falling in love with him. I am not quite sure why, save the sovereign reason she is ready. Also they are the same religion, not so easy in England. He does not know it yet but will feel it soon. He is, to be sure, remarkably handsome and beautifully polite.

"He does not know it yet," Victoria again almost whispered on to the surface of this silence. Making Imogen start at the echo of her own thought with another meaning.

"I feel I do know, you understand," Francis said softly. So good night and best love…W., he thought. He raised his head, looked at Victoria. They looked intently at each other across the room.

"I shall just tidy the kitchen," Imogen murmured, rising. "Have more coffee." But expected no reply.

Francis had shared the letters with them and also the print of the old pussycat, bringing it with him. The sister, by some strange coincidence also called Victoria, was alive in her letter, was vividly there: the feel of the white, furry moth on her neck, the half-amusement, half-annoyance at its crawling over the machine, Imogen saw and felt it all, even the aching fever of that long-distant cold in the head. The letters had completely put out of their minds the cataclysmic happenings of the last weeks. The calling up of these two people dear to Francis seemed of much more urgent importance.

Hence they had not spoken yet of Yalta, about which someone was talking as Imogen switched on the wireless in the kitchen. Mr Churchill, Premier Stalin and President Roosevelt had met, proposing a body called the United Nations; allowing that the French should have a German zone; arranging that Russia should take reparations from Germany and should enter the Far East war when Europe was quelled. The two Western powers had also agreed to Russian plans for Poland, while trying to hold to free elections in that suffering and deeply anti-Russian country. What hope was there of that? It was this that Imogen had expected Francis to talk of, but his heart was otherwise engaged.

Nor had they spoken of the Russian army which instead of taking Berlin (as they had all expected) had stopped short, pushed ahead in the south and were now in Budapest. The conference seemed also to have given the Allies new permissions and incentives to bombing: the Allies had renewed their perpetual onslaughts upon Berlin. And some nights ago, the RAF had flown more than a thousand bombers over the city of Dresden, its population swelled with countless refugees escaping from the approaching Russians, and, it was said, erased it. A firestorm was still raging over miles of the city, it was rumoured the bombed victims were being burnt upon the vast pyres thus made. Imogen had felt a rush of anger, and found that everybody also was similarly sickened. Though the destruction of each other's cities had become a commonplace, opinion was totally outraged by the destruction of Dresden. Prudence and Laura whom she had met over lunch the next day had emanated a pained fury, referred to it with pale rage.

She went back to find an oasis of sweet peace in the drawing room, a kind of promise of hope and happiness, and a tinkling stream of Chopin, whose music Francis adored. Throughout the ballade, the two young people sat glowing shyly at each other. When it was done, Victoria began to talk of what everyone was talking of.

"Did we have to do this, Ma, did we have to destroy Dresden?"

"Why do we all feel it's so much worse than all the other places? Is it the romance of the Meissen, or what?" Imogen countered, puzzled. "It seemed particularly awful that it should be Valentine's Day."

"It's because it's so cold-blooded, when the war's nearly over."

"And everybody, of course, vindictively remembering Coventry," Imogen murmured.

"Was it for morale, do you suppose, destroying German morale? Or would it really help the Russian advance? Anyway they're retreating everywhere, they're beat, the Gerries," Victoria explained.

"Not entirely, oh no. I read somewhere, the chiefs of staff think the war may well go on till the end of the year. They'll fight every inch, won't they?"

Her daughter groaned.

"Mrs Tripp's husband was killed," Imogen went on, in a tone more puzzled than sad. "Over Dresden."

"Oh, Ma. That's the nice lady who loves the sunshine?"

"The same. Comes from Malta."

"Have you seen her, is she devastated?"

Imogen had reached for her knitting, a sock for one of the boys, and studied it with a frown before she looked up.

"No. Composed, dry-eyed, and dignified. I got her alone, to say how sorry I was. She looked at me quite steadily, as if she were confessing. She said, 'You need not feel sorry for me, Mrs Wicklow.' So I just looked steadily back and said, 'I see.' As sympathetically as I could. So difficult."

"But what did you see?"

"I imagine that Flying Officer Tripp was not all that he has been cried up to be. She seemed to be so proud of him, always talked of him as such a hero. But I daresay that was the blind loyalty of a betrayed wife."

"What a beastly shame. How sad."

"Laura said, 'Oh poor Mrs Tripp, what good will the sunshine of Malta do her now?' in her poetical, romantic way. Laura's fond of her, she was so understanding about the old dog. I didn't enlighten Laura. But I hope the sunshine will heal Mrs Tripp, I hope she'll go back quite soon."

"Perhaps she'll find a nice Maltese."

"Perhaps she will." Imogen nodded at her daughter over the half-spectacles.

Francis smiled tenderly at them both.

Imogen rose up suddenly, toddled off into her bedroom and returned with her Dresden piece, a shepherd on his knees wooing, a shepherdess half turned away, bashful, the ground all powdered with flowers. She set it on the low table, between them all.

"There," she said. "So. Let us think of this, not the bombs."

Victoria blushed suddenly and prettily.

"Daddy gave it to you? When you were engaged."

"Yes." Her mother nodded, smiling. "Valentine's Day."

Francis watched them, looked from the girl to her mother. He had grown to love Imogen, her gestures, intuitive like this one, often expressed an underlying symbolic compassion. A hardly acknowledged excitement was rising in his heart: as if life were gently deciding to give, to stop taking away.

"Phallic symbols, all tube trains," observed Tom, watching one disappearing rowdily into a tunnel.

"Be easier for you pointing out what *isn't*," Laura replied.

"Most things are," he laughed.

"Must be in your mind," said she.

"It must be in yours only you won't admit to it."

They were on their way to the place where Tom worked, for he, feeling somewhat skint, had suggested drinks and sandwiches in his room before a concert. They had met for lunch, taken the afternoon off, and had a cold walk along the river embankment. Most people in Tom's building had gone home. Tom clanged to the noisy door of the ancient cage-like lift and pressed the requisite button. A kind of breathy groan, a series of judderings, a whine, as the lift started very sedately into action.

"Sounds like that ghost in galoshes. Were you over here for the ghost in galoshes?"

"No, but I heard about it. It was more like footsteps, ga-losh- ga-losh, wasn't it? What was it anyway, did anyone ever discover?"

"I never heard. Isn't this slow?"

"Sure. Antediluvian, whole building's antediluvian, can't think how it stands up. 'Specially after the bombs shaking it around. But then England's full of rickety old, antediluvian old, ghastly old buildings," he teased.

"Yes, well, we started five or six hundred years before you." She dodged as Tom tweaked her nose.

"Come on, come on," he encouraged the lift, stamping his feet.

The lift heaved a sigh and ground slowly, delicately to a halt, clicking and shivering slightly.

"Oh, come on, oh no," breathed Tom. Blank walls of dirty pale green surrounded the cage, no landing was visible. They were between floors, stuck. Tom pressed the fourth floor button again. Tom pressed all the buttons in turn, waiting duly between each one.

"I'm going to press the down button, hold on."

"Is that safe?"

"'Fraid so," he said. "If she can't go up she won't go down either. Hell," Tom suddenly roared.

"You haven't done the emergency button have you?"

"No more I have."

Tom did it, several times, they waited minutes.

"What does it connect with?"

"Well, it should sound an alarm, shouldn't it, let someone, somewhere, know we're stuck? Not that ancient lifts are my special subject."

Tom suddenly went to the door side of the lift, craned his neck sideways, trying to see up, seized the bars, and shook them with healthy fury and repeated, deafening roars:

"Hi, hi, hi, hi," yelled Tom.

"You look like an angry gorilla at the zoo," Laura laughed. "Cut off from its mate," she added.

He turned back to her, put his hands each side of her head as she leaned against the cage wall, and performed a passable imitation of Dr Jekyll's face turning into the simian features of Mr Hyde as played by Spencer Tracy. Laura recognised the performance, considered it well done, began to laugh with abandon: her mouth spread into the melon grin of a little girl, her eyes glittered, here teeth shone, her nose wrinkled up in amusement, she looked merry, unhampered, carefree as a child. With no plan and no forewarning Tom turned instantly back into himself and planted a hard, determined kiss between her startled lips. Her teeth felt polished as glass, the fugitive tongue tasted sweet, he loved that child's face in its unhurt joy. How good it would be, he suddenly thought, to make Laura happy.

"Sure, that's what I am," he said withdrawing.

She blinked, remembering what she had said.

"You looked about six. There must be a snap of you, looking like that, when you were six?"

"Tom. You've never done that before," she laughed. It was breaking their record.

He sighed, saying with exaggerated patience, "Well I've got to begin somewhere, haven't I? Did you mind?"

"No," Laura said, sounding surprised.

"So may I do it again? From time to time?"

"Yes. I think so."

"Think so, think so," he teased: and pulled her into his arms and kissed her again. The small girl had gone, but what was there was very kissable even while turning anxious.

"Tom: we're stuck in the lift. What're we going to do?" she demanded.

"Cover your ears, I'm going to shout again."

He did so, longer and louder than before. The silence afterwards was the more intense.

"Someone, surely, soon, will want to use the lift," Laura pondered. She was feeling amazed at the lightness in her heart, where sensations were tumbling about weightless.

"So I thought. Shush, listen."

"What?"

"Footsteps?"

Tom roared again. Certainly footsteps distantly. Then a man's voice called, from the landing above.

"What's up? Who's that?"

"It's me, Tom Turner. Lift's stuck. Who's that?"

"It's I, Carter."

"Oh, Cyril, for Christ's sake get someone to this blasted British lift, we're trying to get to a concert, I've got a girl in here, fainting, having hysterics, all sorts, do hurry!"

"Well I'm going home now, so I'll tell the porter."

"Yes, but promise me you'll see him ring for the mechanic, promise me, OK? *Before* you go? Cyril?"

"All right, very well, I'll do that, Turner."

"Tailor's dummy," muttered Tom turning to see Laura subsided on to the floor, leaning against the cage, sitting carefully on her mackintosh, nursing her tumbled heart.

"Playing the part of my fainting girl?"

"May as well be comfortable. There's bound to be a wait."

"Mr Turner?" called the porter soon in sepulchral tones.

"Yes? What's happening?"

"I've rung Percy."

"Percy? Can't *you* do something?"

"No, they say always to ring for Percy. He'll be about half an hour, though, getting here."

"Ought to *be* here, ought to be on duty!"

"Well, latish evening, Mr Turner."

"Blast Percy."

"He'll be as quick as he can I'm sure. Anything I can do for you? How's the young lady?"

"Having a kind of a fit."

"Oh dear, oh tut tut, and I can't get nothing for you, shall I get a doctor, sir, eh, or an ambulance, to be ready?—There now, I can hear her."

Laura smothered her laughter with some difficulty.

"I think she'll recover," called Tom. "If I slap her. Just hurry Percy up."

"I will, sir." They heard him tramp downstairs again.

"So we're stuck. What shall we talk about?" Tom asked sitting down beside her. "We're here for up to an hour I'd say. Let's talk about you."

"Me? Why?"

"You must be interested in you? And so am I. As I have just tried to show you. So why don't I make you talk about you. OK?"

"All right," she said, not averse. "What?" To talk might steady her upside-down heart.

"You're stuck."

"*I'm* stuck?"

"Well, we're both stuck, in this scene. Listen. This tutor, this adored don you lost your heart to? That must be two years ago? Have you seen or heard of him? Other than standing on Didcot station?"

"No."

"Then why are you still stuck?"

"Because I truly loved him I suppose."

Tom believed that this was so, he remembered feeling shut out of paradise. "Did he love you?"

"Nearly, I think. Do you know what I mean? But he's married and broke it off."

171

"Of course I know what you mean. A watershed period. And he decided not. So it's over. So why don't you love someone else?"

"Doesn't it take time to get over it?"

"You've had the time. Know what I think?"

"What?"

"You're hiding behind it. You're frightened of something, so you say I'm still in love with what's-his-name, I can't love anyone else. It's a lovely excuse."

"Well, I haven't loved anyone else."

"Not even the one that made you walk up the wrong escalator." Tom could never forget that incident.

"Oh well, yes," Laura laughed, "in a way, but it was only physical."

"The whole thing's physical, girl, what is sex if not physical, but can you get at why you're so frightened of it? Not that it's at all unusual, lots of girls are, over here, it's this puritan upbringing."

"Well, am I more frightened than most?"

"I thought perhaps you were. Are you frightened of giving birth?"

"I don't think so."

"Are you frightened of the responsibility? Of bringing them up?"

"I never thought much about it."

"Perhaps you're not very maternal? Perhaps all you want is your creative career?"

"I'd rather have someone to love. Anyway I want both."

"So are you afraid of it not lasting, the love not lasting?"

Laura gave a deep sigh.

"Yes, that I am afraid of," said she.

"Because of your parents. Being so wretched? So are you frightened of committing yourself?"

"Maybe."

"But your marriage is only to do with you, and your husband, it is up to you. In your hands. You can't inherit your parents' unhappiness. You just have to trust yourself. Perhaps it's just, you don't trust yourself."

"Perhaps I don't. Yet."

"Well, you've every reason to. You're good-looking, you're young, you're clever. You have to launch out, girl. But it could be you just want yourself to yourself," he added, pondering. "A point of view I entirely understand, and rather share."

Distant tappings impinged upon their ears.

"Hey, hey," Tom said leaping up. "Percy? Percy!" he yelled.

"Yes hang on, sir, I'm working on it," someone called reedily.

The lights went out. "Oh, carry on, London," muttered Tom.

"Sorry to plunge you in the dark," piped the voice.

"In the dark. In a cage," said Tom with disgust.

Laura stood up, groped her way towards Tom, and held on to his arm.

The tappings and clinkings went on.

"Soon be out," said Tom. "Of this stoppage," laughed he. "Do you feel at all liberated?"

"Liberated?"

"By talking about you?"

"Oh. Maybe. Maybe I will." For half a minute, she thought he meant by his kisses, which had certainly cut her heart loose. It was still floating, tugging like a barrage balloon. Anyone would think she had never been kissed before: what was the matter with her?

The lights went up, the lift sighed, wobbled sedately up to the next floor landing.

As he stepped out of the lift, Tom, who certainly felt liberated, said suddenly to himself, I have been waiting about for Laura, marking time too long. From now on, I am going for this girl. But I shall have to go very gingerly, or she may turn and flee again.

"Come on," he said, seizing her hand as they ran along the corridor, "we've got to bolt the sandwiches. Or take them with us."

I t's all going to end," Prudence thought in some amazement. "Quite soon. As Pop predicts."

She sat in a tube train reading an evening paper going home from her class. Throughout April, it had become apparent, this unexpectedly sudden, progressive, all-round crumbling away of the grip of the war: like ice melting, avalanches rushing. A decisive step had been the Yanks getting over the Rhine, finding an unblown bridge at Remagen early in March, ending the struggle started at Arnhem in the autumn. There was a gradual sense dawning of an icy hand beginning to unlock. There were cracks in the ice, there was a foreseeable future; people were beginning to look into the sea of possibilities, to find suggestions within it. A new dawn of personal freedoms lit up the horizon. Her father had drawn attention to all this over the past weeks, this pervasive sense of release.

Today Prudence read of the Allies at long last, after so many months, so many stops and starts, over the River Po, into northern Italy.

She folded the paper and allowed herself to think her own thoughts.

What on earth, I wonder what on earth? I do wonder what on earth has happened to him, Prudence said to herself. It was coming less frequently now, the question about her acquaintance of what was weeks, no, months ago. But she let it come. The distraught man who had come to the class in the autumn and had not, by Prudence, been seen again.

Who had poured out his tragic story and then disappeared rapidly, declaring he was ashamed to have done so. Vanished, it would seem, forever. Was he, the wicked thought once more crossed her mind, some sort of a charlatan, spinning a yarn, fantasising, unable to tell truth from fiction? But no, there was nothing to be gained of prestige in that kind of story; and neither would a charlatan say he was ashamed. For the first few weeks, she had looked forward eagerly to seeing him again, possibly even discussing her work with a man who had been so imaginatively understanding about her hopes and fears. In the New Year, at the start of the term, she had allowed herself to think he might re-appear. He had perhaps "gone under" (as he had half adumbrated) had to stop work, rest, go away. I don't know what'll happen, I'm sure, she remembered him saying. She assumed he was in happier times attached to London University, but he had said he was doing war work.

Had some terrible accident befallen him, as he plunged about London streets at strange hours demented with grief? Had he, in a fit of despair, done away with himself?

Come now, Prudence said, thinking she sounded like Alice, you are being melodramatic, stop it, do. In any event, what is it to you? Well, what it is to me is a person who understood my plans and my future. I shan't forget "Keep that light in your eye". (Prudence had not been reared on *The Pilgrim's Progress* as Laura had, and strangely enough did not know the quotation.) Quite apart from that (her thoughts ran) I felt terribly sorry for him, I feel anxious about him, I would like to know he's all right.

He'll never be all right, she thought: this is the kind of hideous scar which never becomes part of you and unnoticeable, just as the body never quite assimilates a bad flesh wound. Millions of people have had such scarring blows rained upon them during this war: think of that, she told herself. Prudence was too young in years to have experienced the startling resilience of the human heart, systematically calloused by the blows of life. (It was a large cause of hers and Laura's gloom, their youngness.) However, what choice has the heart but to carry on? Unless it decides to die.

Edwin always wanted to know the substance of the manuscript gobbets they had been reading. (Is Pop a scholar manqué, his daughter often wondered?) Margery was more interested in the people. Today, though she had not remembered it for weeks, she asked after "that poor man", perhaps due to currents of thought emanating from her daughter.

"Not there, Mum, no sign," Prudence said. "He's obviously had to give it up."

"I expect he's moved out of reach. Didn't you say he had a home, parents?"

"He spoke of his mother perhaps coming to help him clear the cottage, that's all."

Everything he had said was burnt on Prudence's memory.

"He seemed pretty desperate you know, he may well have gone under," she added.

"Gone under?" Edwin echoed, as if scandalised at such weakness.

"Yes, Pop, got overwhelmed, had a breakdown, had to rest a bit," she said meeting his cold grey eye. "People do." She sounded quite severe, despite her smile.

Edwin had heard they did but was not disposed to forgive them.

He could hardly keep up with the pace of events today, and fell into a kind of bristly, angry shorthand in the diary.

> Roosevelt dead! Truman colourless, no experience, doesn't trust the Russians (who would?) Like some cosmic button, that death, starting off a landslide. Russians hell for leather towards Berlin—(Vienna taken already). Churchill, a cat on hot bricks, thinks they'll get there first, which they will, so thinks I, before the Americans. Germans in thousands laying down arms in the Ruhr. Mödel has shot himself. Führer barricaded in some hole in the city. Monty has Hamburg, Stuttgart gone to the French again. Before you can say knife, the American and Russian boys will be shaking hands over the Elbe. Things will happen fast now.

"I told you it would be over quite soon, didn't I?" Edwin said to his womenfolk: almost as if he had had a hand in it.

Prudence smiled.

Marie seemed forever to be taking messages for Laura from Tom, which rubbed salt into her wound. After one such she said glumly, "That Tom of yours. He's getting serious, isn't he? He's nice; I once let out what my name was. Now he says, is that Marie? You shouldn't let him go. You're very lucky," Marie said tragically.

"Oh Marie. It is a shame," Laura mourned. "Find someone else, love someone else. That's what Tom said to me. About my man I can't have."

"Why does Tom say find someone else when he wants you himself?" demanded Marie with some reason.

"He said that a while ago. How are you so sure he wants me himself?"

"Just the way he asks for you. Besides, he rings up quite often now, doesn't he?"

Does Tom want me himself, Laura wondered? She was waiting the next day to meet Tom off a train at home. Those kisses, so unexpected and so unexpectedly nice with their consequent turmoil in her heart, need not mean anything at all. There had been others, but not invariably after meeting. Tom would suddenly kiss her if he was tickled or touched or felt affectionate: but never simply for his own delectation. Tom is one of the most unpossessive, detached people I know, she thought. Also, Tom is cagey, cautious, not to be caught: he would not venture serious approaches unless a person were ready to receive them. We can talk about anything under the sun, we're not always being sucked towards sex, as with poor Hubert, it was like a whirlpool dragging you in. (She worried about Hubert, who still from time to time rang her up with choked professions of passion.)

It was a Saturday, they were going for a walk. First, Tom had to meet Mamma.

Kitty was well disposed towards Canadians, she had a school friend over there who had married a farmer, and whose large brood looking very like each other kept turning up one after another, all through the war, dressed in the uniform of Princess Patricia's Regiment and come to help fight. She welcomed Tom, dark and quiet, as one in the procession of Laura's friends: and suffered the familiar displacement of a telephone voice by a face.

They climbed the Hurst and entered the silvery crowd of young birches whispering spells at the usual place. Laura missed the General sorely when she came up here: the memory called up the vision of the lovers.

"Once, there was a pair of lovers, sitting in that grassy hollow. They were quite old, Tom, they weren't young at all. They were so happy, there seemed to be a kind of light from them, an aura, you know what I mean. The dog blundered up wagging his tail but they laughed, they didn't mind. They said nothing, they were in their own world."

"Yes, I know what you mean." Tom was thinking of the look on Laura's face in the train from Oxford.

"So what is it, Tom?"

"What is love? O Laura!" he laughed aloud.

"Come on, give me a philosophical disquisition. On what is love?"

"Well, first and earthily, it's animal desire."

"Those two weren't thinking of animal desire, they were in their fifties—and adored each other."

Tom laughed rather tenderly at her innocence.

"The fifties are a field-day for animal desire. But let that pass. When you're young it's simply procreation after all: 'a nice trap nature lays and baited sweetly'." He said this as if it were a quotation.

"Who said that?"

"I said it. In a play I half-wrote. It's highly effective, it makes you think the other person's totally desirable, your fleshly need blinds you. After a year or two you may discover your mistake." Tom looked at her sideways, one eyebrow up.

She laughed. "Oh Tom. Don't you believe in romantic love? Lasting? I believe in the whole thing, I even believe in love at first sight. I've been brought up believing in romantic love," Laura realised, as she said it, slowly.

"Who brought you up believing in romantic love, Laura?"

"My mama. Who else?"

"But your ma, your pa, you've always said, were utterly miserable."

"The unhappiest marriage I know," said Laura. "But my mama still goes on believing in romantic love."

"Perhaps that's why," said Tom darkly. "Fiction dwells on the glories of falling in love and having each other. Not on the acridities afterwards."

"Think of my lovers, over there."

"Yes. Well, so what is it makes it last? It has to be this chemistry thing first. Then it has to be affinity. When people come as close, stay as close, be soul mates, they've got to have far more in common than *not*, haven't they?"

"Yes. So," she propounded, having thought a moment, "it's propinquity (a favourite word of my papa's); chemistry; affinity."

Tom laughed. "Yes. I like that."

"We need a word to mean going on at it, making it work, never giving up?"

"We do. However much you start with, it's hard work, I imagine, all the time."

"So we want a word meaning determination, endless accommodating, making allowances, being kind, being committed?"

"All that, only we want a word the shape of the others. Come on, witty word girl."

They were enjoying the game.

"Wish I had my Roget. Unanimity?"

"Bit impersonal. Probably impossible too."

"Solidarity?"

"Better. Not wide enough?"

"Not heartfelt enough...Amity!" she said. "It's a lovely word, so comfortable and eighteenth-century. Love settled down!"

"OK. We'll have amity."

"Charity!" she cried after a pause. "Amity's settled, charity's active love, working away all the time, enduring!"

"Propinquity, chemistry, affinity, amity, charity! The progress of love," Tom added.

"And what happens," Laura went on "when, if you've exhausted each other, you've discovered all there is to know, to love, to enjoy— charity faileth, after all?"

"Laura, how can I know? I should think you have to keep feeding more in, find more areas to explore. Some people just move on to someone else and start again."

"I'd rather think there were always going to be more things to discover. By virtue of love."

"So would I, romantic girl," Tom said, and kissed her cheek as they walked. "I was down with my aunt last weekend. Ros was there."

"How is she? Still in a stew about not marrying?"

"Yes, desperate, in a flat spin. We went for a walk, which consisted of her going through about a dozen of your friends, your year, and telling me how lucky they all were to be settled. She said everybody is getting married. An obvious exaggeration."

"Who, Tom? Do remember, I want to know."

"How can I? I don't know them. There was a Rachel I think, and a Helen."

Laura shrieked. "Not surprised," she said.

"A Margaret, I believe. And several nicknames. I said if she was keener on getting married than anything else, why didn't she? I told her to get and find someone. Think of them all, flooding out of the forces, they soon will be."

"Tom, do you suppose, you don't suppose…she's interested in you, do you? I mean, you've grown up apart, you're not like close cousins."

Tom considered this proposition with amazed gloom.

"It never crossed my mind," he said. "She asked after you. And your absent heart," Tom smiled at her. My heart that is not there, Laura thought.

"That was kind of her. Can't think why she's so desperate, we're only twenty-three."

Tom reflected.

"She's more single-minded than you. *She* hasn't got any creative urge, she just wants to create her family, I guess. She's had a happy family herself. And she's a much more public person than you, she's social minded, quite keen on politics."

"I know. She read PPE."

"You're a private person, you see," he said quietly, with conviction.

"What you call an introvert?"

"Perhaps. But it's more than that, I think. You may well find you're an artist. Of some kind. The person you marry has got to understand that. Or you will be made unhappy and so will he. Which will be no fun for anyone, least of all you."

Laura thought that Tom was the first person who had understood this about her (which she barely understood herself) and had taken it seriously.

"I wonder how I'm going to do it and earn my living too," she said, her perennial problem.

"It'll have to be in your spare time at first. What line do you want to do?"

"I think I want to tell stories. Only not the same kind as my mother! Novels: thoughtful novels."

"That's clear enough. So practise. All the time."

"Do you? Do you practise?"

"I've got to have a salary of course, too, especially if I marry. So I shall teach philosophy. As soon as I've got this degree."

"So you'll write in your spare time? What will you write?"

"Witty plays. I love the theatre. With good plots, but underlain with philosophical ideas. And experimental. People joining in from the audience. Getting inside the play from outside."

"You can't, it's an art form, you can't burst into it, can you, without breaking the illusion?"

"See what Oxford's done for you," he teased, "put you in a traditional straightjacket. It's what people are going to be doing with drama, putting it back where the audience can join in: and improvising, experimenting with a state of flux. Which way are things going? They can go endless ways."

"A state of flux is what you create *out* of, Chaos. Then shape," observed Laura didactically.

He laughed at her.

"Laura, you're hide-bound, you have to have everything according to ancient rules," he teased. "And you're too timid to break them, yet. You'll have to fight it."

"I know," she agreed, humbly. "I want to go on writing poems, too," she said.

"But you've absolutely no conceit, you dear creature," Tom said fondly, and kissed her again.

Laura thought this was probably untrue, but was grateful all the same.

❦

Laura was at the hairdresser, being led down the space between the two rows of shrouded cubicles, which formed the establishment (all personal privacy having not yet been swept away along with the curtains in hair salons.) A curtain opened, a woman emerged, leaving her victim prey to the vulgar gaze for a split second.

In the mirror of the cubicle Laura saw the pink, innocent, rounded face of Prudence, its child-like quality, which was yet like an old wisdom, its still puppyish plumpness, exaggerated by the wettened hair. On the lino all round her were drifts and curls of burnished gold.

"Prudence!" Laura wailed (though softly.) "Your beautiful hair, what *have* you done, what *have* you let them do?" She held back the curtain with force, as the hairdresser, outraged at the intrusion, tried to close it before she walked away: ladies, thought she, do not wish to be observed as skinned rabbits. But Prudence, damp and cheerful, had no need of concealment, she was like a cherub from a bathtub.

"Laura!" she giggled. "It got too wild, too long to cut it myself. It needed shaping."

"I thought you *always* cut it yourself. What a lot, oh what masses she's cut off, I'd like to collect it." Laura stooped and gathered up a handful of crisp curled gold. Whose hair does it remind me of? she wondered putting it rather sadly into her pocket. It's not flaxen, it's not just fair, it's *gold*.

"Can you have tea afterwards?" she asked.

So they sat in Fuller's near Marble Arch, eating walnut cake with soft yet crisp white icing, one of the oases of the war. (You could not buy them very easily, but you could always eat some there.) Prudence looked like a sculptured Greek god, the short curls coiled down neatly all over her head. She was dying to brush them all out. She realised dimly that her rounded, chubby features could not take sculptured hair.

"It's ages since we've had a meal," she said.

"I know, isn't it? What have you been doing?"

"Pretending to work at the office."

"Me, too, it's winding down, isn't it?"

"It's going to end, you know. Quite soon, Pop says, it's all going to end, the war."

"It's gone on so long, we're used to it," Laura stated.

"So what have *you* been doing? I've rung once or twice, and missed you, for lunch," Prudence explained. "I'm still doing the palaeography. And brooding, on my actual subject, for the research."

"Any nearer?"

"Nothing definite. And you? Any nice new boyfriends?"

"Well, I seem to be seeing a lot of Tom, these days."

"That's your Canadian."

"Yes."

"I always thought he sounded interesting."

"He is. He *is* interesting, and he's funny, and I think he's very clever. He's very understanding. And objective."

"He's doing philosophy and psychology, didn't you say? But originally, is a chemist?"

"Yes. He seems to understand what I'm like. He knows about my writing urge, because partly, he's got it himself."

"Is he fond of you?"

"We get on awfully well. But I don't really know, exactly. He's cagey, he doesn't show much, he kisses me occasionally," she confessed, smiling.

"He won't show much unless you do, will he?"

"Won't commit himself, you mean?"

"Not unless he thinks he's a chance, will he?"

Laura wondered how Prudence could discuss these things with insight having had no experience.

"Are you fond of him?" she said simply.

"Very. In a way," Laura answered in a puzzled tone. Her hand in her pocket fingered the golden hair. It is Gavin's hair, she suddenly realised, Prudence and Gavin have the same burning hair.

Prudence noted the familiar anguish pass over her friend's face.

"You're going to have to forget you-know-who," she said.

"Gavin Kitto? Yes," Laura sighed. "I suppose."

"Tom sounds so nice, so right for you."

"Maybe. Are there any men at your class, or are they all boys?"

"Mostly quite young. There was an older man came once, we talked, he knew all about research. But he never came again, he'd had a tragedy, lost his wife and baby. The Barnet bomb. He told me all about it, before he dashed off."

"How monstrous. Poor man," Laura said appalled. "And you've never seen him since? How long ago?"

"Right at the beginning, in October."

"And you didn't find out who he was?"

"No. I quite expected to see him again. He said, 'See you next week.' He was overwhelmed suddenly at having told me it all, I think. He poured it out, he said it was still compulsive."

"I don't wonder. What can have happened to him?"

"I wish I knew."

"Whatever will Mum and Pop say, about your lovely hair?" Laura mourned, as they rose a minute later.

"I did warn them," Prudence explained, with her apologetic smile.

As events gathered the momentum, which everyone including Edwin had foreseen, that April of 1945 ended in a kind of merciless melodrama, in an obscene puppetry almost calling to mind a Punch and Judy show, as if history must get punch-drunk to present such scenes at all, as if violence more than men could bear might be presented as slapstick.

The avenging Allies, over-running Italy, drove before them the German occupying forces, ever harried by partisans. There was also a secretive major with the pantomime nickname of Popski, an English-speaking, Cambridge educated, Belgian engineer of Russian parentage, leading a private army of a hundred or so loosely attached to the Eighth. They had been playing hide-and-seek with the retreating Germans in the eastern Apennines, convincing them by guile, and the rapid hidden movement of their few armoured jeeps, that they faced a force much larger than their own: and flushing them out of small mountain towns like birds before a beater.

With some of the Germans fled Benito Mussolini (having failed to negotiate with the partisans), joined by his mistress Clara Petacci. Partisan forces came up with them, seized them at Dongo, and the next day shot them both against a wall, sending the bodies to be dumped with others in the Piazza Loreto in Milan, exposed to the indignities served out by the mob, and finally to be hung upside down in front of a garage. Whence after two days the US Army rescued them with Anglo-Saxon disapproval and had them buried in the paupers' part of the cemetery.

The German forces in Italy thereafter surrendered. The news of this fiasco, reaching the greater tyrant in his Berlin redoubt, led, it was soon reported, to his death and that of his mistress, though nobody yet knew how. Many of the Italian resistance forces, their share of the work done, melted away into the bludgeoned countryside, to repair the ravages of war, to recuperate damaged nature, to coax what harvest men could from neglected farms and vineyards and outraged fields. Meanwhile Major Vladimir Péniakoff, or Popski, having sailed five vehicles on landing craft from Chioggia to Venice up the lagoon, moored them on the quay, and drove his jeep at the head of the four others seven times round the Piazzo San Marco in a long-planned gesture of triumph.

Edwin's diary is a blank upon the frenetic last weekend of April: almost as if relief or shock had overwhelmed him. Imogen, appalled at her own sense of vindictive triumph at the fall of the tyrants, took refuge in church; while Franciszek and Victoria, feeling their love grow, walked hand in hand by the Serpentine. (He was telling her how Chopin, born of a Polish mother, had died in some other country, and how his sister caused his heart to be brought back to Warsaw and enshrined in a pillar of a church. He is thinking of *his* sister, thought Victoria, he is thinking that his own heart belongs to Poland! How are we going to manage, she wondered, feeling the first of those cold apprehensions, which assault and chill the betrothed? How will he live here with me? Will those poor ghosts haunt us forever? I wonder if the church with the heart is bombed with the rest? But she said no word, love prevailed.)

On the last day of April, the faces of Big Ben were once more illuminated; and surrender was in the air. Laura sat quietly at home that evening with her mother, the wireless at hand, waiting for the next charade.

"I never could see anything but mindless savagery in desecrating dead bodies," Kitty remarked, looking sadly down her very long nose as she darned a stocking, thinking of the fate of Mussolini.

18

The sirens will not sound again, said the daily papers of the third of May. (Their mechanism had been actually dispensed with.)

A great deal was happening in a very short space of time: so that people felt stunned. The landslide of the last week of April was followed by a rush of events just as cataclysmic.

Milan, Genoa and Venice were by now all freed. Marshal Tito led Yugoslavian Communist partisans into Trieste, to the apprehension of the Western Allies. After the Führer's death, his last-appointed Chief of Staff, Krebs, tried to discuss a partial surrender with the Russian General Chuikov. The attempt was rejected. The notorious Goebbels and his wife poisoned their six children and themselves, as soon as Hitler's death was announced by Admiral Doenitz. These events were the signal for the surrender, on the second of May, of the commander of the garrison of Berlin, with his seventy thousand men, though pockets of Germans fought on for a little throughout the city. Doenitz, who had been appointed head of the Reich in Hitler's will, now attempted to negotiate a partial western surrender, while continuing to fight on in the east: but with this naïve suggestion General Eisenhower would have nothing to do.

On the fourth of May, on Lüneburg Heath, General Montgomery received the formal surrender of all the German forces in the north. Thereafter, Europe waited, London held its breath; for three days

187

rumours and counter-rumours filled the air like the distant echoes of a thunderstorm. A kind of torpor prevailed, people were unable to react with any emotion at all.

Laura sat alone in the office in the early afternoon of the seventh of May, fiddling with papers long since irrelevant, making a feint to be sorting what could now be allowed to be consigned (by her) to destruction: when in came Daisy, her eyes round and blue and solemn behind her spectacles, and no smile upon her face.

"It's just come through on the tape," said Daisy.

"What's just come through on the tape? Anyway, what does that *mean*, I never know what that means?" Laura said irritably.

"You know, the ticker-tape, in the news-room?"

Un-technical Laura did not know and could not imagine. "Well, what?" said she. "What's come through?"

"The end of the war. The surrender, all signed. In Europe, that is. Victory in Europe. But whether we're supposed to be celebrating it, VE day, today, *now*," Daisy repeated with some desperation, "or tomorrow, and next day, no one seems to *know*."

It had been known for weeks that there would be two days' holiday, the second in true army jargon to be called VE+1. Like D-day and its after days.

"Oh," Laura said, gazing at her, equally solemn. There was a sense of vast, blank, yawning, absurd anti-climax behind Laura's consciousness: due partly to the hugeness of the tension released and partly to the uncertainty Daisy suggested. She got up and walked across to look out into the street.

As she watched, a window in the building opposite flew up, a fair head appeared, yelling, laughing, flinging a flutter of torn-up paper, which twirled down to the pavement. Another window opened, another girl's head appeared, and another, and another, till there were laughing faces the whole length of the block opposite, and toilet rolls tumbling out with crude abandon, and torn-up newspaper, and screwed-up balls of typing, and more toilet rolls, and people in the street, suddenly multiplying, looking up at the windows, shouting, waving, tossing things about, laughing, being entangled in lavatory paper, kicking through real paper streamers. It's evidently just come through on everybody's tape, Laura thought in amazement, trying to take it in. They are doing it better than we are.

"Look, Daisy!" called Laura. Daisy came back and looked, a smile spreading across her face.

"When I've told everyone," said Daisy, "I'll make some coffee!"

Slow, quiet, serious and kindly, Laura thought Daisy a rather suitable messenger of peace. Peace? Peace! Here so suddenly after a fortnight's hurtle of events. Yet in another way, peace creeping so slow: like a tide where you must watch a pebble wetten to be aware it came.

Daisy made her coffee and summoned her chickens, who soon gathered, some not long back from lunch. The building was suddenly full of slamming doors and shouting people and opening windows and paper whirling down from above.

"We ought to have had a bottle ready," said Marie. "We were slow." And suddenly thought with anguish of Charles's wine racks in that terrible cellar where she nearly died, which she did not want to think of.

"There'll be plenty of time for that later on," said Mrs Tripp, bravely, considering her circumstances. Imogen Wicklow came padding softly in, her eyebrows up, her green eyes alight.

"Can you believe it, Mrs Wicklow?" Laura asked.

"It is just beginning to dawn upon me," replied she.

"I suppose we can all go home?" asked Miss Richardson nervously, and thinking without much joy of being alone in her room. With all this going on outside.

"Home!" said brave Mrs Tripp. "You're not going home. Not tonight. When the news has got through. Why don't we stay up, get a bite at your nice place, and go to Whitehall? They may make the announcement from there. Or go to the Palace?"

"The Palace?" asked Miss Richardson, appalled.

"That's it, go and shake hands with the King and Queen," put in Marie, her tone more than half-barbed.

"Mrs Tripp's quite right," said Imogen. "People will go up the Mall. To the Palace. Or to Trafalgar Square. Or Piccadilly. That is if it's really VE day."

Miss Richardson's frown deepened.

"That's it. Why hasn't there been a proper announcement? Anyway, I'm not very good in crowds," said she.

"Oh, come on, you'll be all right with me," said Mrs Tripp, badly needing a companion, "we'll stick together." As she thought about it Miss Richardson grew secretly delighted, she could hardly believe Mrs Tripp had time for her. She would be in it, for once, right in it. Whatever news was announced, she would stay and hear.

Mrs Tripp was about, magnanimously, to press Marie to join them when the telephone bell rang. This was Sadie; saying to Marie that she was not to go back home, Sadie would fetch her, they would both be taken by Sadie's Ronald to supper, and then to the fun.

"All right! Yes, thank you, how lovely!" Marie said, her eyes filling with tears. (Ronald being a post-office engineer of uncertain years had never been in uniform, he was reserved.) Ronald would hang on to one on either arm, said Sadie. Oh, how kind, oh how merry the world was going to be, because the war was over.

Mr Gorzinska put his head round the door, looking for Imogen, smiling at them all, unwontedly. The whole office had noticed the change in Mr Gorzinska.

"Francis!"

"Mrs Wicklow!" He was very proper, never would he call her anything else in the office. "May I see you home? I think," he said, looking from the window, "the streets are full, the buses are full, the tubes worse. I greatly want to see you home."

"Of course, my dear, thank you. Not only that, you will stay to supper. I believe there is a bottle of something. Won't Victoria turn up? I should expect so. Laura, what will you do?"

"I shall go home as soon as I can before the crowds get worse," said Laura. "Daisy, what are you going to do?"

"Back to my mum. Like you," admitted Daisy, under her breath, smiling.

"Francis, I wonder, what about Matthew? I wonder if Matthew—"

"Mr Tate will, I believe, have his own plans. But ring him through, perhaps?"

There was no answer from Matthew, Matthew had already made good his escape and was on the way to join his usual cronies, as Francis well knew. (He had seen him go: but was unable to resist the temptation to appear magnanimous in Imogen's eyes.) What night could be better for such a purpose, for general forgiveness, than victory night, Mrs Wicklow had thought: for Matthew's devoted dudgeon had been the deeper since the rumour of Francis and Victoria had reached him.

Prudence came in, pink and gold and smiling.

"Oh Prudence, can you take it *in*?" Laura greeted her.

"Not at all, not a whit, but I had to come down and see you all," Prudence said.

"Are you rushing home?"

"No, it's my class, you see."

"Monday, so it is! He'll cancel it!"

"He won't," laughed Prudence, taking her cup from Daisy. "After all, it's not really VE day yet, is it? Has there been a speech? No!"

Like a school let out, the building quickly emptied. Feeling was beginning to flow. Irene Wainewright hurried back to her rich father's mansion in Hampstead (from which nothing but the exigence of war would have caused her to issue so early each morning for the last three and a half years. Already she was thinking Hooray, I need work no more, I can give in my notice, *Hooray*!) Mr Watson stumped off less willingly, purchased a tiny box of chocolates with his ration (mercifully and by chance not yet spent this month), and prepared with some stoicism to play out the first evening of forced bonhomie with his suspicious wife. He had to push his way to Piccadilly Circus, it was clotted with crowds, there were more people every moment, waiting around, clutching Eros, ready to rejoice, clambering on cars which crawled good-naturedly, waving flags, singing. The nucleus of the crowd commonly starts at Eros, as if to reiterate that love is the start of all.

Laura had thought perhaps Tom might ring, but he had not. As she walked over to Victoria, there were little groups of people gathered in the Park, with a tentative, self-conscious air of rejoicing about them. There were already men selling paper hats and flags and streamers at the station. There were breathless ejaculations on the evening paperboards.

Prudence meanwhile, making her way down to Malet Street, met a steady, pervasive drift of people from the City to the West End. Prudence, against the stream, was glad she had left plenty of time to reach her class. Here, their teacher, supposing (slightly sourly) that he need not contend with the frivolity of advance victory celebrations amongst those of serious mind, assured them nonetheless that they were free to go at once if they chose. (Only one boy did: he slunk off half-smiling to join a throng of other London University students whom he knew to be gathering even now at King's. Bearing their flag they marched in procession up the Strand and through Admiralty Arch to the Palace, where they shouted loyally but in vain for the King. What was his poor Majesty to do, hampered by plans and protocol?) Those frivolous enough amongst the rest of the class would jaunt up to Westminster afterwards to see if the peace had really broken.

Prudence meanwhile had had the greatest difficulty in attending to what she called 'her muttons'. For slipping into a desk at the side almost late, she had seen from the corner of her eye her tragic acquaintance of last autumn. At last. Back. The class over, she thought I must at least go and greet him, ask after him. Collecting her things, she looked up telling herself he would have slid away. But he was walking towards her.

"Oh," Prudence said simply, "how are you? I've worried about you often!"

"That's kind. They sent me away, my doctor packed me off home. My Scottish wilds and my dear people helped. I got a temporary job in Edinburgh. I'm very much better, thank you. What about the news, eh?"

"I still can't believe it. I keep forgetting!"

"Yes. You're not staying up? In town?"

"I thought I'd better rush, there'll be such a scrum. Mum and Pop'll have kittens if I'm late."

"No doubt," he smiled. "I'd like to see you to your tube, please: there'll certainly be a scrum."

"Thank you, you are kind. It's Russell Square. But what are you going to do? Are you staying with friends?"

"No. I've got a dig, temporarily," he explained, "while I finish things off near London."

Prudence was amazed to hear herself say: "Would you like to come home with me, have supper with us? As you're alone? My parents would be pleased. Or do you want to mill with the crowds?"

Would they? Would Mum be pleased? What had possessed her? It was so impulsive and unconsidered, it was not the kind of thing she did, supposing there were not enough food? She would have given much not to have said it.

He paused a moment, considering, which made her feel worse. Poor man, she thought, he doesn't know how to refuse.

"That really is very charming of you. Are you sure they would be pleased? Shan't I be one too many?"

"No, I told them about you. My mother still asks about you from time to time. They will be pleased."

"Thank you," he said. "I'd like to." He had had no plan, it was easy to relinquish the idea of being alone in a crowd.

Even sober Bloomsbury was beginning to be crowded. With a small apology, he took her arm, steering her through the crowds in the Square, over the road, past the hotel, along to the station. The train was not particularly full. Most people were coming *in* to London to join those already gathered in the squares and circuses. Only the few, the outsiders by nature, made for their respective burrows and left the metropolis to its rejoicings. The metropolis, not noticing, swelled, hummed and roared beneath the early summer sky of a fine evening.

"The funny thing is," Prudence said, seated beside him, "I don't know your name! And I'll have to introduce you to my parents!"

He liked her deprecatory giggle of amused laughter.

"I'm Gavin Kitto," he said with his sweet smile.

Prudence felt herself go hot: and then cold. With a shock like a pointed icicle her body of its own accord stiffened.

"I'm Prudence Kyle," she replied quietly: and sat still, recovering her wits, releasing her limbs.

This, then, was Laura's man! This was he for whom Prudence had sometimes seen Laura's violet grey eyes fill with tears; about whom Laura was dreaming when rapt (as she could be) in those absences of mind where even a friend's voice did not penetrate. At this point Prudence the candid, the pellucid, the transparently honest, whose soul was as a mountain tarn, was guilty of a most unusual duplicity. As the words came to her lips, as she prepared to describe to Gavin her friendship with Laura Cardew his pupil, as the sentence sprang to mind she dammed it back, not knowing why, sitting frozen, unable to speak. A minute later Prudence thought: why have I not told him at once that I know Laura? Why should I be so shocked, I wonder? It is unexpected: but it is a kind, a wonderful chance! It is fate being benign, not cruel, for once! I can re-introduce them. I can put this happiness within Laura's reach! Which of them should she tell first? She began to consider: and with considerings the spontaneous statement was again lost. How and when and where best, she wondered, could she manage their re-meeting? She almost smiled, thinking of Laura's incredulous joy. (Though this surely was to presume too much: so far as this man was concerned the feeling might be at an end: nevertheless, nevertheless...) She could not but applaud Laura's choice. He was scholarly, he was sensitive, the sad confession of their first meeting had proved him open and feeling: he was kind, he seemed modest, his face had a peculiar, but now melancholy charm. That he was so sad was natural, with the bitter circumstance he had suffered.

Then she remembered suddenly about Tom: and her excited imaginings were shattered.

Gavin sat there, realising his acceptance of this chance invitation was in accord with his friend Gerald's policy. Just let things happen to you, for a bit: accept everything, float, rest, Gerald had said. Gavin envied him now, tucked away in the safety of his monastery in Midlothian. When not with him, Gavin reverted to his name, Gerald, he could not think of him as Brother Anything except when confronted with the actual figure of his monkish acquaintance: who had wrapped him in his arms as he stood in a sudden gale of dry sobs.

"Oh my dear fellow," he sighed, "we all must learn, soon or late, that the biggest thing in life is death."

At the time Gavin accepted this Delphic utterance as obvious: but as the empty, bereft weeks passed it was not found to be of much immediate help. Gavin was thirty-six, he had his life to lead.

"I feel it's all my fault, I feel it's a judgement on me."

"What are you talking about?"

"There was a girl I taught the year before I had to give up. I fell in love with her, I made her fall in love with me, I think."

"What happened?"

"Oh, nothing. I knew I was leaving college for the duration, I'd never see her again. But it was faithless, faithless to my wife and my son. I feel I'm being punished, worse still, they were punished because of me."

"Why are you feeling guilty, about your marriage? Did anything go wrong?"

"I resented my son, he took everything, all her love and attention."

"I believe many men resent the first son. And you didn't get time properly to recoup it. But you've come to terms with it: or as we used to say, repented of it? As to this girl: you finished it, packed it in?"

"Well, I let it pack itself in when I left."

"Then what are you worrying about? Really, Gavin, how can you entertain, let alone express, such fundamentalist *rubbish*? As that you are being punished? Your grief has made you revert to childishness," Gerald said sternly.

Gavin had felt much relieved realising the truth of this; it was like being shaken.

"I saw the girl once."

"Where? When? By chance?"

"Yes. In London at a concert. I hid, I didn't speak to them, she was with a friend."

"It is harsh to say this now, but when you feel better I should get after her. You are not a man to be alone, I think. Meanwhile, rest, float, and let things happen."

She was with a friend.

Gavin turned his head and studied Prudence. She felt his gaze, and smiled.

"Here we are."

Their silent journey had not embarrassed them.

"Mum! Pop!" she called, as she opened the front door. "I've brought a friend, from the class, who's alone! Mum, this is Gavin Kitto."

Margery had hurried from the kitchen, speechless, but welcoming, for this was so unlike Prudence. Reflecting that it was a good thing she could never prevent herself from cooking enough for Donald "in case", she seized his hand.

"You're very welcome," she said, and retreated.

"No night to be alone," Edwin said shyly, emerging into the hall. "How do you do. What's going on up there? There was already a choking throng when I left."

Leaving him to her father, Prudence followed Margery.

"Mum, I must tell you, it's the one who lost his wife and son. He wanted to see me to the train: I couldn't bear him being alone. His people are in Scotland."

"Prudence! You were right. Get him a drink. Send Eddie—Daddy out to me, I'll explain."

Edwin poured four careful glasses of sherry, first, for them to drink to this importunate peace. Against his usual practice, he left the wireless on. "Then we'll get whatever does come through," he said, going to help Margery.

Prudence was quiet throughout the meal, letting the men talk. Rejoicing in the peace claimed most of their attention. Margery wondered if Prudence was attracted to this quiet, nervous, tragic man with the Scottish name and the golden hair like her own. But Prudence's abstraction was due to her efforts to decide what to do about the revelation she surely must make. Her uncertainty did not resolve itself, but increased. The evening passed with nothing said.

Laura's arrival home considerably earlier than was her usual wont had surprised Kitty, who was back at her desk contending with a bigger batch of agony than usual, soothing some of the minor sorrows of the world with her sane kindness.

"Lolly!" she said, looking up flushed. "You're early. Or am I late?"

Laura looked at her mother, grinning.

"Darling, haven't you actually heard? Haven't you heard the news?"

"No, such a lot of letters. What? Not—?"

"It's over, Mummy, the war's over. Funny Daisy came and announced it like a figure of doom, after it came through on the tape as she calls it—And I felt 'struck all of a heap' just like old Hilda." Old Hilda was Kitty's historic daily in Suffolk.

Laura flung herself down on the sofa, laughing at her mother's long, abashed, sober face. No one seemed able to rejoice upon the instant.

"Oh, Lolly," Kitty said, with much beneath her voice. "I'd better just finish this letter, poor woman."

"People were so funny in the train! Saying *nothing*. We were all grinning, but *saying* nothing. So English. We all ought to have 'suddenly burst out singing'. Yes, you just finish that letter," Laura agreed.

Then Tom rang.

"Laura? Sorry I missed you. Did you go home early?"

"Well, the war's *over*, Tom!"

"I know, I know, but London's boiling with excitement, I hoped we could go and join in and get rowdy."

"But Tom, the proper VE day's tomorrow! I'll meet you tomorrow!"

"Proper, proper! It's tonight it's all boiling over!" said Tom with his usual pragmatism. "You can't stop news even if they don't announce it." He felt exasperated with her rule-keeping, while longing to have her by his side in the throng.

"Oh, Tom, I'm so sorry, do you want me to come back?"

"No, no, don't do that. We'll meet tomorrow." They fixed the time and place.

"Tom, what're you going to do?" Laura wailed enviously.

"Oh, just throw myself into it. Get drunk perhaps!"

The true sequence of events following the fourth of May was pieced together eventually. In the middle of the night of Sunday the sixth— Monday the seventh of May, the signatories of the document of surrender forgathered at the little red school building in Rheims, which had been General Eisenhower's headquarters. The frustrated press from papers all over the world clamoured and clawed outside, not one— (as the man from *The Times* in furious dignity wrote later) by a "most inequitable arrangement of the public relations division"—not one allowed in: not one paper was directly represented at the culminating ceremony. At two-forty-one in the morning the document was signed, General Jodl signing for Germany. At five past three, the first official to leave emerged. This was General Bedell Smith, chief of staff of the Allied Expeditionary Force. As he stepped into his car he was thought to murmur—"Fini la guerre!"

But the official secrecy held. It held because Marshal Stalin wanted the news deferred until after the second signing the next day, the eighth, in Berlin: when the news was to be simultaneously announced by all the leaders at three o'clock in the afternoon. (Had not Mr Stalin thought of the near impossibility of world-wide synchronisation?)

The difficulties of communication in arranging this delicate timing were evidently overwhelming and to hold back news of such world-shaking importance proved impossible. An American newsman was said to have broken the ban. (Did he overhear the English General? Was he as angry as the others at being kept in darkness? Who will ever know?) The news reached New York on the seventh in time for some of the morning papers and was confirmed in the afternoon ones. It was not long in reaching London and Paris. But such was the official eagerness to try to accommodate the Russian notion, that the afternoon and then the evening wore on in London with no official public statement, until the Ministry of Information scotched all hope at nine o'clock.

"…the arrangement could not be completed in time, so that a momentous day could not be brought to its due consummation," lamented *The Times* ponderously on Tuesday. In other words the victory announcement through no precise British fault was bungled, and it could be said that the celebrations went off at half-cock too soon, like a faulty firework. This would be to cast a slur upon what happened, which was simply that people took matters into their own hands and exploded into spontaneous, high-spirited joy and gladness, an immediate expression of universal relief. The same thing had happened in New York and Paris, let the Russians hold it back as they might. Let them keep it on the ninth if they chose. Which they did.

The rejoicings of the seventh had no bad effect upon those of the next day. Though many a person must have felt more in sympathy with the sober and dejected mood of the Poet Laureate's poem (…Not hopeful, therefore, but…the time arrives…) London was, nonetheless, filling up. Laura hurried eagerly to Victoria, where Tom was waiting. Meanwhile the well-known voices of well-known commentators were whipping their hearers at home into the proper, the required mood of rejoicing. London was filling up as it ever had from the days of the medieval kings to the present, filling up for a triumph. From the dull suburbs, people came to swell the joy in battered but glittering London. From Edgware and Finchley, from Archway and Holloway, from Finsbury and Hackney, from Bermondsey and Battersea, from Putney and Acton and Shepherd's Bush and Cricklewood, crowds poured in, their spirits rising with their numbers. They choked the tubes, they halted the buses, and they dammed the streets. London filled up with a vast tide of people, and the rest listening at home could hear it roar. Every now and then the frenetic voice of the BBC commentator, choking to transmit all this warm feeling to his listeners, would pause for breath, would let through a little of the roaring, just a taste of what the people could do. They were on the steps, he went on, they were on the windowsills, they were on the lamp-posts, they were on the statues. Piccadilly Circus had been the hub of it. Now people were everywhere. The Mall was full, the Arch was seething, Whitehall was awash, Trafalgar Square was solid, Westminster Bridge was come to a halt, the river was crowded with craft that hooted, the Embankment was thronged. Everything that day happened as it should. In hot afternoon sun outside the Palace, surrounded by May-time tulips, the Prime Minister's voice (as Big Ben struck three) reminded the people (how incongruously) that the lights went out and the bombs came down, but London could take it. At Westminster the crowds cheered their Parliament, going to church after the speech. In Whitehall, just before six, Mr Churchill emerged in person from the flags on the Ministry of Health balcony to say This is Your Victory...God Bless you All.

Mr Bevin came with him, suggesting to everyone that he was a jolly good fellow. When the faces of Big Ben lit up at night, the Prime Minister came again, conducted the people into "Land of Hope and Glory", and urged them on to the work still ahead, with a sombre aside about the foe in the East. By the time the King's speech was due at nine o'clock, those who had been wise virgins enough early enough (amongst whom were Mrs Tripp and Miss Richardson determined not to miss the real thing despite last night) were pressing the Palace like the waves frilling the edge of a huge sea. The hubbub that had reigned for hours was stilled. People listened in rapt silence wherever they were, it was relayed all over London: a king reminding his countrymen that the enslaved and isolated peoples of Europe had looked to them; and they had not failed. When it was over people's voices flowed together at last into a huge single-hearted roar, like some immense wave rising never to fall, the corporate voice of relief and joy, the throat of London.

The roar turned eventually into the National Anthem: and after the anthem came the chant for the King. The light at last was fading, flares showed, windows lit up, whistles shrilled, rattles clattered, songs spurted up and subsided, demands for the Family became ever more insistent. The sea bobbed with funny hats of every description, prickled with flags, foamed with streamers, was unsteady with surging seal heads and waving Medusa arms. Laura sat within Tom's arm on a stone vantage point, whence they watched the sea as outsiders.

The family came out three times, four small distant figures engulfed in cheering. Once Mr Churchill came with them. The last time people noted the Princesses were not there, supposed they had gone to bed. But they were outside with the people, seeing the Crown from the vantage point of the ordinary man.

There was floodlighting everywhere, not only at the Palace, but at St Paul's (where there had been services of thanks all day). Trafalgar Square, and upon Nelson himself. The National Gallery searchlights beamed along Whitehall, shafts of platinum. Others circled and centred in the sky overhead like the spokes of a huge wheel. Fireworks, rockets, crackers and flashes went up. Bonfires were lit, multiplications of petty Hitlers were burned. People danced and sang all over the capital. The commentators of the BBC were hoarse with describing it.

"Just listen," Kitty exclaimed aloud, sitting alone at home, in the amazed contralto voice, which Laura would recall to the end of her days. "Just listen! To all that cheering!" Kitty had grown beyond minding that there was, sometimes, no one to answer.

19

After VE day, a department devised for the prosecution of the war having lost its sense of purpose, the office became a dying body. And by the last week in May its demise was announced in the press. It was simply a matter of its being wound up.

First its flesh (in the form of a certain number of people like Miss Wainewright who did not by their good fortune have to work at all) fell away: likewise its loads of now obsolete files and redundant memos and questionable monographs, were sent to a department bent on deciding (like Hamlet) if they were to be or not to be. Until, to the heightened imagination of some still left, it seemed to become ever more like an articulated skeleton going through the motions of life. The process was to take months: yet already, click clack, one seemed to hear its bones rattling as the typewriters in the pool chattered with outdated purposes, superseded plans, cancelled necessities, redundant dooms. It would struggle on pale and fleshless till it fell apart.

People went. Or people stayed. Matthew, for instance. Matthew stayed on over that summer, resisting all suggestions that he should be diverted usefully elsewhere—the Treasury for instance?—Matthew shuddered—and suffering no qualms of conscience that the government should support him a little longer while he polished his novel, he looked about him for employment not too uncongenial, practising which he would pursue his primary desire to write. With some cynicism, he later needled his guilty parents as to what they could do to help him to a job of some sort: and settled eventually, at his mother's anxious instigation, for a routine editing job in medical publishing, in a firm which had always had a medical list but was much better known for its interest in avant garde literature. Once in, Matthew thought, I can worm my way elsewhere.

Most of the clerical staff, and the typists, amongst whom were Marie, Mrs Tripp and Miss Richardson, determined to hang on as long as they possibly could (if necessary until the articulated skeleton collapsed in a clacking heap) were found, little by little, alternative niches in permanent ministries: or discovered places for themselves in the better-paid pools of business and industry. Francis Gorzinska approached the British firm which had employed him, and on account of which he had actually sought British citizenship, and found that he was valued enough to be welcomed back as soon as he chose to come; which he deserved.

Mr Watson was less lucky, no such place had been kept for him, he had at least seven years' working life to go, and knew not quite where to turn. "Dewdrop" disappeared at the end of VE week, never to be seen again, Mr Harvald stayed busily in Europe for months to come. Mr Wheedon must hover till all these settlements and dispersals were seen to: but Mr Wheedon was lucky, he had the major share in his family's firm and neither work nor retirement was going to cause him anxiety either way.

One of the first to go was Imogen, who, unlike Matthew, seeing no reason why the British government should pay her money she did not need for work she was not doing, quickly negotiated her release very soon after VE day, and surveyed her life with her usual gratitude mingled with some apprehension of approaching loneliness.

For to Imogen the main virtue of the office had been the alleviation of loneliness, the daily company. She was grateful for all of them, for those who would still come to tea with her, join her for a cinema or a play. She was particularly grateful for Laura and Prudence; Prudence she was sure would never lose touch with her, and of Laura she would hear through her friend. Her children were all saved alive: Harry could go back to his broadcasting, and literary ploys, Willy to his engraving, Victoria (it appeared) into the arms of Francis. Jane and her young would re-appear from India. There would be more grandchildren. She should stay in London, where they all were, or would come. On her own account, her heart burst with thankfulness that the war at hand was over. She had masses said for all her children, she prayed constantly and at length for the end to the unspeakable happenings in the Far East: she agonised in bewildered sorrow over the hideous revelations recently disclosed from Buchenwald.

This morning she sat, at about half past eleven on a weekday with a sense still vibrant of disgraceful idleness and luxury, her coffee finished, her spectacles upon her nose, her cheeks flushed with a mixture of shocked embarrassment and irresistible laughter, reading Matthew's novel. Which she had faithfully promised to do, and must therefore keep her word. Why, she had soon thought, picking her way into the rather badly typed sheets, did I go to such lengths to help to save this? What is this? I can find as yet no story, no structure, what is the dear boy trying to tell us? She could not at first easily distinguish the people, and was very fussed by this, for she did not know which was talking. However, their talk was so uniformly larded with c-s, and f-s, and b-s and b-ls and others, which she had never heard of, that their conversation would not have helped distinguish them anyway. Matthew had typed them all out in full, it was she who imagined them all initialised thus, for decency's sake. Try as she would, alone as she was, she could not read them aloud, even mouth them. Who would publish this? Perhaps in the brave, liberated world of after the war someone really would? Her sense of its being too much, of his going too far, reduced her to a state of shaking laughter, which increasingly incommoded her attention. She had a recurring fantasy of the whole book when published as simply a network, a pattern, a guesswork, of initial letters and dots concealing obscenities. She threw aside the typescript with pouting lips and uncontrollable giggles and made for the kitchen, to get on with lunch for Victoria and Francis.

"What's this, darling Ma?" Victoria said later, transfixed by a page in the text she had opened at random.

"Matthew's novel," Imogen admitted.

"Obscurely poetical. And blatantly obscene," pronounced her daughter with some acumen.

Freedom of choice! Freedom of choice? When the future presented itself as still going to be there, as a country to which they would all inevitably journey, many people were like slaves from a ship battened down under hatches, now emerging, crawling out into the world of open choice, blinking in the sunlight. Some did not like the sunlight, and did not know what to do with it, preferred their wartime job and bonds, tried to crawl back or stay under. For the enforced work, the regular pay, had been a boon to many, particularly women: a vast section of whom had taken and earned their independence from their husbands or parents as workers.

Laura's choice was urgent. No other man had as yet given her the certain and compulsive joy she had possessed but once, although she realised that she was thinking of Tom with increasing fondness. She must find some way, and find it quickly, of earning her own living, for she must not fall back upon her mother. Kitty had enough ado to earn her own upkeep without keeping Laura. For Kitty, nothing was changed by the partial ending of the war and the appearance over the horizon of the future. The sad, unaltered landscape of Kitty's future lay uninvitingly there, a grey country to be courageously illumined by her own efforts. She was alone, she would stay alone: no change in Laurence's standpoint was to be effected by the ending of the war. Laurence would never return, nor would he support her, for they were not legally separated, even less were they likely to be divorced, their religious convictions forbade it.

Kitty was only in her early fifties, Kitty was romantic and loving, and despite Laura's natural involvement in her own urgent decisions, she mourned for her mother. Likewise she was astounded at the way Kitty accepted all this and set about to make her future. Never did she appear bitter or cynical or self-pitying, never did she rail against chance or fortune: for since she believed Providence to overrule them both, what Providence provided she humbly accepted without apparent demur. One did not kick against Providence in Kitty's world. It was an attitude leading to a restful relaxation, Laura decided, rather than to sad resignation. For the miracle was, her mother remained one of the happiest people Laura had ever known.

Kitty meanwhile wished with all her heart that Laura would celebrate the peace by marrying some nice and loving young man, settling down, having her children. Time enough for creative endeavour and new mental interests in all these acres of middle age, motherhood done, which she was plodding through sadly alone herself. She surveyed the battlefield of Laura's boys, back into schooldays. Those fat letters which Laurence disapproved of (she had the greatest difficulty in preventing him opening them and used to grab and hide them herself for Laura if she could) from Cambridge boys, met in the holidays. Laurence eventually forbade them until his daughter was "older". Forbade her to receive letters from boys! How dare he. Then all the Oxford lot, some of whose names she had never mastered. And Godfrey who lasted longer. And the one after the wedding. And poor Hubert. And now this nice Tom. Surely, amongst this legion there should be someone. But alas the older one, she suspected, still eclipsed all the rest, who was out of reach, and not available. Kitty sighed.

So they lived together, this mother and daughter, usually in calm daily happiness, observing each other's plight with mutual sorrow, wondering at each other's inability to improve it, loving each other far more than simply out of habit, but never totally able to see life as the other saw it since they surveyed it with thirty years between.

It was not surprising that Laura eventually looked in the same direction as Matthew, and despite her distaste for regular office life, found a humble job in the lower regions of a publisher's in Bloomsbury. (The pay, to be sure, was derisory, but having come of a family that never had any Laura could not be expected to feel much affection for money.) Here she hoped the general literary ambience would inspire her and further her own inclinations. Her lunches with Prudence would be less frequent, they now worked too far part, but they would meet, regularly if rarely, at some halfway point. Lucky Prudence, Laura thought, seeing her friend blossom and liven at the prospect of her work to come. For Prudence stayed on with the others in the expiring office, conscientiously sorting, destroying, or indexing, doing her time, earning her salary, until in the autumn the university term should start.

Gavin Kitto would have been amazed had he known the dilemma into which his re-appearance had thrown Prudence Kyle. Prudence had missed making that first, obvious, rational revelation about Laura, when he had come to supper, and the longer she thought about it the more complex it seemed to become. It seemed: but it was not. What was complex was due to the nature of Prudence's own feelings, and of these she was not yet properly aware. Kitto was the first man of the right kind, old enough to appeal to a girl who worshipped her father, doing the same work as she was to do, who had showed he understood this, and who had almost inadvertently called upon her pity and sympathy. His long absence had increased rather than diminished her interest. But even the shock of his identity had not revealed to her why she had felt so much, why she had not turned at once in the train and said oh, you taught Laura Cardew, I've been working with her! Prudence's instincts, stronger than her good nature, were saying quite clearly this is your kind of man. She covered her inner ears, she summoned her affection and good will, of course she must tell Laura as soon as possible. But Laura was on the verge, surely, of choosing to fall in love with Tom! Without any personal experience, Prudence knew that there was a certain amount of choice in the decision to go towards a person, in the hope of love. How could she destroy all that (they had been about together a lot, she gathered, since the spring) on the off-chance of this poor man being in the mood yet to woo anyone, even Laura? Surely it was, in itself, unlikely? Should she not simply keep quiet about it? Once Laura's heart was given, and possessed, all that glowing capacity for love, which Prudence was aware of, all that warm ability to show it, would have found its haven. Laura was, had proved herself to be, a faithful girl, not flighty, however many boys she had tried in her comical but ardent pursuit of love. Once settled, she would not be shaken, even by so cruel a trick of time and fate, would she? But supposing she were? Supposing she were to discover that Prudence had hidden the truth of Gavin's circumstances! How would she, Prudence, ever be able to face her friend again? It was impossible to think of. Laura was bound to discover, sooner or later, if her tutor was to re-enter her orbit. Why should he do so, however, Prudence wondered? Because, once settled, Laura would very probably get in touch with him, she had various friends she talked of, Godfrey was one, with whom she had had affairs, with whom she continued to be friends. Laura was warm-hearted: it was one of the qualities Prudence loved her for.

In such agonised and purblind wonderings Prudence continued for several weeks. Gavin came only once more to the class before the long vacation began and the series ended. He told her then how he was involved in the sad task of clearing out the cottage. After that, he would, and more congenially, be getting back to Oxford, picking up the pieces, finding a place to live, preparing to take up his fellowship again. He had looked—not happy, but alive, interested, as he talked of it, it was a profound relief, he said, to have an object.

It was easy therefore for Prudence, drifting back and forth in this dilemma, to find that it was June, it was nearly a month since he had come to see them. To realise that between clearing up at the office and reading around for her own work, she had got nowhere with a problem which might *affect the whole of Laura's future*. Her anxiety began to disturb her concentration.

I shall have to ask Pop, Prudence realised at last, I shall have to tell the parents and talk it all over with them. The decision made, she acted upon it the same night. She was not prepared for the immediate, angry, shocked reaction of her father.

"Prudence! You must tell Laura at once. You should have told *him* on the spot. What prevented you?" he demanded, in an outraged tone such as he seldom used to her.

Edwin in fact was surprised himself at the strength of his reaction. Margery looked at him mildly and thought there will be ructions and flummoxes when Prudence wants to marry. What a pity, Margery thought, about this Gavin Kitto, he would have just been grand for Prudence, and he is a bonny Scot to boot.

"Eddie," she said, "you have missed the point, about this other one, this Tom."

"There is only one clear point at issue," Edwin answered sternly "which is Prudence's obligation to tell Laura."

"Pop, you're perfectly right," Prudence said, feeling relieved. "I see how clear it is to you. But, she's talked very fondly of Tom."

"Is she engaged to Tom, or is there an understanding, in old-fashioned terms?"

"Not that I know of, no. I asked her if she was fond of him: she said very. He sounds so right for her, that's all."

"Only Laura can decide that. We don't know this Oxford man has any intentions of marrying again. Yet. But Laura should decide with her eyes open," Edwin said.

"Yes" Prudence agreed. "Which should I tell first? How do I put them in touch?"

"Tell Laura," Margery pondered. "No, tell Kitto." A pause. "Tell them both together," she cried.

First Prudence, and then Edwin, laughed fondly at her. Neither was exactly sure why, but it helped to reduce the tension.

"After all," Margery said giggling, pleased to have made them laugh, "they may both feel totally different, *now*."

"Laura doesn't—yet—I think," said Prudence.

"She will," Margery pointed out, playing a rearguard action for her daughter and the bonny Scot, "if she gets settled with this Tom."

"I can't let her, without knowing this."

"No," Edwin's voice was gentler now.

"It's a bit ticklish, my approaching him?"

"Ask him to supper again," Margery said at once.

"Prudence would rather do it on her own," Edwin said. She smiled.

"Ask them both to supper," Margery said triumphantly.

They laughed again. Why was it so farcical?

"Too sudden?"

"Yes, too sudden."

"But you could tell them both, beforehand! Who they are to meet? There can't be any harm in that?"

"If there are feelings left between them they won't want to re-meet with us, in public, as it were," Prudence said, imaginatively pondering. "I'll work something out."

"Yes. Don't let it slide any longer though," her father said.

In the event, Prudence wrote a little note. There was a friend of hers whom he had taught, Laura Cardew, she thought he might be interested to meet her again. She had to send it to his college so that it was several days before Gavin Kitto received it. He remembered his sudden sense in the train of having perhaps seen Prudence before, and said yes. At that concert. In another life. Thinking of Gerald's advice, he responded at once. He would be glad to meet her on the day she said in the place she suggested, to hear about this. It was very convenient, thank you, being near the British Museum.

20

While the horizons of peace were defined in ravaged Europe, the Allies withdrawing behind four agreed boundaries within Germany and Austria, and the Control Commission beginning upon their thankless, anonymous tasks, the world watched the Far East.

Daisy, in particular, simple, loving, and not particularly interested in the spectacle of war, kept a desperate, mesmerised eye upon the doings out there in blurred pictures in the papers she took. For early in May the British with the help of Indian divisions had taken Rangoon and recovered Burma: Daisy had reason to think her boy was in Burma.

On a cold Saturday morning in June, Daisy got a telegram: her husband, wounded in the fighting for Pegu on the way to Rangoon had now regrettably died of his wounds.

"I can't feel anything," said pale distressed Daisy, her eyes rounder than ever, to her loving mother trying to cuddle her. "Not anything." She squinted at the indistinguishable face beneath the broad-brimmed jungle hat, in the snap she had received early in the war.

"'Course you can't, pet, you hardly knew him, you didn't have time. You could say it's easier, in a way. I daresay you'll feel it later on."

"Poor Geoff. My poor Geoff. Just think of it, all on his own, feeling so ill."

"Shall I ring his mother, dear? Aren't we supposed to tell her? You're next of kin, see...oh they're not on the phone though are they?"

"No. Fancy telling them," Daisy mourned, a tear coming at this idea. "Got to, though." It was the thought of his parents' shock, which at last made her cry.

"Will they bring him back? What do they do, Mum? I kind of want to see him again, I can hardly remember his face…I can't go back to the office." Daisy suddenly added, "I can't go back, Monday, and there's no need, it's closing down. I'll find a job somewhere else. I can't tell them all, see them all."

Most of her distress was due to not feeling enough sorrow and having to act it. He's my *husband*, and I can hardly picture his *face*, she thought.

"What about all your things?"

"I'll go now, no one will be in today, I'll go and get it all now."

"I'll come with you, ducky."

"Let's go at once, it'll be something to do."

Daisy had married hurriedly, innocently, before her boy left, a young, prudish girl. They had only two nights to consummate it. They had not got very far. Daisy remembered pain, discomfort and shyness. I wish I'd had a baby she thought. Who am I? I'm not really *Mrs* Anything. I ought to be in a right stew, minding, and I'm not. Really, I'm not. She was horrified at herself. In the deserted office she collected her stuff, her pencil case, her shopping bag, her dictionary, her old indoor shoes. She left a sleazy cardigan she rather disliked over the back of her chair, not noticing it. She smiled at the old porter (she had smiled at him for four years) chatting to her mother in the ground floor hall. (She hoped her mother had not told him, but was afraid she had.)

On Monday only her cardigan showed where Daisy had been.

"Oh poor Daisy," Prudence mourned, when Marie told her of the telephone message. "Marie, I didn't even know, I'd totally forgotten, she was Mrs," Prudence said. "Of course she wore a ring."

"Well, we all called her Daisy, didn't we?" said Marie. "And she never talked about him, that I heard. Not like Mrs Tripp did. She did tell me once they only had a weekend and then he was off."

So Daisy's marriage, Prudence reflected, was one of those ghostly things in life that never happens. When she told her mother, Margery was sadly sympathetic. Thousands of girls in the same boat, thousands of ghost marriages. They all rush to get married, very naturally.

Prudence pondered the sad image of a million ghost marriages. Edwin, lifting his head from his diary, said, "It's because the boys want an anchor, they want some stake at home. Someone to clutch on to? Apart from the frantic feeling that they may not—" He broke off, remembering Donald.

"I wonder if you really face the fact you may not come back?"

"Oh yes," said her parents together: who remembered the Great War. But it had never been voiced between her mother and Donald, so far as Prudence knew.

Edwin was noting the strange circumstances of the Czech resurrection.

Wolfed right at the start, almost first, I recall vivid maps of the open German maw round those countries. The Czech resistance rose just before VE day, suffered heavy losses. But when a retreating German division made for Prague, what stood in its way was a General Vlasov and his army, a *non-Communist Russian* who'd been fighting till then for the Germans. He saved Prague. One wouldn't be Vlasov from any point of view, the Russians will savage him, I wonder who holds him now. Allies ordered communist Tito out of Trieste.

All eyes on the Pacific. An island called Okinawa took three months and twenty thousand dead Americans to capture. Hideous repeated bombings of Tokyo thought to have killed far more—and civilians, too. No one seems able to get through to the new Japanese prime minister, an admiral Baron Suzuki, to urge peace, though they *must* be ready to treat. Do the Allies not *want* to?

Sickening, senseless spectacle of men killing each other in thousands, how can anyone propound a *meaning*?

Prudence saw despair in her father's eyes as he tossed the book furiously away.

One late afternoon of a golden summer day Laura, making her way down a narrow street towards her bus stop, lifted her eyes to the window of a tea-shop over the road and was arrested, mouth open in a slight smile, as if some blow had struck to her heart, threatened her very life. So suddenly did she stop that a young man hurrying behind her bumped her slightly as he passed. Laura did not hear his apology nor notice his passing, she stood transfixed.

At the table in the window across the road sat Gavin: he looked older than she remembered, but, unmistakably Gavin, his sweet smile, his expressive hands, his burnished hair, in serious conversation with Prudence: Prudence, pink and smiling and equally fair, throwing back her honey-gold head in a gesture of joy as he spoke, answering, nodding, then suddenly serious.

The vision grew blurred as Laura stood there, was it tears in the eyes, was it the approach of faintness? I shall fall, I shall faint if I cannot sit down, if I fall they will see me. Where can I go, where can I hide? So little could she accept what she saw that she turned her back on it, her eyes tightly closed; and stumbled away from it, stumbled back the way she had come, leaving it behind, relegating it to a world of the impossible; she had not seen Gavin talking intimately to Prudence, she had imagined it, dreamed the whole scene! Her dizzying heartbeats shook her. I must go in somewhere, I must ask to sit down or I shall faint, she thought. Her left hand, groping, found the handle of the door of the shop on the corner. She knew it well, often she had gazed at the things in the window; several times when they were young she and Marian had been brought here, by a school friend of Kitty's who lived in Bloomsbury, who would borrow them for the day, and to crown the fun, buy them a treasure here. Working near it, Laura had greeted it as an old friend, still there, proof against war.

She knew the door handle, she knew the voice of the bell, she stumbled down the step.

"Oh, Mr Jacowitz, may I, may I please sit down!"

For there was a high, hard chair by the counter where the old Jewish proprietor stood, his smooth yellow hands fondling some object with reverent gentleness, his white hair curled streakily on his cheeks. That she knew his name did not surprise him, though he did not recognise her, looking at her with concern, as she sprawled on to the chair, and put her head on the counter.

"My dear young lady, what is it, you feel faint, whatever has happened to upset you? Rest there, recover yourself, there is no hurry in the world."

In a few moments she lifted her head, pale, dazed and breathless.

"I am so sorry," she said, "I had a shock, it made me faint."

Love, he said to himself, it will be some cruel blow of love, she is young, she is sweet, she is sure the end of the world has come, that she will die of it.

"Come round, come through, there is a comfortable chair behind here, what can have happened, to give you such distress?" He led her gently into the room behind, where his ancient handsome, wing chair waited. Laura sank into it.

"Two people, I have seen two people," she said.

"One of whom you love," he supplied, with gentle amusement, as she paused.

"*Both* of whom I love!"

"Together?"

"Together. I did not know they knew each other!"

"Alas."

"It took my breath away."

"It drained the blood from your pretty cheeks. Here is tea, I have just drunk some, it is fresh. And this cup is beautiful." He poured the scented tea into a shallow cup painted with flowers. "It will make you feel better. No one ever died of love, my dear young lady, save in opera. Or Shakespeare."

"Oh, I wish I *could* die!" breathed Laura.

The shop bell rang.

"Look at these beautiful things, which someone has just brought in. Take them into your hands, look at them as you sit here. Stay for a little, you will feel better. Drink some tea."

She obeyed like a child, as he left her.

I cannot believe it, it cannot be true, mourned Laura. How could it happen? I cannot have it happen, it must not be allowed to happen. How can I possibly look at his treasures, she protested, what do they matter? Prudence has met Gavin, Prudence glows and smiles before him, she is falling in love with Gavin, he is delighted with Prudence, my familiar friend. It is as inevitable as doom. They are like each other. They are both golden-haired, she thought inconsequentially. She felt faint again, choking with distress. She took a deep breath. Why am I being so foolish, Laura asked herself, why shouldn't they know each other? He's been working in London, they are both medieval historians. More important, Gavin is married, and would not carry on with our affair. Prudence is my friend, utterly trustworthy, she is also in her way a puritan. Why have I suffered this sight of them as if it were a cataclysmic revelation, why did it make me faint as if I were fetched a deathblow? He is not after all *mine*. Am I so jealous? A great sigh took over within her.

It is because I still love him, she realised. My heart is still tied, my heartstrings are tied: which, tugged, bring exquisite joy or blinding pain. I love him. I am jealous of Prudence even *knowing* him. I wonder when she will tell me that they have met.

With a strange sense of distance, like recalling something faded and far away, she remembered Tom. How *can* I have forgotten about Tom? That proves where my heart is, she thought, with an angry, choking sob. She thought that she might have to tell Tom about this, about what was aroused in her again with such ineluctable force.

She picked up an object from the little Spanish tray Mr Jacowitz had left, held it up into a glint of sunlight, saw nothing, blinked tears away and looked again. A small ornament, she believed it was netsuke, of yellowed ivory. A twig of Holm oak with two acorns lay on top of a cluster of larger ones. She turned it over, and behold! The acorns held minute scenes, whole worlds! A spreading tree near a house with steps by a lake, two sails on the horizon. A pagoda, a twisted bush, a frail fence and again the little ships on the sea. A hut by a shore, smoke curling, a tiny boat on the strand, and three sails, three sails on the water! Each scene an enclosed secret world, the whole piece barely one inch by one and a half. How could any fingers carve those little worlds? Eternities in the palm of the hand. The very thought calmed the mind.

She took up a scent bottle (as she supposed) with a jade stopper upon an ivory dipper: and on the clouded glass of the small flagon-shaped vessel a rose pink creature sprawled, a claw, a pair of eyes, scaly convolutions, fishy fins, impossible to tell if it were one creature or two which writhed around the thing, whether they loved or fought, whether they fought as they loved.

And here was a paper knife. An ivory paper knife, the blade of which was inlaid with a green beetle furnished with unimaginably delicate antennae and bent legs; with a ladybird, wings slit, about to fly; with a butterfly, a bee, a thorned spray, all of mother o' pearl. But its handle! Its handle was a monkey, aggressively mischievous, his hind leg on the back, his face and right arm on the front: his wide mouth, his nostrils, his glinting eyes, his pointed ears, every hair carved! The long right arm stretched down to pluck a rose hip.

And what was this, in a mulberry velvet case the shape of a tiny 'cello? A golden rose lay inside, a spray, with delicate leaves below. She still held it in her hand when the old man came back.

"Ah. You feel better. Look." He showed her how the rosebud was hinged, you could open it, in its heart was scented wadding which some Edwardian girl had sniffed long ago.

"Oh!" There was something so romantically symbolic in the revelation, so sentimental, it made them laugh. "Thank you, I am better, thank you for the tea. I am so sorry."

"*I* am sorry," he bowed slightly. "Take heart, my dear young lady. You are young, the war is almost over. My people, the remnant, will soon be delivered."

Laura looked at him appalled. Speechless and ashamed she stood up.

"No more customers," he said as he prepared to lock the door behind her. "Good night, my dear," said he kindly. Laura whispered her farewell with a watery smile.

She walked bravely down the street. The teashop window was empty.

Why had she not walked straight in, joined them, greeted them? I didn't know you knew each other? She heard herself say. Gavin would rise, seize her hand, smile: Laura, how good to see you again! She thought she could have carried it off, it would have been real, obvious, every day. It was fantasy that drained you, defeated you, killed you.

✣

Laura had tried so hard to say something to Tom, all the evening. But here they were, at Victoria.

"Tom, there's something I've simply got to tell you."

"You've met that teacher of yours again."

Laura gasped. "Tom, how do you always know, you seem to be a kind of a thought reader?"

"Just that star-crossed look on your face. Tell me."

"I only saw him in a teashop. He was with Prudence, my clever friend I've told you about, the one I worked with."

"I know, I know. Prudence the clever, I always call her. What was she doing with him, did you know they knew each other?"

"No, but I guess they met at Prudence's palaeography class. They were just talking with great pleasure and fervour."

"So what? Suppose they were enchanted with their palaeography?" Tom said in some disbelief.

"I know, but…Tom, I felt so sad, and shocked, and jealous, I nearly fainted, I had to go into a shop… . And I thought if I still feel like this about him, how can I not tell you, it felt treacherous… ."

"Treacherous to whom?" asked Tom, precisely.

"Well, to you."

"You and I haven't any fixed understanding yet, Laura. Go on."

"Well, and then I thought how could Prudence be getting involved with a married man, she's so upright, you simply can't imagine it of her, she was adamant with me about it."

"So she may have changed, due to the power of love. Did it look as if she were in love with him?" Tom pursued. "Or did it lead you to wonder whether your tutor is now free?"

"Yes…it did, it does lead on to that," Laura said. Her thoughts had of course reached thus far.

Tom took a deep breath.

"And you don't know about it. However, people can have tea together without being judged involved."

217

"I know, Tom, I know I'm being mad, leaping to conclusions. I'm only telling you because you know about it through Rose, you were sympathetic. And somehow I just had to tell you."

"Yes, I see you had. I'm grateful." Tom thought for a moment. He could not find any logical reason why Laura should assume that circumstances were different. This however, was beyond logic.

"Laura, you must find out. Find out if anything's different. Just pick up the phone, and ring up Prudence the clever, and say what you saw, and ask what the hell's going on," Tom explained, as if she were a child. "Only make it sound casual."

"Oh, Tom. Can I? How can I interfere?"

Tom sighed at the maze-like deviousness of women's feelings, their ponderings too precisely on events.

"For everybody's sake, especially yours, you must find out, girl, what has happened. If anything," said Tom, with urgency and kindness. He had not called her "girl" for ages. It was as if he had stepped back into an earlier room of their acquaintance.

"Though," he added, "I can't think why you're so sure anything's different at all. Unless it's just intuition. It could be, women are famous for it. Meanwhile, you and I are best having a watershed period, you know what I mean, don't you?"

Laura looked at Tom and had never loved him more. The ironical enmeshments of chance would strike her later, at the moment she was too involved with her heart's desires and muddled by her emotions. Here was Tom being a loveable paragon of unhuffy generosity, and Laura while worshipping this unable to alter the situation that brought it forth.

"Oh, Tom," she blurted, throwing herself against him and hugging him. "You're so marvellous, you're so unselfish."

"Hey, hey," said Tom, looking more like a centurion than ever, "I'm just as keen on making the right choice as you are. The essential thing is that we should both be happy. Let's get this over quickly, now. There are plenty of fish in the sea, you go after that big one, if it's flopping about free. You obviously *have* to, Laura. Don't dare worry about me, by the way, I forbid it, I don't need it, it's an insult. We've had a great time this summer. Please, though, let me *know* what happens, I can't suddenly lose all interest in you. Don't cry now, goodnight, darling Laura, let's be like Michael Drayton, you know." He shook her shoulders gently, a familiar gesture of his. He was pale. "Only just let me know," he begged. He kissed her fondly once, her cheek, her lips were wet, and walked quickly away thinking with a twisted smile God in heaven it's she who should be comforting me. Hurrah for the comforts of philosophy, said Tom, though he knew his heart was wounded. It felt cold, or rather it was unable to feel much at all.

Laura watched him go and thought of the poem. She had always loved the way he knew the essential poems. Since there's no help come let us kiss and part. She stared numbly after his disappearing form. All the way home and far into the night she fretted about what she had done, she had lost dear, kind, clever, amusing Tom (probably for good whatever he said about watersheds) with no justification except the glow of this earlier love which had welled up with such bright force again as not to be denied.

Prudence telephoned to Laura in the third week of July.

"Laura! We're all going to Oban for a whole month, for August, isn't it heaven!"

Laura agreed sardonically, knowing neither heaven nor Oban: but it was dearest P's native earth, in so far as any of them ever showed any emotion, they must be over the moon.

"We'd all love it so much if you could come? For a week? Would you think it worth it? Or are you," said Prudence, with most uncharacteristic guile, "on the verge of getting engaged to Tom, and not wanting to leave London?" She had heard Laura gasp, now she heard a deep breath, which was a sigh.

"Tom and I," stated Laura, rather bleakly, "are having what he calls a watershed period, it's his good expression for uncertainty, not knowing quite," she paused. She was not ready to explain its reason, she was caught offguard. Prudence turned her eyes heavenward, almost she sent thanks to an Almighty. "So, oh Prudence! I'd love to come, oh thank you all so much!"

Now Laura sounded almost tearful. They proceeded to discuss dates, and details, and the rail journey, which however you did it was sure to be tedious. This business occupied the front of the mind, and only when it was done, when Prudence had rung off, did the huge brooding question come forward again in Laura's mind. Why didn't I ask her, she said aloud, about meeting Gavin? Why doesn't she tell me? Does she not realise who he is? Surely I have often said his name lately, I know I have. How unlike Prudence not simply to tell me. Oh heart, heart, are you right? Is he somehow at large, is he falling in love with her? The holiday is just a consolation prize, to break it to me gently. From intense joy and excitement, she was plunged into gloom.

Prudence, returning from the telephone, looked pleased.

"So?" said Margery.

"She's thrilled, she'd love to come for a week. What's more, I was awfully subtle, I've found out about Tom."

"What about Tom?"

"She sounded a bit sad, she said things were uncertain, they were not meeting for a little."

"Splendid," Edwin exclaimed, raising his head from his diary.

"So didn't you just *tell* her? What's happened to Kitto?"

"I thought I could do it better, more gently perhaps, when I'm with her, when she joins us."

"Yes," Margery agreed sadly.

Edwin grunted, returning to his page.

Election: due to Labour coming out of coalition, and Churchill forming national interim government. The most protracted election I've ever known: we voted last week, many of the Scots aren't voting till next, and heaven knows when the Service votes will be in. My suspicion, my feeling is, there'll be a kind of manic roar, and a landslide for Labour, which M. will call ingratitude to Churchill. Who managed a party forsooth, at No 10 to say goodbye to the Coalition! (Would obviously rather keep it going.) He says, 'this is a strange, unnatural election' tearing to bits 'many ties of mutual comprehension and comradeship!' Belligerent he may be, needed to be, but he's faithful, he's staunch, he's a bull-dog, he's willed us all along to win the war, with those indomitable early speeches and memorable turns of phrase. Daren't ask Prudence how she exercised her first vote. Laura, she said, barely persuaded to vote at all: 'a-political'! Uninformed, no doubt, and uninterested, I suspect.

Now the 'big Three' posturing at Potsdam (plus Attlee, in case he's in). Wild rumours about Japan, that they have asked Stalin to be mediator, arrange peace.

From Potsdam the three leaders warned Japan solemnly to surrender. Baron Suzuki the old prime minister replied that he had nothing to say in public, a reply which was wrongly taken to mean he scorned all thought of peace. (Far from this, he ardently wanted peace, for the country was at the end of its tether; but with, however, some saving of face and the preserving of the Imperial dynasty.) The misunderstanding caused the Americans to assume that fighting must go on: and much as many of their leaders had come to dislike the idea of Russian intervention at the last gasp of a war that the Americans (with some British) had fought, they knew this resource was there.

In some quarters, including the conference at Potsdam, people knew also that there was another resource.

Two days after the conference met in mid-July, an old woman at a "gas" station near Alamogordo in New Mexico, who was always up in the early hours, saw what she thought to be the sun flip up very early over the horizon and then disappear: to rise again at the proper time. She reported this puzzling apparition to the drained and weary men who bought petrol from her on their way back from some over-night work at the desert-testing site she only dimly knew of. Their half-smiles were unwilling, their replies forced and vague.

T he colours, the colours," sighed Prudence.

The Kyles had returned to their native heath, to the roots of their lives, to what Edwin still could not help feeling a grudge against, as being the source of the oppression of both their childhoods (for he and Margery had lived not far apart). The Kyles had arrived back in Oban all three, Prudence in high spirits, Margery hoping desperately that Donald would be freed to come and join them.

Edwin was surveying the neat grey church the other side of the harbour from the pier.

The Church in Oban is against a backdrop of dark, dark green trees, the afternoon light from the south-west lights up the mass of grey buildings, church, hotels and houses, into sunny steel. The calm water of the bay is often columned with broad silver reflections from the piles of illuminated clouds above the church and the low hills bordering the shore.

Birds' wings are black arrows of shadow above their silver breasts in the blue sky.

Despite all this beauty he felt exasperated dudgeon, for although it was not their church, which was an old Wee Free chapel in a nearby village, but the Episcopalian, it was none the less a bastion of a repressive ideology, they all were. Sunday had proved itself as intractably iron-grey as ever.

It was many years since they had been here all together, as a family. Prudence was a little pretty girl, golden-haired. They had frequented south-coast places for years with the children: and then had come the war.

Prudence was exhilarated to be back. Everyone had greeted her with Scottish neighs of amazement, as if they might have expected the little tiny girl to have stayed frozen so. She was now exceedingly tall, to be sure, and still golden-haired. She looked at the surrounding mountains with ecstasy: calm, eternal and sublimely untouched by the war, fleeting pools of shadow cast upon their green hollows by the glorious procession of billowing cloud which sat piled whitely upon them or chased past them on the fine days. On the wet days all was obliterated.

Edwin thought perhaps they had been wrong to stay with Margery's cousins, who still lived, as he put it to himself, in the closed-in box of their religion. Had they been in lodgings they could have organised their own Sunday without offence (unspoken yet surely there, Prudence acting as a kind of mollifying buffer). But the invitation had been so warm and the welcome so kind, it would have been difficult to refuse. He nonetheless found the small stone cottage oppressive, the bedroom too low-ceilinged and stuffy, he had not slept very well. He would do better, Margery averred, when he was more un-wound. How far away London, the office and the war seemed after a few days, how delicious was the smell of the sea, the sharp, cool northern air morning and evening. He would rather sleep out of doors, he thought. Was it to do with some need that he still had to escape, to elude these deadening tentacles so hatefully remembered and gladly cast off? Perhaps it was. Nevertheless he must be getting rested, he felt himself tonight drifting off into delicious sleep as he thought of their walk into the hills.

In his dream, he continued to walk over the sunny uplands on the short grass and the sweet thyme but at a visionary speed. He was alone, there were even no sheep, he felt a great urgency to get to the visible top of this hill, though he knew there would be another crest and another. The landscape unreeled with the swiftness and silence of a film and he strode, seemingly weightless, over the distance and the height, his new pace and progress convincing him that it had to do with his mission which would be revealed at the summit. All would be revealed and he must only get there, in order to see why he was going. But ridge after ridge rose up; no sooner did he surmount one with this supernatural ease but another was there. He began to think he would never reach the top, never look down from the highest peak. When suddenly he did.

He looked down upon a vast, silent, sinister, dusty reddish-coloured desert. His mind protested at once. For this should be the sea, the sea should stretch silver and glistening, the channel between the mainland and the island. Where had his journey brought him? No sea, no further hills, but a desert from which such heat arose that he could feel it. He could feel the heat upon his face, his skin. His eyes felt it. He narrowed them, waiting. There was nothing to see here, but arid waste. Yet he must wait, he knew he must wait. For the vast, thunderous, distant, evil explosion. A violent, apocalyptic ball of flame leapt up which was soon smothered in cloud. Was it cloud or was it smoke? It grew, it grew as he watched. Its stalk was a thick column tinged with the flame, its cap was a mushroom. He was stifled with terror at this simple shape for he knew it to be obscenely sinister. It grew as he watched. This was the significance of it, he was completely aware, with no one to tell him. That it grew. He did not know what it was or would turn into. Only that, evilly, it grew. There was something to make you shudder in the act of visible growing, some fearful adumbration of unforetellable consequence. Composed of seemingly heavy yet billowing cloud, with its column of fire-devoured stalk and with a great, evil, brain-shaped cap, it grew, spreading ever outwards as it teased apart. It would fill the whole vast desert. This was the significance. In fact it was doing so, it was billowing towards him, up and hot and at him, flaming, he began to choke, he began to struggle, he cried out. He awoke sweating and, too hot, he flung off the bedclothes.

"Eddie?" Margery said sleepily from the other bed.

"Sorry. Nightmare," he muttered. He lay until he cooled off. Now shudderingly cold, he kept tasting the inexplicable evil taste, the devastating ambience of the dream. Much later he fell asleep again.

"...Scientists both American and British," said the Scottish voice of a BBC announcer at the breakfast table in the safe stone kitchen in the cottage of Margery's cousins in Oban, "have at last succeeded in making an atomic bomb. One of these was dropped at twenty past midnight London time on the night of Sunday-Monday upon Hiroshima the Japanese port and army base..."

In Hiroshima it had been just after eight o'clock in the morning. Edwin sat, straining his ears for the cousins exclaimed and talked all through it.

It was Tuesday the seventh of August. Laura was to arrive that day.

The first time Edwin heard a reasoned description of the look of the atomic explosion, he shuddered, for here was his dream.

And even more so the first time he saw a photograph in the papers on the next Monday. It was a rather poor photograph, fuzzy and indistinct: but the evil shape was there.

"Eddie, are you cold?" Margery said on this occasion, seeing him.

He affirmed this, gruffly.

"Well, it is chilly, to be sure. Bring Pop's cardigan," she called to Prudence.

Edwin very much disliked any suggestion of things extrasensory. He resented his mind, his perception, being of an order to do this to him. (His view was precisely that of Laurence Cardew for other reasons.) Yet where else had the vision come from? He was not aware of having read of, or seen, its shape. But he supposed this must be the case. Prudence put his cardigan lovingly round his shoulders and was surprised that in his abstraction he uttered no word in answer to hers.

In the few weeks, following her sight of Prudence with Gavin, Laura had been the tennis ball of her feelings and the victim of her fantasies. She had moved from savage jealousy to the ecstasies of renunciation on behalf of her loved friend, and back again to jealousy and despair. (She had after all been reared in a theology of renunciation, the putting-down of self and its fleshly desires, she was conditioned to this position, it seemed second nature to her to embrace this cross.) In vain, she told herself that Gavin was not free, no such thing as she imagined could possibly happen. She was enveloped in a fantasy that it could, that it was actually doing so. She is meeting him, she is getting to know my person, my beloved teacher! She and I are in some ways alike, our tastes the same. No wonder she likes him! And the two of *them* are the same, their interests, their life, their careers overlapping! It cannot help but happen, I am defeated. Fortunate Prudence, not only her work, but her life mapped out! She was desperately sad also if she had hurt Tom: she could not guess if much, or superficially. Tom had been wise and sensible, he had told her to *find out* if the situation were different. She had missed the chance of asking Prudence over the phone, she had not taken his advice, she had failed to act in a simple, direct way, partly perhaps because she was afraid of what she would discover. After all, Prudence, she sometimes persuaded herself, is far the worthier, far the best for Gavin!

By the time Laura travelled north she felt she knew what had happened: somehow, Gavin was unattached, he had met Prudence, it was *he*, he who was falling in love, he with golden Prudence, he would woo and win and marry her! (Why should he be entertaining any thoughts of me, she mourned?) She schooled herself into having to accept all this: I must stop thinking of him, get free, go on to the next thing, she told herself, it is what Tom has always said. Oh why, why did I tell Tom, she then asked? How foolish, foolish of me to tell Tom! She had been guileless. Will Tom understand, shall we be able to pick up where we left off? Tom may say he's no wish to be second best. Out of all these stormy thoughts emerged one main intention, as she came to join the Kyles: to discuss tactfully, casually, exactly what the situation was, and as soon as opportunity offered.

"So what are they saying in London about these terrible bombs, eh, Laura?" Edwin asked.

They were lapped in glory. The sea, a resplendent scintillating blue, stretched away in a myriad of gently heaving ribs like glistening watered silk. It reflected the sky, as deep and deeper azure. The mainland mountains brooded watchfully, purple grey and green; the highland of Mull, the colour of the sea but velvet in texture, lay ahead; water and air were so crisp Laura felt faint with ecstasy. (And also with her journey: a night and half a day.) They were all going over to Mull for the few days of Laura's visit.

Laura searched her mind for what people had said, looking puzzled.

"I was on the way here, it hadn't happened. Isn't it just another different kind of bomb? That's what I overheard someone say. And that if it stops the war, it's *saving* lives."

"It's more than just a different kind of bomb," said Prudence's stern father. "It's a nuclear explosion, they've managed a controlled nuclear explosion."

"Laura and I," Prudence put in, sweetly apologetic, "don't really understand what that means, Pop."

"They have split the atom. You must have heard about splitting the atom," Edwin said, looking at the clever, comical seagulls hitching a lift on the ferry's mast and rigging. They gleamed in new feather, as they swayed back and forth, they were much brighter than the old worn paint. All the ferries were shabby, dirty, depleted, worn, nothing much could be done to keep them spruce through the war. The services were depleted too, but Margery's relations knew ferry and fishermen, they had found a passage.

And where will splitting the atom lead, said Edwin to himself having silenced the girls, and thinking of his dream? He had told no one of his dream. There was that glorious mass of white, of innocent cloud over the land behind them, and there was that evil growth in the dream. Prudence looked across at her father, close enough to his mind to know that something disturbed him greatly.

On the eighth of August news came that Stalin had, true to a promise at Potsdam, ordered the invasion of Manchuria, held by the Japanese since before the war in Europe. It was China with whom Stalin had been negotiating, no wonder he would not see an emissary from Japan.

On the ninth of August the Americans dropped their third bomb on Nagasaki.

(When it became known later that the aircraft bearing those devastating loads had been blessed by a Catholic priest, Edwin's anger was not assuaged by his scorn, which hissed in him like water on molten metal. Imogen, totally abashed, bewildered yet loyal to her faith, felt like a blind dead stump of a tree lifting up bare arms towards the sun, dying of not understanding.)

On the tenth of August, a BBC report from China announced that the Japanese, faced with the Russians in Manchuria, had agreed to surrender, and described the Chinese crowd weeping with joy and relief in the streets. For their war had begun years ago, with the Japanese depredations in the summer of 1937.

❦

Prudence and Laura, on a bright August morning, walked up a little hill to the nearest cairn overlooking the bay of Uisken near to which they had lodgings.

The war, then, was over, all but the arguments and the signing. This day and this place were so celestial that the news of the bombs seemed distant and unreal. They knew as yet no hideous details. Their habitual gloom about the war was hidden in present glory. Young, and at the fresh start of their interrupted lives, they were full of their own concerns.

Now, Laura thought, this is the time, here's my chance. She climbed the hill beside her friend and said with calm:

"Well, how are you, dearest P, how are you getting on with your work, with your plans? The news has made us forget everything."

"Oh, I think I've met my fate, met my man!" laughed Prudence breathlessly, tossing back her gold and shaggy hair. It had grown longer again, and she looked more like herself. Oh my prophetic soul, Laura sighed.

"Do tell me," she said aloud. "How exciting!"

"I think he's going to be perfect, really. In a way I wonder if it's because maybe I'm a bit like him. In character I mean. Looking at things from the wings always."

"Yes, you do do that, I think. Does he?"

"And seeing all round things; I mean, in a way not really letting myself get involved or feel much, like you do. You feel things so enormously, Laura."

Laura wondered how these two were going to manage at all if they were not prepared to feel things. She had not realised this about Gavin,

228

that he did not get involved or feel things: indeed she would not have said it was true, she was prepared to wager he was beginning to feel quite deeply for her when he bravely broke it all up. But Prudence perhaps was speaking of him as the scholar.

"This is a person of such clear-cut intellect," Prudence was chattering on, "it's disgraceful conceit that I could compare myself with him at all, you'll laugh at me, quite rightly."

"No; you've got a clear-cut intellect, too."

"—but I'm sure it's a kind of sympathy with his way of seeing that draws me to him. And then he's got this deliciously simple but mordaunt kind of humour, it shows in his letters."

"I would say that was quite a good description of your own sense of humour," Laura put in, in measured tones, wondering at the rate and amount of correspondence Prudence's remark suggested.

"Anyway, I'm beginning to feel so excited, I can't wait for it to begin."

"It sounds as if it *has* begun!" said Laura.

"In a way, in a way, but I'm nowhere near close enough to him yet to see what it is I want to pursue, what I actually need to do to come up with it, and what the possible gaps are I could fill. Until I've read a whole heap more."

"Read?" exclaimed Laura, at a standstill. "Prudence, do please tell me who it is we're talking about?"

"John of Salisbury," said Prudence, glowing. "You know, Thomas Becket's friend. He's a wonderful man, a wonderful subject, lots to do; I haven't quite defined what, yet, as I say."

Laura, her breath taken, knew not whether to laugh or cry.

"Prudence!" she said mainly laughing, "I thought you meant a MAN, you know, a real man, now, a boyfriend, a suitor, a possible husband! I thought you were going to tell me, at *last*, about Gavin Kitto. I saw you together, you see, I saw you in that teashop. And when you went on saying nothing about it, I got absolutely convinced you were falling in love with each other, you're so suitable! (Are you, by any chance?) And then I thought no, how could they, Gavin wouldn't carry on like that, Gavin's married and you're so upright."

"Dearest Laura!" Prudence exclaimed. "Why didn't you *tell* me, say you'd seen us? What a lot of anguish it would have saved."

"But why didn't *you* tell *me*? *What* anguish?" Laura demanded, at sea.

The spirit of Tom hovered about. Pussy-footing around, he said, what can you expect but a complexity of cat's cradles. "I was worrying about Tom. You sounded as if you were hopeful, getting fond, when we talked."

Laura was puzzled.

"We were, I think. What's Tom got to do with it? When I saw Gavin with you, the whole thing came welling back, I had to tell Tom, well, he guessed really."

"*That's* why the watershed time!"

"Yes. How is Gavin, anyway? I suppose you met at that class. He must be so thrilled, planning to get back to Oxford? You both looked rather happy, I thought: though he looked *much* older, I realised, than that time I saw him from the train. What were you talking about? John of Salisbury?"

"Partly. He was interested, he did slightly push me in this direction, as well as my own supervisor. Mostly, though, we were talking about Laura Cardew."

They were both breathless now with the last scramble.

"Why?" Laura said glumly.

"Let's get to the top of this hill and reach that cairn, because I'm getting puffed. And I've got something so important to tell you."

They turned at the top, they surveyed the glittering sea, the wheeling birds, a distant string of tiny clouds.

"What?" Laura said urgently, panting a little.

Prudence waited, fetching her breath. She put her left hand over Laura's right, as they stood there side by side.

"Gavin has been widowed, Laura," she said. "Both his wife and his child were killed in the Barnet bomb."

There was a minute of total silence save for the sound of their breath. Into this silence, a sea bird placed a shriek like a dagger, a long agonised call, turning into a proliferation of quick gasping sobs.

Laura sat down on the short turf amongst thyme and lichened stones, put her head on her bent knees and began to weep. She had much to make her weep. Prudence let her weep herself out, and shed a tear or two in sympathy.

"Poor Gavin," Laura wailed at last, as her shaking ceased.

"He's pulled himself up, Laura. He's getting better. It's nearly a year you know. Not that I suppose you're ever really better from such a thing. He says he would very much like to see you. Come on," Prudence said, hauling her friend up, "let's put stones on the cairn. For new things."

"Did he tell you about it?"

"Yes, every detail. Don't you remember, I told you? It was the first time I met him." It was burnt upon Prudence's memory.

"Oh yes, I understand, how strange, *that* was Gavin."

"I didn't know who he was."

"No. I remember."

"I'll tell you all he told me, later."

"Yes. Please."

They put their stones on the cairn, choosing what they thought were shapely, significant ones. Then they ran dangerously down the hill, sideways, like goats.

In bed that night, with a sense of release, of crooked places about to be made plain, of a hope so huge that it was fearful, Laura sighed. And wept again. And giggled over all her wasted renunciation. If Prudence was in love with anyone she was in love with John of Salisbury. Hundreds of years ago, safely, safely, dustily dead. Secretary to Becket (Laura thought she remembered), later Bishop of Chartres. Not romantic (like Peter Abelard), not the bold and fiery martyr like Thomas: but the stylist, the humanist, the scholar of his age. And yet, probably similar to dearest Prudence in his outlook. Dear, kind Prudence, whose thoughts had been for *her*, Laura, all the time, and Gavin has said he wants to see me, he has said he wants to meet me! The ecstasy of this kept her hours awake, joy being a more potent insomniac than sorrow.

She was not altogether right about Prudence: who lay not very far off also awake, profoundly relieved that the tangle was loosed, but feeling a tenderness in the heart like a fading bruise. She was barely aware of the fact that she would never be the same again, that something had opened inside her. Love had touched her at last.

22

The war was over. From the dot-dot-dot-dash of the victory chords—(none of these young people, Laura would think several years on, hearing a college orchestra launching rather raggedly into Beethoven's Fifth Symphony, can have any idea what these bars must always mean to us)—from the V-signs, the bulldog jaws, the terrors, the deaths, the losses and privations, to the hysteria of victory itself: it was over.

Japan had been forced to what her Emperor called the endurance of the unendurable by the dropping of the two Bombs, whose incalculable damage cast long evil shadows into the future, to be indeed never calculated. A pilot, flying over Nagasaki twelve hours after, while the city was still a mass of flames, reported that it was like looking over the rim of a volcano in process of eruption. (Edwin, still in his highland retreat, had noted this in the paper of the thirteenth of August and recognised it as the continuation of his nightmare.) Someone else much later recalled that the place where Hiroshima had been had looked like a sea of black, boiling lava.

The morning papers of the fourteenth were still reporting no answer from Japan: but at midnight, the prime minister had eventually broadcast the news, saying, "The last of our enemies is laid low." Many people did not hear him. Many set off to work on the fifteenth of August not knowing that final victory had dawned. Amongst them Laura, just back from Scotland, who reached her office to find two colleagues poring over a paper, having fallen into the same trap. The timing on this occasion was felicitous, coinciding with the long-arranged opening of Parliament: the King and Queen were to drive in state, a good deal of peacetime ceremonial was to be restored.

"Well, come on, we can't just stay here, it's a holiday. Let's go and see what's happening."

"Let's go up to Whitehall, anyway, even if we can't get near. Someone'll come out on a balcony!"

"I'm not very good at crowds, I believe," Laura had said to her new office companions. She remembered the VE day crowd: but they had been on the fringe of it, she and Tom. She must ring Tom up, soon, and tell him. He would say, "Good luck, Laura." She felt a sudden piercing nostalgia for dear, unworried Tom. She had exiled herself from Tom, she must wait in limbo.

But nonetheless here she was against her nature, she thought, persuaded because it was so historic. In a swaying, jabbering confluence of people in which they were at first loosely cocooned. Very soon the whole thing began to take on the nature of a dream, a baddish dream, and she herself watching herself from somewhere outside it.

Come on, Laura, keep up, don't get separated, hang on to me. I can't reach you, Laura thinks, I'm trying to keep up, I'm trying.

The press, the weight, the awful sense of the multitude becoming an entity, the many-headed multitude, one great hideous monster with some terrible and unpredictable life of its own in which those waving beetle or tortoise heads are nothing, have no power, no will of their own! Where are you? Can't even see you, some rude thrusting shoulder has burrowed between my friends and me, my body is borne along unwillingly by heavier and heavier pressure into the depth of the crowd, which is rushing towards the Whitehall buildings like a flood. When we arrived we were on the edge, the outside, and I was all right, I can bear being on the edge. But I cannot bear the increasing depth of the sea of heads, seal heads, necking and stretching further and further behind me.

Laura looks over her shoulder, sees them all pushing, pressing, swaying, sees herself getting deeper and deeper, can't do it.

"I'll have to get out, I'll have to go," she calls to her friends.

"Oh Laura, we're quite near, keep up!"

More and more heads, shoulders, bodies keep thrusting in between. "I'm just going to burrow out," she calls, "don't worry, I'll be all right!" She takes a look behind her over the heaving mass, craning to see where the dry land of the empty road is nearest, turns her left shoulder into the throng and burrows. "Excuse me, I feel faint, I must get out. Let me through please or I shall faint." (Pushing, burrowing against Papa's black stomach. *Black* stomach? says Tom.) "Let me through, please." Push in the left shoulder, the right shoulder, if they can push with their shoulders so can you, everyone for himself. "Let me through please or I shall faint," (*and be trampled underfoot*).

Her progress is barely heeded for all eyes are on Whitehall windows and balconies. She pushes with increasing relief as the pressure becomes lighter. Now there is even a foot or two between people, they fill up her room, their mesmerised eyes upon balconies where public figures will eventually appear and shout and gesture. They close over her space like an incoming tide devouring and annihilating a pool.

Oh thank goodness, says Laura, able to walk normally. She is herself, escaped from the multitude she has regained control. She scuttles with relief up Whitehall against the last comers and through into the Park, happy to be against the stream, on the edge, on the outside. Crowds line the Mall, waiting for the King and Queen: she, an outsider, alone at last in St James's. Her face is still wet with tears of fear, but she laughs with relief.

Whatever made me think I could do that, Laura said, shrugging her shoulders, walking freely and leisurely round the water and the cheerful wedge-tailed ducks quite unconscious of war and peace. She turned and looked across the park at the distant, sunlit, stagey backdrop of Whitehall where she had nearly gone under.

It took another two weeks to have the peace signed and sealed. But, after long negotiations and deltas of misunderstanding caused by the different attitudes and assumptions of West and East and the wish to save both the Japanese Emperor and the Japanese face on the part of some; and the bitter intention to punish to the full the victors of Pearl Harbour on the part of others, it was declared finished.

Things had been signed on board a ship in Tokyo Bay. (Many Japanese fought on for weeks, unaware or unwilling to stop.) From the invasion of Poland, the second of September 1939, to now, the second of September 1945, was exactly six years.

Nothing is solved, nothing is solved anywhere, Laura thought, striding up to the Hurst on a September Sunday, soon afterwards, and leaning against one of the girlish silver birches. The war may be over but it decides nothing, For most people nothing is suddenly better, for millions of people everything is in ruins, what the war has caused will never be remedied. History has to make a milestone out of the second of September 1945. How we have all lived, simply for the war to be over! Wars do not solve things, but they have to be fought. How could we not have fought the war? We had to fight this war. An image came of the war as a six-year hole in time through which millions had fallen out of sight: millions more on the cruel edges of the hole that had opened in history would try unavailingly to crawl back into the sunlight. Laura could not be aware of the unspeakable details of the vision, standing in the birches on the Hurst: (thinking of the General, remembering Tom). She would become aware of some of them as the years passed, inexorably revealing metres of terrible film, millions of words of unbelievable description. Fearful scenes from captured films would be burnt upon her memory, would haunt her till she died. A well-dressed Jew, protesting mildly at being manhandled in a queue, beaten almost to death upon the spot and never seen again. The cynical filming of an old man in the Warsaw ghetto dying up against a wall in a niche, white-bearded, black-hatted, the photographer returning again and again to report death's progress (I hope the old man flew straight to Abraham's bosom, Laura thought, or whatever is its philosophical equivalent.) A young soldier having to bulldoze the liquefaction of bodies at a camp to give them burial holding his handkerchief to his horrified face. For before the Holocaust was to be called the unspeakable, was to become the paramount symbol of man's evil, it was to be spoken of, seen, examined, handled, experienced in stark actuality by any who were willing to make that brutal journey.

It was probably Imogen who reminded Francis that divine Bach, lordly Beethoven, beloved Mozart came out of that same country. Many people were saying it, appalled and grasping at hope.

Laura and Prudence in this six years had grown from schoolgirls to women. But neither did Laura in so many words think of this then. She turned and hurried home to tea, with Kitty, whose thankfulness for the ending of the war (which certainly solved nothing for her) was commensurate with her greater maturity, longer perspectives and habitual charity. She was cheerful too, since Laura had told her of Prudence's revelation. She was nursing a secret hope, though saying not a word. It was as if they waited together, precariously, two delicate water beetles on the surface of a lake of silence.

My dear Laura,

said the letter in the writing she had once known so well.

> Prudence Kyle tells me you know about what has happened to me. If you can do with a person still rather shaken, I should greatly like to meet you again. Your friend says she thinks you would welcome this. If so, will you come and see me? I am back, living in college for now. You'll find me in the same rooms! Sixish this Friday? Or Saturday? Let me know. We can go out for something to eat.

> Yours, Gavin Kitto

> Dear Gavin,

she wrote unable to believe it.

> I will be glad to come to Oxford on Friday. And will find my way up the usual stair.

> Yours Laura

She crept up rather softly; the bare treads of the staircases had always made her feel conspicuous. (The men thundered down them, and girls would clatter wildly on their high heels.) She had every reason to tread gently today: she hoped she was not treading on her dreams.

He had left the inner door slightly ajar as usual and she slipped in before he heard her. He stood by the window, a very tall, very thin, slightly unstraight figure, a back view that had often caused Laura's heart to pound and now did so again. The burnished head (that hair she had recognised as Prudence's) was bent slightly sideways, the droop of the shoulders seemed to proclaim both grief and uncertainty.

Gavin turned from the window and looked at her. She still has the heavens in her eyes, he thought.

All he needs at first is comfort thought Laura.

"Gavin."

"Laura."

Their smiles were nervous, they were very shy of each other. Do I shake hands with her, he wondered? He held out both hands.

"Thank you for coming, Laura. It's good to see you again."

With deliberation, with some dread, but with an excitement she had forgotten which nearly stifled her she walked towards him and let him take her hands.

"I don't know how to say how sorry I am for you."

He held her hands for a moment against his heart.

"I know. I'll tell you about it later. But not yet. Here, sit down, in your usual chair, and have some sherry." He did not say then that Prudence had described, in another brief note, the scene on the hilltop.

As they sat and drank and talked she considered him. She considered Gavin Kitto, the man, the real person, the features of his face, the wide, generous mouth, below the shapely nostrils, the tilted nose. She was right in thinking that he looked much older: yet you could not call a man still so young "battered". He looked "shaken" rather, it was his own word, a golden poplar in a gale.

Her impression and the poetical image she found for it were truer than she knew. The obstreperous confidence of his late twenties and early thirties which had delighted Laura the undergraduate had deserted him. The golden-ness, the comical assurance were for the moment gone: the person who could kneel on Bodley's stairs, where was he?

He had been stricken to his foundations. Almost, he needed rebuilding. The shaking had laid bare the deep faults in the structure of his early years, as such great quakes do. He often *felt* like a poplar in a gale. Fortunately for her, Laura was too inexperienced to be aware of all the detailed implications of this. But as she sat watching him, catching sometimes the amused and carefree look of earlier years, she knew that she had love to offer. Her love was still there, had always been there, not even dormant: she believed in love, why, it was about the only thing she did believe in. She sensed also that she must go softly, she must wait, she must let things grow slowly, she would be like Solveig. She must curb her ardour, be gentle and circumspect. As Prudence would be.

"Would it be good," he was saying, "if we could meet, quite often, Laura, if we could just see how we go? Would you like that? You will have to make allowances for a lamed man. Sometimes," he hesitated, "I must just tell you this—I seem to be unable to *feel anything—at all*—" He sounded puzzled. "But I would be so glad if we could meet?"

"I would like that very much," she replied in measured tones. As Prudence might have done. (But the look she gave him was warm, loving, confident with hope.)

How can I live up to such heart-breaking expectancy? Gavin wondered, feeling panic. She was always a stargazer. I will comfort him. But I will make him love me for myself, Laura thought.

When he went to get ready for taking her out, Laura walked over and looked at the photograph more closely, which she had seen from her chair.

The girl was dark, placid, with the heavy happiness of motherhood in her smile, a great rope of black hair lay in a shapely fall over one shoulder, on the other arm sat the child, looking sunny-haired like Gavin and gleeful, holding out a hand. They are gone, they are dead, their lives have been *stolen*, all her joy and care cut off, finished; all the baby's future, his promise, (great cleverness, perhaps) his share of life denied, unhappened. She must have loved him, she probably loved him to distraction (as I will). Where is that love, where is she gone, and the bright-faced boy? Because you are gone, poor girl, I have this chance of great joy, how strange a thought is that. I shall not forget.

"Perhaps I ought to put the photos away?" Gavin said doubtfully, standing behind her.

"Oh no, no, they are part of it, they have to be part of you, they must be part of you, always," Laura exclaimed instinctively, without thought. "Don't you talk to her?"

"You mean, it may be that is their only life? Now?"

"About that I don't know," said she. "Do you?"

"No. Well, I do talk to her," he said. "Let's go."

23

Y ou've met? You're on your way?" Prudence asked, thinking she had never seen Laura look happy in this way before.

"We've met. In the same rooms, up the same stair! Terribly gingerly, I think we're both nervous. But it's glorious."

"It'll be all right. Don't rush it. It probably won't be all that fast, or easy."

"I've discovered that. Oh, Prudence, I'm so grateful to you!"

"Not I! A lucky chance! I expect he would have sought you out anyway."

"Would I have been engaged to Tom?" They looked at each other questioning.

"What happened," Prudence asked, "about nice Tom?"

"You know he asked me to let him know? So I rang after you told me about Gavin. He said there, instinct, intuition, how amazing, you knew. It must be meant, as your ma would say. Go on Laura. Good luck...or words to that effect. He said let him know what happens. I will, too."

"He really is a treasure, that Tom."

"Yes he is" Laura agreed. "He calls you Prudence the clever, by the way...So how's the office? The ranks are thinning?" Laura asked.

"Assuredly. The latest news is Mrs Tripp."

"*Dear* Mrs Tripp," Laura burst in and wondered why her eyes filled suddenly. The General, the darling old General, of course.

"Flew last weekend. Back to Malta."

"Good, good. Was she thrilled?"

"Yes, bless her, she really was. You know, Mrs Wicklow discovered she has parents still alive there, she was going 'home'."

As the office continued its dwindle to a skeleton, Prudence would pass on the details when she met Laura. Marie was still there, a trace bitter Prudence thought, hoping for a transfer to the Ministry of Health. Marie, Laura felt, will always evoke that place, these two years, Marie will always interest me.

So far on that the echoes were faint, and she felt uncertainty, Laura sees Marie sitting alone on a bollard at a picturesque Suffolk watering place, sombre, the fair hair too bright. But it *is* Marie. I ought to go up and say Marie? It must be you! Is it shyness that I don't? Or is it that those years are sealed in their own curiously nostalgic cocoon? A strange thing, nostalgia for a war.

And Miss Richardson was known to have found herself a safe, dull job local to her lodging: a job where she dealt with Breed Units and clothes "kewpons" and other manifestations of developing post-war stringency. And where she fell in love with the handsome manager of the grocery department of her large local store, who would occasionally give her an ounce more butter, a rasher more bacon. And Irene Wainewright? And Mr Watson? Both had disappeared, Prudence knew not where. Mr Gorzinska, of course, was going to marry Mrs Wicklow's daughter, wasn't *that* good? Mrs Wicklow was delighted, and Prudence was to meet Victoria soon. Matthew, now, what has happened to Matthew?

"Matthew works quite near me, I sometimes see him pass," Laura says: thinking of his penny-sized face on his taut neck, his air of getting his own back.

Mr Harvald goes and comes to Europe.

"And you, dearest P, when does your term start?" Laura asks. "Not that terms affect you now."

"Early October," Prudence answers with glee. Prudence has long since found her way into the Reading Room of the British Museum and like thousands before her sits happily intent under the Dome. The Blitz-bombed museum gallery will steadily be restored to peacetime normality: but the Dome—like the Windmill Theatre—never closed. The service of the Reading Room was maintained during the war amidst unprecedented difficulties. The Dome had some tragi-comical adventures and no mistake, offering as it does the perfect air-raid target. Once a bull's-eye was scored by an oil bomb, which crashed through the Dome spilling its oil outside to burn harmlessly, but bringing with it a shower of bricks one of which demolished the lamp on the superintendent's central table. Stranger yet and stranger, two dud bombs on two different days came through the same hole... .

Prudence reads. John of Salisbury begins to put on almost flesh and blood, at least intellect and character.

"I should think the whole thing'll collapse soon, won't it? The office I mean."

"They're still busy finding places for everyone, but it can't keep going much longer."

The block will revert to residences, resume its "luxury". The builders will come to see to all that hastily, temporarily repaired bomb damage. The carpenters to renew maltreated floors and shelves. The plumbers. All those unsavoury bathrooms and lavatories, and failed fresh-air machines. The painters: all will be pastel clean and decent for new owners and tenants. The people will come back to take a Mayfair flat, the war being over. What a relief, my dear, get the furniture out again...got our London pied-á-terre going, come any time, come for a bed, don't forget... ."

"I've got to walk down to Chatham House," Prudence was saying, finishing her coffee. "With a note. Will you come?"

"I'll come. It's a nice day. No hurry to get back."

Laura waited in idle interest, in the dim carpeted foyer of Chatham House in the far corner of St James's Square, while Prudence disappeared to deliver her message. Waiting too, and hovering (she

242

noticed from the corner of her eye), was a man, a slight, fey, young-middle-aged man, in lovat green tweed, with a greyish green trilby of deep velour firmly upon his head at a dashing angle. How odd, that he had not removed his hat. He was now speaking to somebody, accosting her as she walked to the door. Laura could not hear what was said, but caught the shocked expression on the face of the retreating woman, as she hurried out.

"That's it," Prudence said reappearing to join Laura and making briskly for the circular door. Laura followed.

"Excuse me," said the man in the soft green trilby. "Pardon me," he said in a husky, singsong and conspiratorial voice, the tones of which raised immediate echoes in their memories. "Allow me to acquaint you of the fact," there was no mistaking that Irish "t", "allow me to tell you what I know to be the truth."

Prudence had pulled up sharply in consternation, for he was barring the way. Laura studied him with interest. From his pale, somewhat twisted face, there looked out a blue eye and a grey one. Remarkable. Like Miss Peel, at school. He fixed these disparate eyes upon them with a hypnotic gleam, almost one expected him to put forth a skinny hand and stop their progress, like the Ancient Mariner.

"Hitler is not dead, you know. Hitler is not dead at all. Hitler will return. This is the truth. And I know it." Prudence shot a pink and furious glance at Laura, and dodged out of his way; Laura looked at the Irishman in silent surprise and followed. As she pushed through the door, she saw him advance upon somebody else with his cataclysmic information. Laura hurried after Prudence.

Prudence's slim legs, clad in nylon stockings (unheard of as yet in England and a rare present even from America), showed disapproval in every rapid, shining stride, as she led the way smartly round the Square upon her high heels. (The heels, too, were a recent habit, meant to dispel any suspicion that she was a bluestocking.) Laura scampered after her almost panting, this being partly due to a breathless bout of sudden laughter which she was unable to control. It was something about the solemn shocked horror of Prudence's expression, something about her outraged hurrying frame, bent forward, that motherly promising bosom quaking with unwonted rage, that had made Laura laugh.

Prudence looked down at Laura (she was a full two inches taller and the high heels made it worse) in prudish disbelief at her frivolity, then exploded with anxiety and anger.

"Wretched creature," she burst out, "how dare he?"

"Lord Haw-Haw, of course, *that's* what he sounded like," Laura gulped.

There had been a picture in the press of William Joyce, being carried into a British General Hospital at Luneburg. He was half-smiling, his eyes were closed, he was clean-shaven, looked almost bald. And totally passive.

"What does he think he gains?"

"Attention, dearest P. Yours," Laura spluttered, "and public horror. Just what he hoped for. Do stop galloping," she begged.

Certainly Hitler the person was dead, as common sense and scholars were to prove: what evil would live after him was brooding still in the future.

Prudence's face turned quickly into that smile, ironic but sweet, which Laura would remember as long as she lived. She stopped galloping at once. Very soon Laura's laughter had engulfed her. By the steps of the London Library (which was to nurture them both in their different paths) they staggered, leaning against a wall, and laughed: Prudence and Laura sprawled near the peeling portico, the gold-haired and the dark. Was it a sudden, clearer relief for the end of the war, the start of peace, the new life ahead, caused by the ludicrous man's statement? Whatever it was, the laughter was healing, was memorable.

It was mid-December, London exuded that smell of exhaust fumes, cold air, hot air, restaurant food and fog, which makes city people feel at home. It also, to Laura, held the indefinable atmosphere of expectancy, which precedes any Christmas, a flavour, a sense in the heart, a light in ancient memory of times past, times to come. This, by the nature of things, was a special Christmas, this the first Christmas of peace. Her own horizons glistened with hope. She and Gavin had met as often as they could, she catching the familiar train when he suggested it at a weekend, he dashing to town for some scholarly purpose, when they would meet for a meal. After two or three meetings, he had begun to kiss her (an event for which she had yearned) with gentle, rather brotherly kisses, her very shyness of her own increasing longing making her unable to turn them into anything more passionate. Each was so wary, so careful, of the other's feelings: he is exhausted at the end of a week, she would think; she is sensibly wanting to be sure what she feels before she lets go, he would tell himself. For Laura had kept to her plan of gentle carefulness, of not revealing all her heart, all she felt. She felt increasingly much as the weeks passed, as they learnt to know each other again, in such a different ambience from the months of their first friendship as tutor and pupil.

It had been a busy, muddled term that he had just passed: strange things were happening at the universities. War-hardened undergraduates appeared, men in their middle twenties and more, with wives and babies and old motor-cars, needing flats, lodgings, not college rooms; or men with wounds, and memories; jostling for places with the ordinary herd of excited schoolboys and girls. All this had called for new attitudes, different administration in the colleges; young but pre-war fellows like Gavin were as involved as anyone. Pressures of work always distanced him; she had watched anxieties about college duties, or his own research, or teaching problems, prey upon him. Grief, and she thought sometimes guilt, still haunted him. She had learned at these times to retreat, to be unobtrusive, even when she wanted to cry, look at me, notice me!

None of all this shook her determination to love him. As the weeks went on, she rejoiced in the increasing tenderness of his occasional long, quiet embraces when they breathed together, or the excitement when he greeted her with a wild, laughing hug, shouting, lifting her off her feet. Once or twice, he had kissed her long and searchingly on the mouth. Her own hunger was now intense, she wondered how long she could conceal it. She longed for him to want her, to make love to her, she longed to give herself to him. She would not run away from *him*, and the memory of her apprehension was strange to her. What was he doing, waiting so long? Was he still not sure, was he still too harrowed, was he simply *too busy*, overwhelmed with the hard work of his college life starting again? Sometimes she felt ashamed of her passion, sometimes she was amused at it. Prudence, coolly inexperienced, who yet seemed to know increasingly all about it, tried to make her laugh at it. Perhaps when the term is over, when he has more leisure, perhaps then, Laura thought, he will woo me in his orderly, premeditated way, perhaps he is even now thinking about times, dates, opportunities, who knew? Laura would smile ruefully then, thinking I have waited three years, I can wait a few weeks more. Well, now the term *was* over. She longed for him to *give his mind to it*! (Scholars, Prudence replied to this, are noted for having their minds on other things.) She was to meet him this evening, Gavin had said, in the forecourt of the British Museum, quite near where she worked.

As to Gavin, he had been puzzled sometime by her ironic coolness, wondered if she felt as tentative and uncertain as he sometimes did of his own feelings and hers? At all costs he must not *assume* things. He tried not to have a million other subjects on his mind when they met, but often had. Where were, what were, his feelings? Sometimes, as he had said to her, he thought there was no heart there. He would think worriedly am I sure I can love her, and go on loving her, do I trust her to love me? I can't bear to be hurt again. And how could he offer a girl his life to share if his heart were, at times, to do this disappearing trick, softly and suddenly vanish away? Had he better not stick to his scholarship, become the old-fashioned bachelor don? Ponder well, he remembered once saying to her, out of the blue. They should both ponder well. He was standing now halfway up the wide steps in the dark, peering into the lighted entrance hall, in case she was waiting inside and he had missed her. She came through the gate in the black railings by the sentry-box, and saw him before he saw her, one of the outside lamps lighting his much loved figure and his hair. She forgot caution, she flung off constraint, he was there already (early) in the dark waiting for her, her heart's delight and heaven's best!

"Gavin!" she called, between laughing and crying.

He heard and turned. When he saw her pale face alight, watched her break into a run, his heart did a great roar, his heart turned clean over (when had he thought he had no heart?) his heart re-asserted itself like a lion, and they ran joyfully into each other's arms.

Also by Pauline Hunter Blair

The Nelson Boy

An Imaginative Reconstruction of A Great Man's Childhood

Horatio Nelson is one of Britain's great heroes and his later life is well documented. Pauline Hunter Blair offers us a rare chance to explore his childhood – through painstaking research and imaginative but plausible reconstruction. The scene is set in Burnham Thorpe, north Norfolk still (in its rural parts) very much the same. The rector, Edmund Nelson, is to be papa to eight youngsters, and his wife Catherine Nelson (of a family a smidge higher in the social scale) is the busiest of mothers. From this quiverful of children there begins to fly one, outstanding in spirit, wits, and character, who would fly far

Six well-authenticated anecdotes put milestones across Horace's childhood and boyhood: losing himself at Hilborough (where his paternal granny lived); riding to school through deep snow with William; finding the 'rare' bird's nest; picking a sprig of yew from the churchyard tree at dead of night; catching the measles at school at North Walsham; where he also, chiefly for his friends, stripped the master's pear-tree and never owned up. (Was this one reason why he was so keen to leave school aged just over twelve and a half and go into the navy?)

The *Norwich Mercury* and The *Norfolk Gazette* of the time have provided an actual background tapestry of events, but the family's participation in them has to be largely imagined. (Nowhere does the author describe Horace's involvement in an event if that were circumstantially impossible.) We know the people, the neighbours, Horace was fond of when a child from the letters he wrote, the messages he sent, the enquiries he made as an adult, and thus the author lets them people his childhood.

£16.95 ISBN 0-9536317-0-2

A Thorough Seaman

The Ships' Logs of Horatio Nelson's Early Voyages Imaginatively Explored

Before Horatio Nelson was eighteen, he had sailed towards all points of the compass: as captain's servant, coxswain of the captain's gig, able-bodied seaman, foretop man, and midshipman.

After Chatham, he sailed to the West Indies on a sugar ship, the *Mary Ann*, when he must have first revelled in the glorious trade winds. Her captain was a trusted naval friend of his uncle's, now commanding this merchantman, for whom perhaps the boy developed a loving admiration which almost caused his naval ambitions to falter. Safely back in the Medway and Thames, he learned their tides, channels, sand banks and landmarks or points of departure: on one occasion very probably under a Lt Boyles, who sounds like his old friend of Burnham days.

When news of an Arctic voyage to seek a north-east passage to the Pole fired his imagination, he was off in a converted bomb-ketch, aptly named the *Carcase*, to foggy, frosty wastes, encountering floating structures of ice, padding white bears, walrus, and a million sea birds. Six tempests on the way home initiated him into the buffeting manners of the rough North Sea.

HMS *Seahorse* then carried him south, round the Cape, across the Indian Ocean to Madras, and the Bay of Bengal to Calcutta; then to Ceylon, to Bombay, and up the Persian Gulf. They were once involved in a minor but possibly explicable exchange of fire, off the Malabar coast, with some ships of one Hyder Ali, out from Mangalore; his first taste of a skirmish.

HMS *Dolphin* and her kind captain carried him home from Bombay, a sad victim of malaria, and not expected to make England. But on the way, miraculously, he recovered, as we all know.

Logs of all but the first of these voyages exist, so that we can follow the events. Of his relations with captains, officers, masters and friends we know less and must imagine more.

£16.95 ISBN 0-9536317-1-0

Available from Church Farm House, Bottisham, Cambridge, CB5 9BA